Flying Angels

By Danielle Steel

FLYING ANGELS · THE BUTLER · COMPLICATIONS · NINE LIVES
FINDING ASHLEY · THE AFFAIR · NEIGHBORS · ALL THAT GLITTERS
ROYAL · DADDY'S GIRLS · THE WEDDING DRESS · THE NUMBERS GAME
MORAL COMPASS · SPY · CHILD'S PLAY · THE DARK SIDE · LOST AND FOUND
BLESSING IN DISGUISE · SILENT NIGHT · TURNING POINT · BEAUCHAMP HALL
IN HIS FATHER'S FOOTSTEPS · THE GOOD FIGHT · THE CAST
ACCIDENTAL HEROES · FALL FROM GRACE · PAST PERFECT · FAIRYTALE
THE RIGHT TIME · THE DUCHESS · AGAINST ALL ODDS · DANGEROUS GAME
THE MISTRESS · THE AWARD · RUSHING WATERS · MAGIC · THE APARTMENT
PROPERTY OF A NOBLEWOMAN · BLUE · PRECIOUS GIFTS · UNDERCOVER
COUNTRY · PRODIGAL SON · PEGASUS · A PERFECT LIFE · POWER PLAY
WINNERS · FIRST SIGHT · UNTIL THE END OF TIME · THE SINS OF THE MOTHER
FRIENDS FOREVER · BETRAYAL · HOTEL VENDÔME · HAPPY BIRTHDAY
44 CHARLES STREET · LEGACY · FAMILY TIES · BIG GIRL
SOUTHERN LIGHTS · MATTERS OF THE HEART · ONE DAY AT A TIME
A GOOD WOMAN · ROGUE · HONOR THYSELF · AMAZING GRACE
BUNGALOW 2 · SISTERS · H.R.H. · COMING OUT · THE HOUSE
TOXIC BACHELORS · MIRACLE · IMPOSSIBLE · ECHOES · SECOND CHANCE
RANSOM · SAFE HARBOUR · JOHNNY ANGEL · DATING GAME
ANSWERED PRAYERS · SUNSET IN ST. TROPEZ · THE COTTAGE · THE KISS
LEAP OF FAITH · LONE EAGLE · JOURNEY · THE HOUSE ON HOPE STREET
THE WEDDING · IRRESISTIBLE FORCES · GRANNY DAN · BITTERSWEET
MIRROR IMAGE · THE KLONE AND I · THE LONG ROAD HOME · THE GHOST
SPECIAL DELIVERY · THE RANCH · SILENT HONOR · MALICE
FIVE DAYS IN PARIS · LIGHTNING · WINGS · THE GIFT · ACCIDENT
VANISHED · MIXED BLESSINGS · JEWELS · NO GREATER LOVE
HEARTBEAT · MESSAGE FROM NAM · DADDY · STAR · ZOYA
KALEIDOSCOPE · FINE THINGS · WANDERLUST · SECRETS
FAMILY ALBUM · FULL CIRCLE · CHANGES · THURSTON HOUSE
CROSSINGS · ONCE IN A LIFETIME · A PERFECT STRANGER
REMEMBRANCE · PALOMINO · LOVE: *POEMS* · THE RING · LOVING
TO LOVE AGAIN · SUMMER'S END · SEASON OF PASSION · THE PROMISE
NOW AND FOREVER · PASSION'S PROMISE · GOING HOME

Nonfiction

EXPECT A MIRACLE: *Quotations to Live and Love By*
PURE JOY: *The Dogs We Love*
A GIFT OF HOPE: *Helping the Homeless*
HIS BRIGHT LIGHT: *The Story of Nick Traina*

For Children

PRETTY MINNIE IN PARIS
PRETTY MINNIE IN HOLLYWOOD

DANIELLE STEEL

Flying Angels

A Novel

Delacorte Press | New York

Published in the United States by Delacorte Press,
an imprint of Random House,
a division of Penguin Random House LLC, New York.

DELACORTE PRESS and the HOUSE colophon are registered trademarks of Penguin Random House LLC.

Hardback ISBN 978-1-984-82155-3
Ebook ISBN 978-1-984-82156-0

Printed in the United States of America on acid-free paper

randomhousebooks.com

2 4 6 8 9 7 5 3 1

First Edition

To my beloved children,
Beatrix, Trevor, Todd, Nick,
Samantha, Victoria, Vanessa,
Maxx, and Zara,

May the challenges and the hard times
in your lives
prove to be blessings
and bring you closer
to those you love.

I wish you courage, strength, wisdom,
good fortune, joy,
and lives filled with love
and good people to love,
protect, and comfort you.

                    With all my heart and love,
                              Mom / d.s.

"Love makes us brave."

Flying Angels

Chapter 1

It was a big day for the Parker family, on a perfect morning in June 1938. Audrey had set her mother's clothes out for her the night before, the blue-gray silk suit she wore whenever she had something important to go to and felt well enough to go out. It didn't get more important than this. Ellen's son, Audrey's brother, William Edward Parker, was graduating from Annapolis Naval Academy, as an ensign, like his father and grandfather before him. Ellen was only sorry that her late husband and father-in-law wouldn't be there to see it. She and Audrey were the only family Will had now. Unlike his father and grandfather, Will was more interested in planes than ships. His next stop was basic flight training at the Naval Air Station at Pensacola in Florida. He was going to be a navy pilot. He would receive more advanced flight training after that, and eventually would become an expert at taking off and landing on an aircraft carrier. He had earned a Bachelor of Science degree.

His father, Captain Francis Parker, had died three years before of a brain tumor. His grandfather, who had died when Will and Audrey were very young, was only a dim memory now, a tall man in a uniform with a lot of braid on it: three-star Vice Admiral Jeremiah Parker. They were a distinguished naval family, and there had never been any question about Will following in their footsteps. It was an unspoken law in their household, Parker men went to Annapolis, and Will wouldn't have dared do otherwise. He wouldn't have wanted to disappoint his grandfather or his dad, even though they were no longer there to see it. He would be wearing his dress white uniform for the graduation ceremony.

Her parents' illnesses had had an impact on Audrey's life. Only months after Audrey's father had died, after his painful deterioration from cancer, her mother had begun exhibiting strange symptoms: muscle weakness, a lack of balance, and trembling hands. Both Ellen and Audrey thought it was caused by nerves at first, but then she had been diagnosed with the early stages of Parkinson's disease. The doctors had explained to them that it was a progressive illness that would eventually leave her severely impaired, bedridden, and unable to walk. Hopefully that would be a long way off.

For two years before that, Audrey had helped take care of her father during the advancing stages of his illness until he died. As a result, she had developed an unusual seriousness and maturity for her age, and seemed much older now than her eighteen years. She had spent five years nursing her parents, which had ultimately affected her life choices. Her social life had become almost nonexistent while her parents were ill. She had no time to see friends, and rarely dated. While her classmates were having fun during their high school years, Audrey had to be responsible far beyond her true age, and act as support system and unofficial nurse. Her only distraction was the books she read, which kept her from being lonely and provided an escape from the daily realities she faced. She was graduating from high school in a week and was starting nursing school in September. She'd never had a lifetime ambition to become a nurse, but knowing the long, slow degenerative process her mother had ahead of her, Audrey wanted to be able to help her and take care of her, and hopefully extend her mother's life.

She had no resentment for the years she had already spent first helping with her father's care, and then her mother's. She'd given up a great deal for them, her ballet classes, sports, parties, and hanging out with other girls. She'd only been on a few dates, had nervously gone to senior prom, and worried so much about leaving her mother home alone that she had apologized to her date and left early. He'd been nice about it at the time but didn't call her again. For a girl of eighteen, Audrey had already sacrificed a lot for her parents, accepted it as her duty to them, and didn't resent it.

She was a pretty girl with a slim figure, long dark hair, and a delicate face. Her sky-blue eyes were serious, as she kept an eye on her mother, worried that she would fall and hurt herself. It had happened a few times, and they all knew it would happen again. It was the nature of her illness, which had advanced slowly but steadily in the past few years.

Audrey had grown up in Annapolis, a pretty town on the Chesapeake Bay. Her father had taken her and her brother sailing on weekends, and now she and Will sometimes went out in their small sailboat alone. She trusted him completely, and they were both good sailors. She looked up to him as her hero, and he provided her with the only distraction she engaged in, sailing and going to dinner with him occasionally. He brought her magazines and little gifts. She had adored him since they were children. He teased her and made her laugh, which made their burdens seem lighter to Audrey. She thought he was the perfect big brother.

Audrey had a few friends at school, but there was little time to spend with them since she always rushed home after school to help her mother. The friendships dwindled away as a result. She would have liked to spend time with her old girlfriends, but her life was one of responsibility and duty, which left no time for anything else. She was an excellent student. Her mother had been startled and touched when she decided to go to nursing school. Audrey had a gentle nature and a very nurturing side, which made nursing appeal to her, even beyond her mother's illness. Whatever her motivation for going, Ellen thought she'd make an excellent nurse one day. She had a natural gift for medicine, and caring for others.

Audrey was sad that her brother would be going away for basic flight training. She loved having him nearby. He made everything seem lighter to her when she saw him. He lived in the dorms, but came home frequently to have a meal with her and their mother, or to take Audrey out for an hour. All of that was going to change now. After basic training, he'd be stationed somewhere else. She felt as though their days as a family were over. In a sense, Will had become her only friend. His leaving was going to be a loss and hardship for her.

She tried not to think of it as she helped her mother dress for the graduation ceremony. Ellen looked lovely in her blue-gray silk suit, and sat waiting on the couch in the living room for Audrey to dress hurriedly. She was wearing a red cotton suit, and was unaware of how beautiful she looked as she helped her mother stand and walk to the front door with her awkward halting gait. She held her mother's arm firmly, helped her into the car, and drove them to the Yard, which was what everyone called the campus. Audrey had recently gotten her driver's license and was a careful driver. She was responsible in all things, and enjoyed driving and the sense of freedom it gave her. She felt very grown up at the wheel of the family car. Both women were smiling as they took their places and waited for the graduation to begin.

When he appeared in the procession of graduating students, Will looked as tall and handsome as their father had been: six feet four, with straight blond hair that was neatly trimmed, and broad shoulders. He was wearing his dress white uniform. He was graduating with honors, which was no surprise to either of them. The graduates marched in while the Annapolis band played. President Roosevelt was the commencement speaker, and there were several other speeches. The diplomas were handed out, after which, as dictated by tradition, all the graduates threw their hats in the air in jubilation, clapped each other on the back, and there was a brief moment of pandemonium. The ceremony ended when they all sang "Navy Blue and Gold," and Audrey saw that her mother was crying. It was an emotional moment for both of them, and William was beaming when he came to find them afterwards.

He promised to meet up with his friends again later in the day and helped walk his mother to the car in the parking lot. He drove them to Reynolds Tavern, where there were graduates having lunch with their families at almost every table.

Ellen couldn't believe how quickly Will's Annapolis years had sped past them. His father had died during Will's freshman year, and the next three years had been a blur to Ellen, and to Audrey too, while she worried about her mother and learned how to care for her and address her increasing needs. And soon Will would be a navy pilot. He was twenty-two years old, and looked every inch like what an Annapolis graduate should look like. He was the perfect all-American boy. Tall, ramrod straight, a powerful athlete with a bright mind, broad smile, and kind heart. In Ellen and Audrey's eyes, he was the perfect son and brother, and his father would have been proud of him too.

He drove them home after lunch, and Audrey could see that he was eager to meet up with his friends again. They all had plans for that night, and she knew that Will would be seeing the girl he had been dating most recently. She was a beautiful local girl, but he wasn't serious about her. Will loved to have fun, and he had big plans that centered more around airplanes than women for the moment. He'd always had an easy time meeting women, but he was careful not to get too deeply involved. His father had warned him about that. Will wanted a career in the navy, and he had years ahead of him before he'd want to settle down. Several of his classmates were already engaged, and there were a number of weddings planned in the next few months. Will thought that at their age, it would be more of a burden than an asset. He had no interest in marriage for the next many years. He couldn't wait to start flight school and was excited to become a lieutenant eventually. This was only the first step in what he hoped would be a long, distinguished career like his father's and grandfather's. There had been talk of tensions rising in Europe, and a possible war coming, but even if there was one, they were certain the United States would never get into it. They had learned that lesson once, with the last war. Never again.

It was four in the afternoon when Will left them. He told his mother he'd be home late, and not to worry about him. There were half a dozen parties he knew about and wanted to go to. He had waited a lifetime for this day and was determined to enjoy it to the fullest. Audrey was sure he'd come home drunk, but he'd try not to wake them. It had been a beautiful day, and she smiled when Will kissed her on the cheek and left a few minutes later. For an instant, she envied him the freedom he would have now. It was so different being a man. He could do whatever he wanted, and always would. She had so much less independence as a woman, and it would have been that way even if her mother wasn't sick. As a young single girl, Audrey's life was much more restricted than Will's. And even one day if she married, she would never have the freedom her brother did. He could go and do and be whatever he chose. The same opportunities weren't available to women.

She and her mother had a quiet dinner at the kitchen table that night. Her mother looked exhausted by the emotions and exertions of the day, and she was grateful when Audrey helped her up the stairs and put her to bed at eight o'clock. She was asleep minutes later, and Audrey went to her own room, listening to the silence in the house. She could hear a dog barking in the distance and a car honking. She could imagine the graduates going from party to party that night, celebrating. Their graduation from Annapolis was a huge accomplishment and an important rite of passage. Audrey knew that nothing in her life would ever be like that, neither her own high school graduation in a week, nor her graduation from nursing school in three years, which would be a quiet, ladylike event. Annapolis was a very, very big deal, and would win Will the respect of his peers and superiors for the rest of his life. Nothing Audrey had achieved, or ever would, would compare to it, in her eyes or the eyes of others. She knew how much it had meant to her mother. She'd been smiling when she fell asleep. Will had done it. He had fulfilled their father's dream. Will had known what was expected of him ever since he was a small child. He had never wavered for an instant. The navy was going to be his life, and planes his passion. The navy was what their family did, and what was expected of him.

Will went to Audrey's high school graduation, just as she had gone to his at Annapolis. He had stood tall and proud and handsome in his uniform, and had taken care of their mother while Audrey went through the ritual of getting her diploma. Her mother wasn't well that day, and she wasn't up to lunch. She had nearly fallen twice on their way into the auditorium, and they went home right after the ceremony so their mother could lie down. Audrey said she didn't mind, but Will felt bad that there was no celebration for her. She hardly had time to say goodbye to her friends before she had to rush off to help her mother. The other girls were going out to lunch with their families, as they had with Will, but Ellen was too frail and unsteady for a restaurant that day. The other girls were kind to her when she left hurriedly, but Audrey knew she was already an outsider, and had been for years, being stuck at home with her mother so much of the time. It was a sacrifice Audrey had made willingly, which Will admired her for.

Will spoke to her quietly after she took a tray of food up to their mother's room, and he found her in the kitchen in her frilly white dress, with daisies braided into her hair. She looked innocent and young, and as though she didn't have a care in the world. Audrey had a way of putting a positive spin on everything. There was nothing mournful about her.

"Are you okay?" he asked her gently, and she nodded with a smile. He couldn't help noticing how beautiful she was, and he hoped she would have a more exciting life one day. "I'm sorry we didn't get to take you to lunch," he said, and genuinely meant it.

"It's fine, I don't mind." She looked unruffled and peaceful. "Mom hasn't felt well for the past few days. I don't think her new medicine is working." They had tried everything available to them, but none of the medications for Parkinson's really worked for her.

"I worry about you after I leave," Will said softly. He wanted her to have a life, but their mother was so ill.

"We'll be fine," she reassured him. They had already arranged for a nurse to check on her mother twice a day after Audrey started nursing school. Their father had carefully set aside savings for them for years, and they had his pension, so they had enough for all their needs, a nice home, and for Audrey's school. "I'm going to miss you, but you can't sit here for the rest of your life," Audrey said to him fairly, and they both knew it was true. The days of being all to-gether and having Will near at hand were over. He was a grown-up now, soon to be a navy pilot. That sounded very grown up to her, and to Will. Their father had hoped Will would be the captain of a ship one day, and that his boyhood passion for airplanes would fade. But planes were where Will's heart was, and he intended to live his dream to the fullest. And both his mother and sister wanted him to.

He also knew that eventually taking care of their mother would become too much for Audrey to manage on her own, but that time hadn't come yet, and he hoped it wouldn't for a long time, for all their sakes. It saddened him profoundly to see how his mother's health had degenerated, and how much more hampered she was every year. He thought it noble of Audrey to go to nursing school so she could care for Ellen more efficiently, but it was so typical of Audrey. She was always doing for others and willing to sacrifice herself for them. She had given up her youth to do so, and never complained. To Audrey, the glass was always half full, and she met every challenge with love and enthusiasm, which filled Will with admiration for her, and gratitude.

Two weeks after Audrey's graduation, Will left for Florida to begin basic training. He had no time to call them regularly, so communi-cation from him was sporadic, but he sounded ecstatic, almost eu-phoric, whenever they did hear from him. He loved what he was doing, and everything he was learning about flying planes. His dream had come true.

Ellen tried to encourage Audrey to spend time with her old school friends in July and August, to catch up with them, and not lose touch entirely, but many of them were traveling with their families, or had gone to their summer homes, and wouldn't be back until after Labor Day. A few had gotten married right after graduation. And she planned to call one or two to see them in the fall. In the meantime, she was used to keeping busy on her own, and was good at it, with her books and errands for her mother.

Audrey swam at a country club they belonged to, when she could get her mother to go with her. She even got Ellen into the pool a few times, which made her mother feel better afterwards. Audrey gave her mother long gentle massages, and they even managed to go shopping a few times to get her some things she needed for school. As August ended and September began, Audrey was excited about the adventure ahead of her with nursing school. It wasn't going to be as dazzling as Will's, learning to fly fighter planes. He had started with an N3N Canary, a "Yellow Peril," as he called it. It was a biplane built by the navy, and he had graduated to more sophisticated planes by the end of the summer. The navy's goal was to "train superb pilots."

But Audrey was excited by what lay ahead for her too. It wasn't just a training course to learn how to care for her mother. She would be a real nurse, if she chose to be, and was looking forward to the people she would meet in the process. This would no longer be just a bunch of silly kids in high school. These would be serious young women with career goals.

She was impressed by how mature they seemed on the first day of school. They were going to spend much of the first term in the classroom, which Will did during his flight training too, learning about aerodynamics and the complicated calculations he had to know how to make. And even during their first term, Audrey would be meeting and dealing with real patients under close supervision.

On Audrey's first day of classes, she glanced around the room and saw half a dozen girls she would have liked to meet. They all looked older than she was and seemed very sophisticated to her. She suddenly felt small and inexperienced at life. She felt like she might have a panic attack as she observed the girl sitting next to her. She was beautiful and seemed so poised and adult. She was wearing a gray wool skirt, a white blouse, and plain, simple black high heels. She looked more like a secretary in an office than a nursing student. She had blond hair and big blue eyes. There was a halo of soft curls near her face, and her hair was pulled back tightly in a bun. Audrey was wearing an old navy blue suit of her mother's that Ellen had loaned her when she'd turned sixteen and needed something to wear when her school took them to a performance of *Swan Lake* in Baltimore. Her mother had let her keep the suit afterwards. She was wearing a small string of pearls her mother had just given her when she turned eighteen, as a symbol of her adulthood. The pearls said she was no longer a girl but a woman.

Audrey glanced sideways at her neighbor, who smiled at her. They didn't speak to each other until the first break, and then she turned to Audrey with a warm look.

"Hi, I'm Lizzie Hatton. From Boston. Where are you from?" Some of the girls were local, but many weren't, like Lizzie.

"Here. I've lived here all my life," Audrey said shyly.

"Everyone in my family is a doctor or nurse. I didn't get in to nursing school in Boston, so I wound up here." She seemed mildly embarrassed as she said it. Her grades had slipped a little during senior year. She was having too much fun and didn't really care about nursing school. She mentioned that she was living in the dorm.

"Mine are all sailors," Audrey said with a grin. "My father was a captain, my grandfather was a vice admiral, and my brother is a navy pilot."

"That sounds interesting. What does your mom do?" Lizzie was intrigued by Audrey, who seemed very self-possessed, cool and collected, much more so than Lizzie felt.

"Nothing. She's sick. But she didn't work before that."

"Mine is a nurse. My father's a doctor, and so are my grandfather and uncle. My older brother is in medical school at Yale, and my younger brother is premed at BU. I wanted to go to medical school too, and they had a fit. According to my father, it's fine for a woman to be a nurse, but not a doctor. I told him that's an antiquated point of view. All they really want me to do is get married and have babies. They think nursing school is a suitable activity while I look for a husband." Lizzie looked annoyed as she said it.

"Is that what your mom did?" Audrey asked her.

"More or less, but she doesn't put it that way. After they got married, she helped in my father's office until she had us. She quit when my older brother Greg was born. Now she volunteers at a hospital twice a week. She's a Gray Lady with the Red Cross."

"Why wouldn't they let you go to med school?" That sounded puzzling to Audrey. She thought Lizzie was an interesting girl. And she was excited to be talking to someone her age. She hadn't had time for a close friend since her parents got sick.

"They said it takes too many years of study for a woman to become a doctor, and men don't want to marry women who work or have a career. That's probably true. So maybe we'll wind up spinsters after we're nurses," she said, laughing. There was something bright and bold about Lizzie that Audrey liked.

"But your father married your mother, and she was a nurse."

"I don't think she ever intended it as a career forever," Lizzie admitted. "Just until she married."

"I'm here to learn how to take better care of my mother. She has Parkinson's," Audrey confided in her. She was enjoying the exchange and confidences immensely.

"That's serious," Lizzie commented. "So you're not going to work as a nurse after you graduate?" That seemed too limited to Lizzie. It did to Audrey too, when she said it out loud. Her life of dedication to her mother was hard to explain, and what her father had left them meant she didn't have to work, as long as they were careful. Neither Audrey nor her mother were extravagant.

"I'll have to decide when I graduate. It will depend on how my mother is by then." They knew her condition would continue to deteriorate in the coming years.

They had lunch in the cafeteria together and met several of the other girls. Lizzie was nineteen, a year older than Audrey, and several of the girls were a few years older than they were. As it turned out, Audrey was the youngest in the group. A few of them were the daughters of doctors, like Lizzie, or their mothers were nurses. Medicine seemed to run in families, from what Audrey observed.

She didn't tell anyone else that her mother was sick. Lizzie seemed particularly confident while meeting their fellow students, and all the girls were excited about meeting each other and making friends.

Audrey rushed home when classes ended, to see her mother. Mrs. Beavis, the nurse they'd hired, had come twice that day, as promised, to check on Ellen and make her lunch. Ellen was happy to see Audrey at the end of the day and asked her all about school. Nothing earth-shattering had happened so far. They'd been given a book on hospital protocols. They had to learn the basic instruments for surgery for an appendectomy by the next day. Eventually they would know all the instruments and rules.

"I think I'd like to be an OR nurse," Lizzie had said earlier, after they'd been given the assignment.

"I'd be too afraid to make a mistake," Audrey said nervously. "Maybe pediatrics, if I'm not taking care of my mother," she'd said softly, because that would mean her mother had died. There were no cures for Parkinson's, and she wasn't going to get better, only worse. Audrey intended to be at her side as long as she lived.

Ellen had had a better day, and cooked dinner for Audrey and herself that night. It was almost like the old days before she got sick, except she looked so frail now. Audrey told her about Lizzie and her medical family, and Ellen enjoyed hearing about her day. Some of Ellen's old friends dropped by to see her once in a while, but she had little to occupy her, and how well she felt varied from day to day. Sometimes she could go out with Audrey to do errands, or even have lunch at a restaurant. At other times, she could hardly get out of bed. The effect of the medicine she took was erratic. Everything they used to treat Parkinson's seemed so experimental.

Walking was hard for her. She had developed an unsteady gait of tiny short steps and had to use all her energy to propel herself forward. It had been shocking for Audrey and Will to see how she had deteriorated in the past two and a half years. They had thought it was psychological at first, a reaction to their father's death, until she was diagnosed with Parkinson's. The prognosis and the fact that nothing could be done about it was devastating. There had been some progressive treatments used in France, but they had not proved effective. Surgical interventions had been attempted in some cases, but they had not made any great improvement in the patients either. Ellen simply had to live with it as best she could.

She was brave about it, and Audrey was determined to do all she could to improve the quality of her mother's life and support her. Ellen's care fell to Audrey, not to Will, who was expected to embark on his naval career as soon as he graduated. That had always been the plan, and his mother's illness didn't change that. But it changed everything for Audrey, who had hoped to go to college, but now nursing school seemed like a wiser course and would help her be more useful to her mother. Audrey intended to apply herself and learn all she could.

For Lizzie Hatton, nursing school was second best, and seemed like a poor consolation prize instead of going to medical school like her brothers. But it cheered her to have met Audrey. After the first two weeks of classes, Audrey invited her to their home for Sunday night dinner. Ellen thought her a lovely young woman. After the two girls cleaned up the kitchen after dinner, they went to Audrey's bedroom to talk and giggle, like other girls their age. Audrey thoroughly enjoyed her budding friendship with Lizzie. And Lizzie had loved being in a real home for an evening. She came from a close-knit family, and she missed them, particularly her two older brothers, Greg and Henry, who teased her relentlessly when they were home. She enjoyed the warm welcome that Audrey and her mother extended her.

She noticed a photograph of Will in his uniform on Audrey's desk, and looked at it closely.

"Wow! He's gorgeous. Who is that, your boyfriend?" Audrey laughed.

"I've never had a boyfriend." She grinned at her new friend. "That's Will, my brother."

"Where is he now?" Lizzie asked.

"He's in flight training. They're sending him to Nevada or New Mexico or somewhere now for combat training, and then to Hawaii to learn to land on aircraft carriers."

"Does he have a girlfriend?"

"No. He's in love with the planes he flies. It's all he thinks about. My father was that way about ships. For Will, it's planes. I miss him." She looked wistful for a moment, and then smiled at her friend. She wondered for an instant if Will would be attracted to Lizzie if he met her, or if he'd think she was too young because she was a friend of his little sister. But Lizzie was a strikingly pretty girl, with her soft blond curls and sky-blue eyes. She was taller than Audrey, and she had a perfect figure. She was athletic and had played a lot of sports with her brothers when she was younger. Women had always been drawn to Will, and he had dated a lot of pretty girls in high school, and while he attended Annapolis, but it was never serious with him. Flying was all-important to him, and he had no intention of letting a relationship interfere with that, at least not for a long time.

In their first year of nursing school, Lizzie and Audrey learned a great deal about their future profession. Both were good students, and they helped each other study for exams. They began working with actual patients in the first few months and were proud of their white student uniforms. After three months they received their first starched caps. They both took their studies seriously.

Lizzie invited Audrey home to Boston for a weekend during spring break. Audrey had hesitated, not wanting to leave her mother, but Mrs. Beavis had agreed to stay with her for two days. Ellen's condition had been stable for a while, but she caught a bad cold, and it had laid her low for more than a month. She had lost strength and some mobility afterwards. Whenever she got sick, the symptoms of her disease got slightly worse.

By the summer, after Audrey's first year of nursing school, Ellen was well enough to go away to the seaside with Audrey for a week, which raised her spirits. Will got leave and joined them for part of it. It was wonderful being together again.

Lizzie went home for the summer, to stay at her family's summer home in Maine. Both girls came back to Annapolis at the end of August feeling rested and ready to start their second year of nursing school. They were assigned to the hospital and were usually on different rotations. Audrey spent a month in the maternity ward, while Lizzie went to orthopedics, followed by a stint in pediatrics, including the nursery. By then Audrey had done a rotation in the TB ward. Their training exposed them to all the specialties, and once they graduated, they would have the choice of working in a hospital, a doctor's office, or private-duty nursing, which was essentially what Audrey did for her mother. She had learned some additional treatments and techniques to make her mother more comfortable, which Ellen was grateful for. She was impressed by how much Audrey had learned.

Lizzie was in particularly good spirits when she returned to Annapolis and moved back into the dorm of the nursing school. She'd had a brief but fun summer romance with the older brother of an old friend. He was working at a summer job in Boston and came to his family's home in Maine on weekends. It wasn't serious, and they had both agreed that long-distance relationships were too hard so they didn't try to prolong it. He was going into his senior year at Dartmouth, and was planning to work for a bank when he graduated. He was a nice boy and they'd spent some good times together, even if the romance didn't have a future.

Lizzie wasn't absolutely sure that she wanted to go back to Boston when she graduated, and she talked to Audrey sometimes about going to work in New York if she could find a job there. She wanted to see more of the world than just Boston. She talked about California too, but that seemed like it was on another planet, and for now she had nursing school to finish in Annapolis, before she made any big decisions about her future. Audrey admired her spirit of adventure. Lizzie always said that if her parents wouldn't let her pursue the career path she really wanted as a doctor, they couldn't keep her tied to Boston forever too. The life she would have there would be entirely predictable: a job as a nurse in a hospital or a doctor's office, a husband as soon as she could find one, and children immediately thereafter. She wanted more out of life than that. Her options seemed numerous to Audrey, whose future would be even narrower, living at home and caring for her mother.

Neither of the girls had a revolutionary spirit. They were expected to follow their family traditions. They talked about it sometimes late at night, when Lizzie spent the night at the Parkers' and they talked about their futures. Lizzie didn't want a life entirely designed for her by her parents. They had already stopped her from doing the one thing she wanted: medical school. She wanted a voice in the rest, to make her own decisions.

The week they started their second-year classes in nursing school, war was declared in Europe. Both girls followed it with interest, with the reassurance from the White House that America would not be drawn into it. President Roosevelt assured the American public that they would not participate in another war in Europe. But it was concerning anyway, to read about what was happening. Will came home on leave at Thanksgiving, and said he was sorry America was determined not to get involved. The country didn't want to engage in another war. He was still an ensign. He had had some combat training by then, and he would have loved to engage in the war in Europe.

Lizzie was spending Thanksgiving with them, with her parents' permission. She was in awe of Will when she met him. Tall, handsome, glamorous, exciting. At twenty-three, in his uniform, he looked like a movie star to her. She was twenty and a very pretty girl, but he treated her no differently than he did his younger sister, teasing them both like children. Ellen and Audrey were thrilled to see him. He had just been transferred to the Naval Air Station in San Diego, California, and he loved it there. He volunteered no information about his love life and answered none of his sister's questions on the subject. But it was easy to guess that he was dating all the girls he wanted and had time for. Flying remained the love of his life and was his main focus. He was flying a North American SNJ by then. It was a single-engine fighter trainer. It had two seats, one for the pilot and the other for an instructor. It was a thrill to fly and Will loved flying it.

He had a quiet, serious conversation with Audrey about their mother before he left on Sunday night to return to his base. It had been a warm, easygoing family weekend, and Lizzie loved being part of it. The Parkers seemed to get along better than she did with her parents, although she was very close to her brothers.

While he was there, Will had noticed that their mother could no longer get out of a sitting position without help. Her arms seemed weaker, and walking had become even more difficult for her. Audrey had to go into the bathroom with her, and bathe her, to make sure she didn't fall. Her muscles had gotten weaker, but her mind was sharp and clear.

"How do you think Mom really is?" he asked with deep concern. It was sad to see her slipping deeper into her illness, and less able to do things for herself. He could see the life his sister had in store for her. Audrey never complained about it. They both wanted their mother to live for many years, but sooner or later, Audrey's whole life would center around their mother, and caring for her. The skills she had acquired in nursing school were already serving her well.

"It's pretty much what you see. She's going to have to be in a wheelchair all the time soon. She can hardly walk, and she falls a lot." She had fallen out of her wheelchair just that morning in the safety of her bedroom. Audrey was wondering when they would have to move her to the only downstairs bedroom, Will's old room, because she couldn't negotiate the stairs. "She still tries to do as much as she can for herself, but she's lost a lot of muscle control in her hands this year," Audrey said as gently as she could. She knew it was hard for her brother to see Ellen like this.

"She's lucky she has you," he said in a choked voice. They'd been told that eventually even her breathing would be affected, and a cold could kill her if it turned into pneumonia, which it easily could.

"We just have to do everything we can for her, for as long as we can. In a year and a half, I'll have finished nursing school, and I can be home with her all the time." Now that she was in it, she loved nursing school, and everything it had taught her, about more than just caring for her mother. It felt like the right calling for her, just as flying was for Will. She had discovered a passion for nursing, unlike Lizzie, who still wished she could become a doctor, not just a nurse. But Lizzie was enjoying school too, more than she'd expected to, and her friendship with Audrey made it even better for both of them.

"You'll tell me if you ever think I need to come home to see her . . . if . . . if she gets really bad . . ." Will said. Audrey knew he was afraid of her dying without him seeing her again.

"Of course," Audrey said, and they hugged each other, knowing that one day, maybe not too far off, they would each be all the other had. It was heartbreaking to think about.

Ellen cried when Will left that night, and Will and Audrey had tears in their eyes. Lizzie had gone back to the dorm at the nursing school by then. She'd been totally dazzled by Will and was frustrated that she could tell he considered her a child. She felt like one with him. She wanted him to think of her as a femme fatale. He lived in a far more adult world than they did, in the sleepy safety of his hometown. Being a navy pilot had opened up new worlds to him, and he had the life that most young men dreamed of: freedom, flying fabulous fighter planes, the envy and admiration of his peers, and all the girls he wanted. True to the times and their circumstances, his life was very different from his sister's dutiful, dedicated existence, devoted to caring for their invalid mother. But luckily for Audrey, she had discovered her passion. She loved everything about nursing. Being able to use it for her mother was an additional gift now, but no longer her only reason for going to nursing school. She had found her calling and her niche. The moment she put her uniform and cap on, she came alive. Just like Will when he got into his plane and took to the skies.

Chapter 2

B oth Lizzie and Audrey were shocked by how fast the time had flown when they graduated. Three years had sped by. Audrey was twenty-one, and Lizzie twenty-two, and suddenly they were actually nurses and grown women, in proper pale blue uniforms and starched white caps that identified them by their school. They had gotten their nursing pins when they got their diplomas at their graduation ceremony. But little had changed in their lives, despite being nurses now. Lizzie had dated an assortment of young men, rarely more than a few times. Many of the girls she'd gone to high school with had gotten married, some had had their first babies. Lizzie didn't feel ready for any of it. She wanted to live a little before she settled down. She had finally finished school, and she wanted to enjoy life and have some fun after three years of intense studies. As usual, before she could come up with a plan for herself for after graduation, her father had done it for her. He secured a job for her at Massachusetts General Hospital in Boston, where he hospitalized his patients and operated. She hadn't settled on a specialty yet, so he had gotten her a job in a female post-surgical ward, which he thought would be good experience for her. She knew he expected her to be grateful to him, but instead she was angry, and vented to Audrey right before graduation.

"They *always* do that to me, *always*! Both of them! They decide what's best for me, and that's the end of it. They don't even discuss it with me. I'm not a child anymore. I went to nursing school to make them happy, and I'm glad I did, because I met you, and nursing is a decent job, and as close to a medical career as I'm ever going to get. I'd rather do that than be a teacher or a secretary. But I wanted to apply for a job in New York, and without even asking me, my father got me a job in Boston. He doesn't do that to my brothers."

"Maybe he does," Audrey said gently. She felt sorry for her. Lizzie had her own ideas and wanted to be her own person. "Greg is a doctor, and Henry is in medical school. Maybe they didn't want to be doctors, and they did it for him," she suggested. "It's like Will. Nobody ever questioned that he would enlist in the navy. It was expected of him because of my father and grandfather. And if he couldn't fly planes in the navy, he'd be miserable. I don't think he gives a damn about ships, the way my father did."

"My parents have my whole life mapped out for me," Lizzie said angrily. "And just watch, if I'm not engaged in a year, they'll be having a fit. I have a nursing degree. Now they're going to want me to get married and have kids. It's what my mother did. Don't I ever get a voice in my own life?" She had tears in her eyes, but she knew that Audrey's lot was even harder, alone with her slowly dying mother, with no one to help her, and her only brother three thousand miles away, playing ace pilot in California. It seemed so unfair to Lizzie. "It's 1941, not 1910. Nothing ever changes for women. They say it does, but it doesn't. I should have gone to medical school, and to hell with it if my father had a fit." But she couldn't have paid for it, and her parents had paid for nursing school. Her father had refused to pay for medical school for her, only her brothers.

"Maybe you will one day," Audrey said, trying to calm her.

"Maybe I should find a job here, or in Baltimore. At least I'd be close to you. I'm going to miss you so damn much." They had been together constantly for three years. The tears spilled down Lizzie's cheeks then, and the two women hugged, thinking of their futures, which weren't what either of them wanted. Audrey had no choice. She wouldn't abandon her mother, and Lizzie couldn't fight her overpowering father, and her mother agreed with whatever he wanted. Their entire family followed his lead in all things. Her brothers never challenged him either. Neither had she so far. She was due to start the job he'd found for her in Boston in two weeks. They expected her to live at home, which was what proper young women did. She would have liked to get her own apartment, possibly with some other nurses, but she knew her parents would never let her do it. She would be living under their roof until she married. And Audrey had to live with her mother anyway. She hadn't applied for any nursing jobs. She had her life cut out for her too. She would be at home, nursing her mother.

Ellen was entirely aware of the sacrifices Audrey made, and grateful for them. She stunned Audrey with the graduation present she offered her. She told her about it the night before graduation.

"I want you to make plans for a vacation, Audrey," she told her firmly. "I'll pay for you and a friend. I want you to fly to Hawaii. I've already spoken to Will about it, he is stationed in Hawaii now and loves it. He says he can take some leave to escort you around. I assume you'll want to take Lizzie, but that's up to you. I want you to have a real vacation, in a beautiful place. And not sometime in the distant future that never happens. Figure it out. Mrs. Beavis can stay with me for a week or ten days. I already asked her and she agreed. And you go kick up your heels. You've earned it. I'm very proud of you for getting your nursing degree, especially since I know you did it for me. But now it's *your* turn. So figure out when. You can fly to California from New York, and from there to Oahu on Pan Am. I've already put the money aside for the trip, and I won't take no for an answer!" Audrey looked at her in astonishment, and rushed to the phone to call Lizzie in her dorm and tell her about it.

"And you're coming with me!" Audrey said, talking a mile a minute. "It's my graduation gift, and she's paying for me to take a friend. And you're it. So find out when the hospital will let you take a week off. And Will said he'll arrange to take leave then, and he'll escort us around."

"Oh my God, I can't believe it. I would die to go there," and to spend a week with Audrey's brother, which Audrey suspected. He had never shown anything more than brotherly interest in Lizzie, but she hoped that maybe now that she'd graduated, he would treat her like a grown woman. And whether he did or not, she couldn't wait to go somewhere exotic and tropical like Hawaii. It was an incredibly generous gift, and even more so because Mrs. Parker wanted Audrey to take a friend with her.

Both girls were dreaming of it when they went to sleep that night. And graduation the next day was deeply emotional. Will hadn't been able to come, since he was in an advanced combat training program for two weeks that he couldn't get out of. And Ellen made a heroic effort to see her daughter graduate. She had to be strapped into her wheelchair so she wouldn't fall out, and Mrs. Beavis came with them. Audrey suspected it might be the last time her mother would be able to leave the house, but Ellen wasn't going to miss her daughter's graduation any more than she would have missed Will's from Annapolis three years before. Nothing, and no illness, was going to deprive her of this moment. She was profoundly proud of Audrey, who had passed her exams at the top of her class, with Lizzie not far behind her. Ellen had come to love her too, as a dear girl and a wonderful friend to Audrey, her *only* friend. The two young women were a staunch support to each other.

Lizzie's parents had come to the graduation with both her brothers. Her father looked stern and proud as he watched her graduate, and her mother had tears in her eyes when Lizzie accepted her nursing pin and diploma. It brought back memories of her own graduation.

Lizzie told her parents about the invitation to Hawaii right after the ceremony, and was still elated at the prospect.

"We'll see," her mother said quietly. "We'll talk about it." Her response hit Lizzie like a bucket of cold water, and she stopped and stared at her mother. They were not going to do this to her again,

31

infantilize her and tell her what she could and couldn't do. She was a grown woman.

"No, Mother, we won't 'talk about it.' I'm going. I don't know when yet, I'll have to figure that out at work, but I've been invited and I'm going." There was iron in her voice, and both her parents could hear it. It was a new side of her they had never seen before.

"That's a long way to go, and you'd be two girls alone," her mother said, looking nervous.

"It sounds fantastic to me, and Audrey's brother will take leave and chaperone us. I'm going," she said, and turned away then, as her brother Henry winked at her.

"You tell 'em, Sis," he whispered, and she nodded. They negotiated with their mother, but none of them ever stood up to their father. Henry had wanted to study architecture but was continuing medical school in the fall instead. Only Greg really wanted a medical career, and he had been influenced by their father to go into orthopedics instead of pediatrics, because orthopedic surgery was more lucrative. Benjamin Hatton, their father, was a force to be reckoned with. But Lizzie wasn't going to let anyone take her vacation with Audrey away from her. It was the most exciting thing that had ever happened to her, and a chance to spend a week with a dazzling guy she'd had a crush on for two years. Whatever happened, nothing could induce her to miss it.

The two girls introduced their parents to each other. The Hattons were touched when they met Ellen, and saw how ill she was, and how proud she was of her daughter. It gave them a deeper insight into Audrey. Ellen was happy to meet them, and elated over Lizzie's graduation too.

Lizzie left for Boston with her family that night, after three years in Annapolis, and her parting from Audrey and her mother was a tearful one. Audrey had never felt as alone in her life as she did after Lizzie left. She was the best friend Audrey had ever had, and Audrey was even more grateful to her mother for the fabulous graduation trip she had offered them. She couldn't wait to see Will when they went. He hadn't been home in months. Hawaii was a long way away and he was busy flying planes all the time now.

Lizzie's job at Massachusetts General Hospital was as boring as she had feared it would be. The post-op female ward was full of women who had had hysterectomies or other procedures that weren't very interesting medically, and most of the time it felt like maid service to Lizzie. She had a knack for diagnosis, and got no opportunity to use it in her current job. A week after she started, she explained to her supervisor that she had a long-standing "family obligation" in Hawaii, and had to fly there for about a week sometime in the near future. They weren't delighted at the idea, but agreed to give her the time as unpaid vacation in November, before Thanksgiving. They asked her to work on Thanksgiving Day to compensate for it, as a goodwill gesture, so someone else could have the day off. She readily agreed. She called Audrey immediately and told her. Ellen was as excited as they were. She had wanted to do something special for Audrey, knowing full well how much her daughter did for her, and how much Audrey sacrificed taking care of her full-time. It wasn't a fulfilling or happy life for a young girl, but she did it gladly for her mother. Audrey was thrilled at the prospect of such a generous vacation with her best friend, and the chance to spend a week with Will.

They made their plans and booked their flights on United from New York to San Francisco, and on Pan Am from San Francisco to Honolulu. It made the most sense to leave from New York, and Lizzie and Audrey were going to meet there on Thursday night, November sixth, the night before they left on their big adventure. Just flying Pan Am was going to be an extraordinary luxury for both of them, but Ellen had insisted. Neither she nor Audrey spent much money, and they weren't frivolous, but this time, Ellen wanted to go all out, to give her an unforgettable vacation as her graduation present. They were flying west on Friday, November seventh, and flying back on Sunday, November sixteenth to San Francisco, and to New York on Monday. Lizzie could go back to work at the hospital in Boston the day after, and Audrey would take the train to Baltimore the night they landed in New York.

Will had suggested they stay at the Royal Hawaiian Hotel in Honolulu, and he was taking the week off so he could shepherd them around. He was looking forward to it too. The girls were going to be flying into gorgeous warm weather on a lush tropical island, and they shopped for it accordingly in their respective cities. They needed shorts and bathing suits, sundresses and sandals, and some pretty, lightweight dresses to wear out to dinner. Both girls arrived in New York with a suitcase full of their new summery wardrobes.

They met at the Hudson Hotel, an all-female hotel their parents approved of. They spent the night in New York on Thursday night, giggling with excitement about the trip, and called Ellen to tell her that all was going smoothly so far. The next morning, on Friday, they took a bus to LaGuardia Airport, and boarded the United flight to San Francisco, for the first leg of their trip. They were going to spend the night at the Fairmont Hotel, and catch the plane to Honolulu the next day.

They both noticed the very attractive stewards on the United flight. They looked more like movie stars to the young nurses. And there was a stewardess on the flight, who told them she was a nurse when they chatted with her.

"We should have done that," Lizzie said to Audrey in a whisper after the stewardess walked by in her trim uniform, with her matching hat. She looked like a model.

"Done what?" Audrey asked her.

"Become stewardesses. I heard recently that they have to be nurses. And I can tell you that she's having a lot more fun than I am on the post-op ward, and their uniforms are way cuter."

Audrey laughed. "I'd have to have a complete makeover. She looks like she came from a modeling agency. No one in our class at nursing school looked like that," she reminded Lizzie.

"You'd look great in the hat and uniform. I don't know why I never thought of that. This looks like a fun job."

"It's probably harder than it looks," Audrey said practically. But it certainly did look glamorous. Audrey knew she couldn't have left her mother and done it. This was the first time in six years she'd been away from Ellen for more than a day or two, and it had taken meticulous planning to make sure that she'd be cared for by a nurse for the entire time. Mrs. Beavis was taking no time off while Audrey was gone.

Audrey loved the sensation of flying, and looking down at the scenery below, even though the flight was turbulent for some of the time. Neither of the girls was afraid, although several passengers were. The service was impeccable, and the food delicious. Audrey and Lizzie chatted with the stewardess again during the flight, and said that they were nurses too. The United stewardess said how much she loved her job. She said she had never needed her nurse's training in the year she'd worked for United. The medical issues she tended to were minor, like an infant with an earache, or helping someone who was airsick. But other than that, there had never been medical assistance required on her flights, although it could happen.

They said they were going to Honolulu, and Beth, the stewardess, told them how much they were going to love it and that it was a tropical paradise. She had been there once and said it was unforgettable.

"My brother's stationed there. He's a navy pilot," Audrey volunteered. "He loves it. I don't think he'll ever want to come back." They chatted for a few more minutes, and then Audrey and Lizzie went back to their seats for the remainder of the flight. Audrey read a book, and Lizzie went to sleep. They landed in San Francisco and took a cab to the Fairmont Hotel on Nob Hill. They had dinner at the hotel and went to bed early so they'd be fresh for their long flight to Honolulu the next day.

They boarded the Pan Am flight the next day, at Treasure Island, and were in awe when they saw the enormous Boeing 314 Clipper. It was the largest airliner of its time. Normally it could carry seventy-four passengers, but only carried twenty-five on the long flight to

Hawaii. All passengers traveled first class on the flight. There was a festive atmosphere as soon as they got on the plane. Other passengers were going on vacation too, and it was a delight to leave cold wintry weather, and head for bright sun and white sandy beaches. They could hardly wait to land. And in the meantime, the flight itself was memorable. The four stewards met their every need. The Clipper had an upper flight deck, a lower cabin divided into five seating compartments, a large lounge that converted into a dining room, and a bridal suite. The flight took sixteen hours and flew overnight.

The Clipper glided smoothly on the water when it landed on Sunday morning after the luxurious flight. They stopped in front of the terminal, and two beautiful Polynesian girls were waiting to give each passenger a flower lei. The sky was a bright cameo blue, the weather warm. It was dazzling. When Audrey looked up, she saw her brother walking toward her in his white summer uniform. He lifted her right off her feet when he hugged her, and he smiled when he saw Lizzie. Audrey noticed a look pass between them that was different from the way he had looked at her before. Lizzie's long blond hair hung down her back in gentle waves. She was wearing a light blue dress the color of her eyes, and the dress molded her figure without being vulgar. He walked both women out of the airport, looking proud.

He had brought a car to drive them to their hotel, which they hadn't expected. As soon as they checked in and put their bags in their room, he took them to the terrace for lunch, where they ordered drinks with umbrellas in them. They chatted and laughed all through lunch. Audrey and Lizzie had slept well on the flight so they weren't tired. Will was excited to be with them. He was attentive to his sister, but his eyes kept wandering toward Lizzie, and she basked in the warmth of his attention. She could sense how attracted he was to her, and he was no longer treating her like a child. His sister had grown up and so had Lizzie, and now they had a whole week to be together, and discover the wonders of Hawaii. He promised to take them on a tour of Honolulu and Ford Island, the base where he was stationed, the next day. He was flying in formation in an air show the following Saturday, the day before they left, so they would see him fly.

After lunch, Will had to go back to the base for a while, and Audrey and Lizzie went to change to go swimming. He promised to come back for dinner at the luau at the hotel that night.

Audrey lay on the beach with Lizzie that afternoon, unable to believe the fantastic experience they were having, thanks to her mother. Lizzie looked like she had stars in her eyes after lunch with Will. So far, the island paradise had lived up to its reputation, and Will had provided a warm welcome. Both girls giggled and laughed, talking about the days ahead as they lay on the beach.

"It's going to be a great week," Audrey said as she closed her eyes in the bright sun. And Lizzie lay silent and smiling, thinking of Will. She felt dizzy every time she thought of him. As they lay on the beach at Waikiki, the future had never looked brighter, or their dreams sweeter. Life couldn't have been more perfect.

Chapter 3

The Royal Hawaiian Hotel, where they were staying, was right on Waikiki Beach. Their room had a balcony, called a lanai, where they had breakfast the next morning, and then they went downstairs and took a long walk on the beach. By ten-thirty, they were lying in the sun, working on their suntans, and swimming in the surf. Then they went back to their room to shower and dress for lunch. For dinner that night, Lizzie borrowed one of Audrey's dresses, which she liked better than her own, although it was a little short for her. They both looked fresh and young and beautiful when Will met them in the lobby. He stayed late for drinks with them afterwards. He couldn't tear himself away. The girls stayed up late, but were up early for a swim in the morning. Will returned to take them to lunch at the Moana Hotel, and then drove them around the island, and stopped for them to admire the view from all the famous places. At the end of the afternoon, he took them to Ford Island Naval Base, where he lived. The harbor was full of navy ships, and there were sailors and officers in whites everywhere. The insignia on Will's uniform identified him as a pilot, which made him something of a star when others recognized it. He was the section leader of the formation he flew in.

"We don't have as many pilots as the Air Force," he boasted to his sister as he showed them around. "But we're better," he said, laughing. Audrey could tell he meant it. He had been a navy pilot for three years by then, almost three and a half, and was in advanced aircraft carrier flight training. He was twenty-five years old and so handsome he took Lizzie's breath away whenever she looked at him. He had been a perfect gentleman since they arrived, but there was something about the way he looked at her that told her that he liked her, more than just as his little sister's best friend.

He took them back to their hotel at the end of the day, and the three of them swam in the pool. He teased and played mostly with Lizzie, and chased her under water. At one point, she opened her eyes and looked at him, and they were both smiling. They were breathless when they came up for air and he gently put his arms around her.

"You've changed," he said softly to her.

"No, I haven't. I just grew up." He nodded and didn't say anything when they left the pool. He said he'd be back to take them to dinner. Audrey had noticed the exchange between them, and she wondered if Will was going to start something with Lizzie. He had never had a serious girlfriend before, not that she knew of. But he seemed very taken with Lizzie. Audrey knew that Lizzie had had a crush on him for years. She would have liked nothing better than for the two of them to fall in love with each other, but that seemed like a lot to hope for, with only a week's vacation together. But they were all having fun anyway.

Lizzie dressed carefully for dinner that night, and wore a strapless white dress that showed off her figure, with her blond hair in a neat bun, a string of pearls around her neck, and sexy high-heeled silver sandals. Audrey wore a turquoise silk dress that showed off the tan she'd started working on the day before. With her fair skin, Lizzie had to be more careful that she didn't burn. Audrey intended to be as tanned as she could get by the time they left.

They went to a small favorite restaurant of Will's that night, and afterwards he drove them to a lookout point on Diamond Head to admire the view in the moonlight. Audrey had the distinct impression that he would have kissed Lizzie if she hadn't been there, and she tried to walk ahead a little distance so they could have a few minutes of privacy to say whatever they wanted. She thought she saw them holding hands for a minute. But they let go as soon as she walked toward them. They had drinks on the terrace that night, and after a few sips Audrey said she was tired and going back to their room. Lizzie stayed for a few minutes and went for a walk on the beach with Will. She was back in their room half an hour later, and Audrey smiled at her when she walked in.

"Is my brother behaving, or shouldn't I ask that question?" she teased her, and Lizzie smiled and nodded with a mysterious look.

"He's a pretty wonderful guy, Aud."

"I know, he's my brother. I just want him to be nice to you and realize how great you are too."

"He hasn't done or said anything he shouldn't," Lizzie reassured her.

"I hope not. This is only our second night here." Audrey laughed at her.

The romance continued to blossom as the days unfurled like the petals of a flower. He took them to every place he thought they'd enjoy. Waterfalls, exquisite beaches, a forest of delicately scented tropical flowers, his favorite haunts and restaurants, Lau Yee Chai, his favorite Chinese restaurant, and the soda fountain at Benson Smith drugstore, a favorite meeting place for locals, and a night-club where they went dancing. He invited one of his fellow pilots that night so Audrey had someone to dance with, and they all had a good time together. In part, he wanted Audrey to have a wonderful time, it was his way of thanking her for all that she had given up to take care of their mother. And he wanted Lizzie to have a vacation she'd remember forever. He didn't know why he hadn't noticed it before, but he felt as though he had met the woman of his life, and he didn't want the week to end. He had never felt that way about anyone before. After only a few days, he could see spending the rest of his life with her, when he eventually settled down. But it was too soon for either of them. He was thinking of coming back to see her at Christmas, but hadn't said anything to her about it yet. Two days before they left, on a late-night walk down Waikiki Beach in the moonlight, he kissed her, and she melted into his arms. Other than flying, he had never had a sensation like it before, nor had she. She told Audrey about it the next day, and Audrey beamed.

"If you two wind up together, I'll be the happiest woman alive. But he still has a lot of flying to do. He's not ready to settle down yet, but he will be one day." She was hopeful that something serious would come of it.

"I know that. I'm not ready either," Lizzie said thoughtfully. "I want to do something useful with my life, other than emptying bedpans in a post-op ward. I want to do something that makes a difference in the world."

"So do I," Audrey said wistfully. But it was only a distant dream for her.

"You already are," Lizzie said gently. "What you're doing for your mother matters, Aud. You'll always be glad you did it."

"I know. Maybe one day I can use what we learned for others. When the time is right. And in the meantime, I want my brother to fall so madly in love with you that he never lets you go, and we can be sisters forever. Maybe he already has fallen in love with you," she said hopefully.

"So he says," Lizzie said with a cautious smile and a giggle. "Thank you for bringing me with you."

"I wouldn't have come without you. I love my brother, but it would have gotten pretty boring here very quickly without you, and he wouldn't have taken just me to all those places," Audrey said, and they both laughed.

They had to be at the base by noon to watch him fly in formation in the navy demonstration they were putting on that day. People were already lining the beaches in anticipation. Will had told them just where to go on the base, and two of his friends were supposed to join them and look after them.

They got to the base on time, and met up with Will's friends, and the formation Will flew in took their breath away. Will was the section leader and they were flying ten feet apart in Grumman F4F Wildcats. A tiny mistaken move or variation and all the planes would have plummeted together with tragic results. Lizzie was mesmerized, and Audrey was so proud of him as she watched. He was back with them an hour later, having put on an incredible show.

"That was quite something," Lizzie said when he rejoined them.

"Just a little entertainment for the locals." He smiled modestly and leaned over and kissed Lizzie on the cheek.

"You scared me to death," she admitted. "That trick where you all looked like you were going to crash and then pulled out of it flipped my stomach over."

"Mine too," he teased her, "or it used to. We've never had an accident in any of my formations. Flying is the most exciting thing in the world . . . or it was, until you came along," he said and she nodded. She felt that way about him too. It had all happened so fast, and she and Audrey were leaving the next day. He told her that night that he would try to get some time off at Christmas, or right after, to come to see her in Boston. "I'll be counting the hours until I see you again, Lizzie," he said, and kissed her passionately that night, before she left him and went back to her room, where Audrey was waiting. They were all packed and leaving in the morning for the flight to San Francisco. Will had promised to take them to the airport. It had been the most wonderful week of Lizzie's life, and Audrey's too. Her mother had given them the best vacation and graduation gift she could ever have imagined. Ellen had spared nothing for them. A week with her brother had meant a lot to Audrey too. They had only seen each other during brief, infrequent visits in recent years. A whole week with him had been a luxury she knew she would treasure forever. And Lizzie would too.

He took them to the airport the next day, and helped them check in for the Pan Am flight. They stood outside the terminal afterwards, with the tropical flowers all around them. He put a gardenia lei around Lizzie's neck, and then a bright fuchsia one around Audrey's. He kissed Lizzie openly in front of his sister and the other passengers, and Audrey went to buy a red and yellow lei safely nestled in a plastic box for her mother. The flight was announced then, and they walked across the tarmac to the plane. Lizzie turned to wave at him a few times, and stopped as she entered the plane to wave at him for a last time. Audrey did too. Both girls stood together waving at him, as the tall, handsome young navy pilot waved his long arms, and then they disappeared. He stood there looking bereft until the big plane took off, taking with it the woman he knew he would marry one day. He had never felt as lonely in his life as he did when he drove away. All he wanted to do now was see her again. Lizzie had cried when the plane took off, and Audrey held her hand, smiling at her. For all three of them, it had been the best trip of their lives. And the fragrance of the leis followed them all the way to New York. After the United flight from San Francisco the next day, they landed at LaGuardia on Monday night, and Lizzie hopped a short flight to Boston so she could get to work on time the next morning. Audrey took a cab into the city to Pennsylvania Station, where she took a train to Baltimore, and a cab to Annapolis. She walked into her house very late that night. Her mother had woken in the middle of the night and Mrs. Beavis was settling her again. Ellen looked pale and tired but smiled when she saw her daughter. Audrey had a deep tan, and was wearing the lei Will had given her. Her mother looked instantly peaceful and pleased. She was happy to see her, and Audrey looked young and beautiful.

"Welcome home. How was it?" she asked, as Audrey kissed her.

"Oh, Mom, it was the best ever. You can't even imagine how great it was. We even saw Will fly yesterday. You gave me, and Lizzie, the best gift of our lives." She was going to tell her mother about Will and Lizzie later, but it was too late that night. It had been a long trip from San Francisco to Annapolis, and she felt like she was on another planet now. The trip to Hawaii seemed like a dream. When she went to her room she got the lei for her mother out of its box in her suitcase where she had carefully put it for the flight to San Francisco. It was still fragrant and beautiful, and she put it next to her mother's bed as Ellen drifted off to sleep with a smile.

Helping to serve her patients lunch in the post-op ward the day after they got home, Lizzie felt like she was in a daze, but she smiled every time she thought of Will. She could see her future now. Maybe her parents had been right after all. Marriage and children no longer sounded like such a bad idea, even if it had meant giving up medical school. If she had gone to medical school, she would never have met Audrey or her brother, and would never have gone to Hawaii. She had put the lei carefully on her bed table the night before. Its delicate fragrance filled the room and reminded her of Will.

She had a long shift that day, and she wasn't going to finish until nine o'clock that night. But she didn't care. She would have worked twenty-four hours straight if she had to. The love they had discovered in Hawaii gave her the strength and courage to conquer the world. She wasn't going to tell her parents about it yet. She didn't want to give them a chance to examine it, or him, under a microscope, or pick it apart. She wasn't sure that a navy pilot was what they had in mind for her. But she knew how much she loved him, and how right it was. That was good enough for her for now.

For the next week, Audrey and Lizzie called each other every chance they got, when Lizzie wasn't on duty at the hospital. Audrey told her mother about Will and Lizzie, and all Ellen said was that she hoped it would last. They were both very young, and would be apart a lot for the next few years. She hoped that they would have the fortitude to stick with it, and stand by each other. She already loved Lizzie, so she was pleased. And not entirely surprised. Lizzie had been young before, when Will first met her. But at twenty-two, Ellen thought she was old enough for a serious love now. She was sorry that Audrey hadn't at least had a brief flirtation in Hawaii, but Audrey didn't seem to mind. She was so happy for her brother and her best friend that it seemed even better than a romance of her own.

Thanksgiving was on Thursday of that week. Lizzie had to work and Audrey and her mother shared a quiet turkey dinner. The holiday paled this year in comparison to the Hawaiian vacation.

The first letter Will wrote to Lizzie took two weeks to reach her from Honolulu, and he had written to her the day she left. She pounced on it as soon as it arrived, and his letter made her smile and laugh. He told her how much he had fallen in love with her, and that he had never felt this way in his life. She answered him the night she got his letter. She had been waiting to hear from him first, and she reciprocated all his feelings, and told him what she'd been doing since she left. She opened the letter twice before she sent it, to add lengthy PS's and mailed it the next morning on her way to work. It was the first of December, which reminded her that Christmas was just around the corner.

She wondered if Will really would be able to get leave sometime during the holidays. He had said he would try. He hadn't been planning to come back, since his leaves were usually short. But now everything was different, and he had said again in his letter that he would do his best to come to Boston as soon as he could, even if it was only for a few days. He was going to try and catch a military flight. They were notoriously uncomfortable, but he would have come strapped to the fuselage if he had to. And he wanted to meet her parents, so they would know he was serious about her. He was an honorable man, and he wanted to start building a solid future with Lizzie.

She worked double shifts for three days that week, but even that didn't faze her. Thoughts of Will filled her mind during every waking hour, and the images of their time together in Honolulu were as vivid as the days and nights had been when she was there. She could still feel his lips on hers.

She had the weekend off and spent Saturday doing laundry and starching her uniforms. She took a nap, read some magazines, and called Audrey, who was busy bathing her mother with Mrs. Beavis and shampooing her hair, so she couldn't talk. She promised to call back later, but she never did. Her mother had cramps in her legs so

Audrey massaged them late into the night, and by then, she knew it was too late to call Lizzie. She would have woken the whole house if she did.

Audrey called Lizzie back on Sunday morning, but she had gone to church with her parents, which she occasionally did, now that she was living at home again. She did it mostly to humor her parents, since it meant a lot to her mother.

Audrey spent the morning writing checks for her mother, to pay their bills. Ellen's handwriting was barely legible now, and she had trouble holding a pen, just as she did a fork and knife. Her mind was still clear and acute, but everything that involved motor skills— walking, writing, feeding herself, dialing a phone, even lifting a glass to her lips—was hard for her, and required Audrey's help.

Audrey finished writing the checks at noon, and went to make her mother's lunch. She had just put it on a plate an hour later. The phone rang as soon as she did. It was Lizzie, and Audrey was happy to hear her.

"We've been missing each other for two days. I'm sorry I didn't call back last night." She was smiling, wanting to chat with her for a minute, when Lizzie cut through what she said in a voice that was filled with terror.

"The Japanese just bombed Hawaii, Pearl Harbor." They had gone there with Will to look at the navy ships. "I heard it on the radio. It's still going on. Oh my God, Aud . . . oh my God . . . please God, don't let Will be there today." It was just after eight A.M. in Hawaii, and neither of them knew what he was planning to do that

49

day. Then Audrey remembered that he sometimes went out to work on his plane on the weekends, and he had always been an early riser, even as a kid, and especially once he was in the military.

"I have to feed Mom, and I don't want to tell her. Not until we know more about it. I'll call you back after she eats lunch. And Lizzie . . . pray . . ."

Lizzie felt too paralyzed with fear to even speak, and just hung up and went back to the radio her parents were listening to. It sounded terrible. There were explosions and fires. One ship had been bombed four times. Lizzie sat listening, deathly pale, her hands clenched in her lap.

Audrey's hands were shaking while she fed her mother, but Ellen didn't notice, as she chatted to Audrey, who nodded and smiled and tried to act as though everything was normal, but nothing was. Ellen seemed to take forever to eat, and Audrey hurried back to the kitchen as soon as she could get away. She closed the door and turned the radio on just loud enough to hear, but not so her mother could hear it in the downstairs bedroom she slept in now.

The news was terrifying. The attacks continued and the USS *Arizona* was sinking. Its fully loaded fuel tanks were feeding the explosions, according to the news commentator. And worst of all for Audrey, the airfields had been bombed too. It had been a vicious attack, which would have far-reaching effects. But all Audrey could think of was her brother, praying that somehow he had been far enough from the attack to be spared. She sat in the kitchen for an hour, listening to the news. The attack lasted less than two hours, the report on the radio was confusing as to whether nineteen or twenty ships had been destroyed. The early estimate was that thousands had been killed, and maybe as many as a thousand people injured. As she listened, they said that several hundred planes had been destroyed and the airfield decimated. They confirmed that the USS *Arizona* had sunk after being attacked four times by Japanese bombers, and the ship had taken many men, who had been unable to escape, down with it.

It was after three when Audrey called Lizzie. Her voice was shaking, and Lizzie was crying.

"We just have to wait and see what we hear now," Audrey said, trying to sound stronger than she felt. "He probably won't be able to get in touch with us for a while. It must be chaos there. The navy will contact us if he's injured, or worse. Lizzie, we just have to believe that he's okay."

"What if he isn't?" Lizzie sobbed.

"He has to be. We all love him too much to lose him." But so did thousands of other parents, children, and men and women who had loved ones in Hawaii and would be waiting for news now. Audrey felt guilty keeping it from her mother. She would find out sooner or later. She listened to the radio at times, she read the newspapers, and she had a right to know that her son might be in danger. Audrey told her as calmly as she could, but the news was shocking. Audrey told her that the American naval base in Hawaii had been attacked. Ellen looked stunned, and asked Audrey to bring the radio in so they could listen together. Everything they heard on the radio was terrifying, and everyone in the country was wondering if the Japanese would bomb other American cities next.

Ellen and Audrey were awake until late that night, and the next day President Roosevelt asked Congress to declare war on the Japanese. Shortly after they heard his speech to the American people, the doorbell rang, and Audrey opened it with a pounding heart. They weren't expecting anyone, and Mrs. Beavis was with her mother. Two naval officers stood at the door when she opened it. Audrey felt faint for a minute.

"Is Mrs. Parker home, Mrs. Ellen Parker?" they asked politely. Audrey had grown up with naval officers around her all her life, and she recognized immediately that one of them was a captain, the same rank as her father, and the other one was an officer of the Navy Air Force. She was sure that they knew who her father was, and that her grandfather had been a vice admiral, which was why they had sent such high-ranking officers. She was terrified of what they were going to tell her, and she was afraid to ask. She didn't want to know. She wanted him to be alive, even if he was injured. He was only twenty-five years old and such a bright shining star, they couldn't lose him. He was turning twenty-six in a few weeks.

"My mother isn't well," Audrey said in a choked voice, but Audrey knew she couldn't protect her from this, and her mother wouldn't want her to. She had a right to be there. "She's bedridden. I'll bring her in." They sat down on the edge of the couch, and Audrey felt as though the longer she could keep them from telling them the news, the longer Will would be alive. She walked into her mother's downstairs bedroom and told her that there were two officers waiting to speak to her. They both knew what it meant, or could mean. That he was wounded or dead. Ellen looked panicked and her hands were shaking violently, but she asked Audrey and Mrs. Beavis to get her into her wheelchair and wheel her into the living room to see them. She was wearing a navy housedress with pink flowers on it, which Audrey knew she would remember for the rest of her life. She had blue velvet slippers on her feet.

Audrey wheeled her into the living room, and turned her to face the officers as they stood to greet her. She introduced Audrey to them, which Audrey hadn't thought to do herself. Their speech was brief and formal and as compassionate as they could make it. The Navy Air Force officer delivered the news they were both dreading. Will had been killed in the second wave of the attack, at the airfield. He had been working on his plane, and had used an antiaircraft gun from the plane to try and bring one of the Japanese planes down, but they got him first. They had an eyewitness report from a pilot who had been there and been injured. He had survived it and Will hadn't.

"He died honorably in battle, Mrs. Parker, and will be awarded a medal posthumously to show his country's gratitude," the captain said. "He was one of our finest pilots. I met him myself last year. He was a fine young man. We extend the navy's sympathy, and the president's. We are very sorry. His body will be flown home when we can get the aircraft over there to do it. There isn't a functioning plane on the ground there right now. We lost two thousand, four hundred men yesterday, and there are over a thousand wounded. Ships and planes destroyed, sunken ships. It may take awhile to bring him home, but we'll bring him back as soon as we can."

Both men wanted to shake her hand, but saw that it wasn't possible, so they shook Audrey's and left a few minutes later. She wondered how many homes they were going to that day, how many hearts they would have to break, as the bearers of the worst possible tidings anyone could hear. She put her arms around her mother, and they cried together. Audrey still couldn't believe her brother was gone. She had last seen him only three weeks ago to the day, and was even more grateful to her mother for making the trip to Honolulu possible. As she thought it, she realized she would have to tell Lizzie, and she couldn't even put her arms around her. But she had to know in case his name appeared in a newspaper on a list of those killed.

She and Mrs. Beavis got Ellen into bed, and Audrey brought her a cup of tea. Ellen didn't want it. She just lay there with her eyes closed, shaking from head to foot, with tears running down her cheeks, sobbing, as Audrey gently stroked her arm.

Mrs. Beavis got her to take her medicine, and she finally fell asleep. Audrey went out to the kitchen then, and dialed Lizzie's number in Boston. She answered immediately. She'd known instinctively that Audrey would call her. Lizzie wasn't working that day, and her father had canceled his patients for the day. The whole country was holding its breath, waiting to hear what would happen next. All anyone knew was what had happened at Pearl Harbor and that the country was at war with Japan. It had been twenty-four years since America had entered a war. They had gotten into the last one before Audrey and Lizzie were born, so they had never lived it firsthand. The United States had only been in it briefly, but had suffered tremendous losses. This was all new to them.

Lizzie didn't ask her any questions and waited for Audrey to speak.

"The navy came to see us," she said in a dead voice. "He died trying to defend the airfield. He was killed by the Japanese. They're sending his body home when they can." Audrey's voice sounded hollow to her own ears, as Lizzie sank into a chair and cried quietly. Her parents saw what was happening and could guess she had just had terrible news. "I'm sorry, Lizzie," Audrey said, crying. "He loved you. I know that for sure. You're the only girl he ever loved. He would have married you. He told me so. I love you. I'm so sorry, for all of us," she said, and then broke into sobs and had to hang up. Lizzie's father walked over and put a hand on her shoulder, as her mother stared at her in dismay. Lizzie was dissolving in front of them.

"Someone you knew well?" he asked her, and she nodded.

"Audrey Parker's brother. Will," she added. She wanted to say his name so they could hear it, and she looked up at her father with the shards of her broken heart spilling from her eyes. "I loved him, Daddy. He was a wonderful person."

"I'm sure he was," he said sympathetically. "It'll be hard on his mother. She's widowed, isn't she?" Lizzie nodded. They had met at Lizzie and Audrey's nursing school graduation, so he knew how ill she was.

"Audrey takes care of her."

"I'm sorry. Let me know if there's anything we can do, for either of them." He didn't react to her telling him she loved Will. He wasn't sure what she meant by it, but it was no time to ask when she was so upset.

She did the only thing she could think of then. It was the only place she wanted to be, with the family he loved and who loved him. She belonged with them now.

Lizzie packed a bag and went to Pennsylvania Station, and took a train to Annapolis that night. She arrived at the house at eleven o'clock and rang the doorbell. Audrey opened the door and they sank into each other's arms, mourning the boy they had all loved so much. The boy who wanted to fly and had loved planes all his life. The country was at war and he was one of the first casualties. Audrey wondered if her mother would survive it, if any of them would. He was so young and so handsome and such a good person, brother, and son. He would have been good to Lizzie, if he'd had time to do so. And now he was gone. Audrey couldn't imagine what life would be like from this day on, without him, and neither could Lizzie. Their lives would be forever changed, more than either of them could even imagine.

Chapter 4

Lizzie spent the week in Annapolis with Audrey and Ellen. She needed to be with them. They all sat in Will's boyhood room and cried, looking at pictures of him. It was inconceivable to them that he wasn't coming back, and even more so to his mother. Lizzie could still feel his lips, and his arms around her. It was all so fresh in her mind, and now, three weeks later, he was dead. It had all been so brief and so powerful. She couldn't imagine life without him, or a future she would care about. What she did now no longer mattered to her. Her father called and reminded her that she had to go back to work at the hospital, but she didn't care if they fired her. She hated her job anyway. He used his influence to get her a leave of absence. He said he felt very sad for the Parkers, but he told Lizzie she had to be back in Boston by the end of the week to pick up the threads of her own life again. He had no idea how deeply she had loved Will, or what promises they had made each other.

They still had no news of when his body would be returned when she finally left Annapolis on Sunday, a week after the attack on Pearl Harbor. Everyone was talking about war having been declared, and what it meant. Boys were going to be drafted, since the draft had been instated a year before. Thousands had already enlisted that week as a patriotic gesture, and she suspected that her own brothers would join the army now too. Her older brother, Greg, could go as a doctor in the medical corps, but Henry had only just started medical school, and she had no idea what they would do with him, or where he would be sent. America would join the war in Europe now too. Some men would be sent to the Pacific, and others to Europe. The country was in chaos, waiting to hear what would happen next. Those who had enlisted would be sent to basic training soon.

The atmosphere at the hospital was somber when Lizzie went back to work. Some doctors were talking about enlisting. Others were going to wait to be drafted. Some of the nurses were talking about enlisting too, which surprised Lizzie. She hadn't thought about the nurses that would be needed too, not just physicians.

She went through the motions at work and barely spoke to her parents at night. She felt as though a part of her had died with Will on the airfield at Pearl Harbor.

Ellen and Audrey didn't celebrate Christmas, and Lizzie worked on the holiday in Boston. She had nothing to celebrate that year. There was a jubilant mood among those who had enlisted and wanted to celebrate before going off to basic training. Lizzie already knew how it ended, and she couldn't let herself be swept along. She kept to herself at work, and took care of her patients, but there was nothing she cared about now.

They finally sent Will's body back shortly after Christmas. There were so many bodies to send home to families all over the country, and others who had gone down with their ships in the harbor and remained there. Divers brought up as many as they could, but there were a vast number they hadn't reached yet.

Lizzie went back to Annapolis for the small funeral service Audrey arranged for her brother. His classmates from Annapolis were all over the world now. His childhood friends had moved on too, and a bigger funeral would have been too much for her mother. Audrey, Ellen, and Lizzie and a few of their old friends attended the service in the church Audrey and Will had gone to as children. Ellen hadn't been well enough to go to church for years, and Audrey no longer saw her old high school friends. She was too busy taking care of her mother. Lizzie was her closest friend. They buried Will in the cemetery at Annapolis with his father. Will's grandfather and grandmother were there too. There would be a place for Ellen next to her husband, Francis, when she died. It was grimly depressing standing at the cemetery, as they lowered Will's casket into the ground, and two navy pilots handed Ellen the flag from his casket. Her hands trembled violently as she took it and pressed it to her chest.

They went back to the house for a quiet meal afterwards, and Lizzie shocked Audrey with what she told her after they put Audrey's mother to bed. Her health had deteriorated markedly since the Japanese attack on Pearl Harbor and Will's death. It was as though she didn't care enough to put up a fight anymore. Audrey was fighting to keep her stable, but Ellen didn't seem to care one way or another. Lizzie could understand how she felt, and Audrey did too.

They were sitting at the kitchen table drinking a glass of wine when Lizzie told her. Lizzie looked tired and had lost weight in the last month, and the light had gone out of her eyes, as though everything was dark inside her. Audrey didn't look much better, but she was busy with her mother. They were both young to have suffered so much loss.

"I'm going to enlist," Lizzie said so quietly that Audrey didn't hear her at first, and then it hit her.

"You're *what*?"

"I'm going to enlist in the army as a nurse." She said it as simply as though she had said, "I'm going to the store tomorrow to buy a quart of milk."

"They're not drafting women, Lizzie, for heaven's sake." Audrey was shocked.

"Maybe they will eventually. Probably not. I've got nothing else to do, and at least I'll serve some useful purpose. I'm not doing anyone any good emptying bedpans in Boston and living with my parents. Why not use what we learned in nursing school? When you see what happened in Hawaii and what a mess it was, how many wounded there were; they're going to need as many medical personnel as they can get. I'm not married, I don't have kids. I have no reason to stay home. I'd rather go where they need me and do someone some good. The patients I take care of won't miss me. They can get plenty of old nurses to do what I do. I might as well enlist now and let them send me where I'll be useful. I've been thinking about it, and it really makes sense." Nothing else did now. She was calm and matter-of-fact about it, and Audrey could tell she had made up her mind. She could also tell that Lizzie didn't really care if she lived or died at the moment, which worried Audrey.

"Have you told your parents yet?"

"No, I'm sure they'll have a fit when I do. But I don't really care. They won the battle against medical school. They won't win this one. I know I'm right. The army is going to need as many nurses as they can get. Lots of nurses are married and have kids and can't go. I can. I have nothing to hold me back. My brothers will be going, so why shouldn't I?" And she wanted to honor Will in some important way.

"Aren't you scared, Lizzie?" Audrey asked her, and Lizzie shook her head. She looked like a different person since Will had died. She seemed empty and cold. All the joy and life and hope had gone out of her.

"No, I'm not scared. They probably won't put nurses on the front lines anyway. I'm going to tell my parents when I go back to Boston now, and then I'll sign up." Audrey wasn't sure if she was right or not, but she didn't want to lose her closest friend. She couldn't think of joining her, because she had her mother to take care of.

"Where would you go?"

"Wherever they send me. They'll probably send a lot of the wounded back to the States. They might not send me anywhere, except an army base somewhere in the U.S. Either way, I'm willing to go."

"I'm impressed," Audrey said quietly.

"It just feels right. The country is at war. I think young people should go. Women as well as men." She believed in equality for men and women, which wasn't a popular point of view.

They talked about it some more that night, but Audrey could tell she'd made up her mind. It wasn't entirely a patriotic decision. It was more of a practical one. She felt useless where she was and wanted to serve the men who would fall in battle in the coming months. She saw a need looming on the horizon, for nurses as well as soldiers, and she wanted to make her contribution to fill it. And she was wasting her abilities in her current job.

Audrey hugged her tight when Lizzie left to go back to Boston. She suddenly had the feeling that she didn't know when they would see each other again.

"Let me know what you're doing," Audrey said, and Lizzie smiled at her for the first time in days.

"I'm not going to go sneaking off. I'll come see you before they send me anywhere."

She left a few minutes later.

Her parents were talking in the kitchen when she got home that night. She walked in and sat down with them with a serious expression.

"I have something to tell you," she said quietly. She suddenly looked older and more grown up. Something about her had changed in the last month. She had already been different when she came back from Honolulu with Audrey, and her parents didn't know what it was. "I'm going to enlist in the army, as a nurse." She said it calmly and waited for their reaction. She knew there would be one and the storm hit quickly.

"Are you crazy? They're not going to be drafting women," her father told her.

"Maybe they should, Dad. I want to do my patriotic duty. They're going to need nurses, lots of them, to treat the wounded." She figured it was a better tack than saying that she hated her job and had nothing better to do, and that she didn't mind risking her life, now that Will was dead. She didn't care about her future without him now anyway. "I'm young. I'm a nurse. People like me are the ones who should go. I don't have kids, I'm not married. They'll need medical personnel. I just wanted to let you know that's what I'm going to do." Her mother was too amazed to even speak.

They both looked shocked as they stared at her and couldn't seem to come up with a convincing argument to dissuade her. "When are you planning to do it?" her father asked in a hoarse voice. She was enlisting sooner than either of her brothers.

"Soon. In the next few days. I'm not vital in my job. They can manage without me. I'll let you know as soon as I know when I'm leaving," she said calmly, and then reached out and held their hands.

"I think it's a crazy idea, Lizzie," her father said quietly. He knew that arguing with her wasn't going to work. Not this time.

"Yeah, like my wanting to go to medical school was crazy, huh?"

"Are you punishing me for not letting you go?" he asked, looking worried. She was a headstrong girl, and he knew he had underestimated her before, even though she had given in and gone to nursing school. And now look at what she was doing.

"I'm not punishing you." Life had done that to her more than any human could have, when she lost Will. Now she had to find a way to live without him, without their dreams. She had no dreams now, just a job to do. She was well equipped for the job as a nurse, so why not do it?

"You're not scared of where they'll send you?" her mother asked her finally.

She shook her head in answer. "Not at all." They could see that she wasn't, and they admired her for it. She was a gutsy young woman. Her father had spoken to both his sons since war was declared, and both were afraid of where they might be sent and what would happen. His daughter wasn't, and she was willing to offer herself up. He wondered if maybe she was right, and he was sure they wouldn't send nurses too close to the battlefields, so he wasn't too worried about her. His sons would be in greater danger, but he thought it was brave of her anyway.

"Let me know what they tell you, Lizzie," he said, as her mother dabbed at her eyes. Lizzie stood up and hugged them both. And as Ben Hatton hugged her, he couldn't help being proud that his daughter would be the first in their family to enlist, even before his sons. She was quite a girl. He said as much to Lizzie's mother that night. She thought it was a terrible decision, and was angry at her husband for not stopping their daughter.

"We can't fight her on everything, Alice. We stopped her from going to medical school, which just didn't make sense to me, even if she might have been a good doctor. I'm sure she would have. And now she wants to do her patriotic duty and serve her country when we're at war. I'll tell you something. If we tried to stop her on this, she'd walk right past us and out that door anyway." He had seen it in her eyes that night, and he wasn't wrong. Nothing was going to stop Lizzie. She had no reason to be there, and nothing worthwhile to do at home. She was going where she was needed, which actually sounded like the right idea to him. She was the youngest of his children, and just a girl, but she had more guts than any of them.

Lizzie called in sick to work the next day and went to the recruiting office. It was jammed, and she had a three-hour wait before they called her number. She signed up and filled out all the papers she had to. She had brought her nursing certificate with her, and proof that she had graduated as a registered nurse. They told her to come back in two weeks for her physical. She would be notified after that if she was acceptable to be inducted into the army, then given a date to report for four weeks of instruction and training in military protocol and procedures. She would be sent to a military base after that. It all sounded very simple and very direct. She notified the hospital the next day, and told them that her leaving would depend on whether she passed the army physical, but there was no reason why she shouldn't. She was athletic and in good health. The nursing supervisor was impressed when Lizzie told her she had enlisted.

"I guess others will too eventually. It's brave of you, Elizabeth."

"Not really," Lizzie said quietly. "It just felt like the right thing to do, for a lot of reasons."

She called Audrey and told her that night.

"I just hope they don't send you anywhere too far away," or where she'd be in danger. Audrey hoped they'd keep her in the States. Lizzie thought it was likely they would, but she was willing to go anywhere. "I'm going to miss you, if I can't see you." Audrey doubted that she'd be able to leave her mother again. Ellen's health had deteriorated sharply since Will's death. The shock of it had hit her hard.

"Will I have to salute when I see you?" Audrey teased her, trying to make light of it. She was sad thinking about Lizzie going away.

"I'm not even sure that nurses get a rank. And no one's going to get rich on the pay. I think the people doing it, like me, are doing it because they figure they owe it to our country. And someone will have to take care of the wounded, so it might as well be me. There's no glory in it, and no glamour, from everything I've heard. It's a lot of hard work. That's what I need right now." They both knew she had a broken heart, and she was trying to put it to good use, to serve others. There was merit in that. It was an ugly war, and it had already cost them both too much.

Chapter 5

When Audrey and Lizzie had entered nursing school in September 1938, earnestly intending to apply themselves to their nursing studies, Alexandra Whitman White was on the cusp of the most exciting time of her life. An aristocratic, almost regal-looking, statuesque blonde with striking, movie star good looks, she was preparing for her first official social season in New York. Related to Astors and Vanderbilts on both sides, with Morgan cousins, and distantly related to the Roosevelts, she was going to be presented to society at the same cotillion where her mother and grandmother had come out. In the week after the cotillion, her parents would be giving her her own private ball in their mansion on Fifth Avenue. Her sister Charlotte had gone through the same process five years earlier, with considerable success. She had met her future husband at a friend's coming-out ball in the same season. They were engaged within six months, married the following Christmas, and were now happily married with three little girls.

The purpose of making one's debut in previous centuries was to bring young ladies out of the seclusion of the "schoolroom" at home and help them find suitable husbands in the same social set. It was the accepted way of finding a husband then, and some brilliant matches—and equally brilliant and often lucrative mergers between important wealthy families—were made. The couples barely knew each other when they married. A similar system had existed in England for centuries, among the aristocracy. Ideally, there were no unfortunate surprises, and decent marriages were the result, although that wasn't always the case. Alex White's older sister, Charlotte, was very happy with her husband, a prominent New York banker from a blue-blooded family like theirs. Alex and Charlotte's father, Robert White, was a banker too. Banking was thought to be the only truly respectable career for a gentleman. None of the women of Alex's mother's generation worked. They had no reason to, and it would have been considered inappropriate. The few women who had jobs or careers were severely criticized, and they rarely married. Nothing in their earlier education had prepared them to work. It was considered more important for them to have a solid understanding of art, appreciate theater, opera, and the ballet, run an elegant home, and speak several languages. Alex spoke fluent French, and passable German and Italian, taught to her by her nannies while she was growing up. Her mother, Astrid, and her friends were involved in charitable committees to benefit those less fortunate. It was a value system based on traditions that had existed for generations.

Alex was excited about her debut. She loved going to parties and had envied her older sister all the special events and balls she went to when she came out. Alex had a gregarious nature, and at thirteen, she had sat upstairs on the landing the night of the ball their parents gave her sister, Charlotte, wishing that she could be downstairs dancing with the guests and wearing a fabulous white gown.

Astrid had selected and ordered Alex's debut dress with her in Paris that summer at Patou. It was a wispy creation in white organza, and Alex couldn't wait to wear it. She had another one for her own ball, which they had bought in New York. She was going to wear her dark hair swept up for the first time. She had two escorts for the cotillion, as was the tradition, and her private ball was going to be spectacular. It was going to be the most exciting time of her life, and she felt like Cinderella every time she thought about it. What she loved about it was the dancing, the party, and the hundreds of people present when she curtsied. What she didn't like about it was the idea that she was expected to find a husband, marry within a year or two, and start having babies. It would be even worse if she had to move to Connecticut, as Charlotte had, or to a horse farm in New Jersey and ride all the time. Alex hated horses, and she had no desire to marry for several years. She had known the boys coming to her party since they were in third or fourth grade, and they seemed ridiculous to her. She had no desire for children, or at least not for a long time. She had wanted to go to college, as a few of her more progressive friends had, and her parents had decided it was unnecessary. Neither Alex's mother nor her sister had gone to college, nor had either of her grandmothers. Her sister Charlotte was perfectly happy never having gone to college, and just being a wife.

Alex had shocked her parents at seventeen, when she volunteered at a well-known hospital, and then at the Foundling Hospital, helping to care for the babies there. Her mother had explained to her that charity work was something you did on a committee, not actually working with the patients or the poor. You did things that benefited them, you didn't ever actually meet them. Alex had realized then that she was different from her family, and she had no idea why. But she was still excited about her debut. She was eighteen when she came out as a debutante, and although she went to every party she was invited to, and had a wonderful time, she didn't meet a single boy she thought was interesting, and none of them snagged her heart. It was an exhausting year of constant parties. And by her second season, the war had begun in Europe a few months before in September 1939. Although it didn't affect any of them personally, it bothered Alex that another deb season had begun, while people were suffering in Europe during a war. That seemed so wrong to her. She had continued her hospital volunteer work despite her mother's objections. Her father had agreed to let her continue it. And after her second season as a deb, with no engagement in sight, she didn't want another season. She regretted more than ever not having gone to college, and allowing her parents to talk her out of it. Her mother told her that overeducated women did not appeal to men, which seemed odd to Alex too. Why wouldn't a man want an educated, intelligent wife, or one with a career?

After her second season, her volunteer work at the hospital no longer seemed like enough to her. Without consulting anyone this time, she signed up for an accelerated course at a nursing school in the city. It was January of 1940, and she was scheduled to graduate in June of 1942. Alex was thrilled with what she'd done. Her mother tried to convince her to withdraw, and her father said it might be simpler if she did, rather than upset her mother, but Alex refused. She was nineteen years old, and her sister suggested that it was some form of belated adolescent rebellion. Whatever the reason for it in the first place, Alex loved her nursing classes and did well.

When the Japanese attacked Pearl Harbor in December of 1941, Alex had six months of nursing school left and the country was at war. Alex had only one goal after that, which she discussed with no one. She knew what the reaction would be, but she had a mind of her own, and knew how to get what she wanted.

She graduated from nursing school. She was twenty-one years old, and two days after she graduated, she enlisted in the army as a nurse, with the army nurses' corps. With a war on, it seemed the only right thing to do. She told her parents the same day, and her mother cried all night. Her debut was almost four years behind her by then. There wasn't a single man in her world that she wanted to marry, and she didn't see why she should. She'd been happy living with her parents at home in New York all through nursing school. She had gone out with all the men she wanted to, at least once, and found none of them particularly interesting. All she wanted to do was be a nurse and take care of the wounded sent back from the war. There were many of them and would be more. She had a particular interest in psychiatry, which sounded even worse to her parents, if she intended to work in mental hospitals after the war.

She was told when she enlisted that she would take a four-week military nurses' training course, to learn the military protocols and how the army worked. Since she had expressed an interest in psychiatry, there was an additional training course for that. Then she would be sent to the base where she'd be stationed, to work at a hospital there. It was exactly what Alex had wanted, and she had no regrets whatsoever. Her sister came in from Connecticut to try to talk her out of it, and she explained to Charlotte that it wasn't something she could change her mind about, like a dinner party. She had signed legally binding documents, and if she passed the physical, she would become an army nurse.

Charlotte went back to Connecticut in a huff, and her father resigned himself to the inevitable. It didn't seem like a noble choice to him, but more like youthful folly, and he just prayed that they didn't send her anywhere dangerous and just kept her in the States. He thought it likely they would. He had read somewhere that the army didn't know what to do with their nurses, and were keeping them in the States for the time being. But he wasn't pleased with what she'd done. And more than his wife and older daughter, he fully understood that the papers Alex had signed were legally binding, and she would have to go through with it, much to his dismay.

The day Alexandra left for her army nurses' training class was a day of mourning for them. Her father came alone to see her off at the station. He wished her luck, and she saw with surprise that there were tears in his eyes as the train pulled away. She wondered at times how she came to be related to them. She always felt like a stranger in their midst, and more than ever now.

After Lizzie Hatton passed the army physical, and was notified, she left for her four-week training class in early March. She managed to squeeze in a few days in Annapolis with Audrey and her mother, who was bedridden now and could no longer get up. Ellen had trouble breathing, and Audrey lived in terror that she'd catch a cold, which could kill her. She slept in the same room with her now, on a cot, so she could hear her mother breathing at night.

Lizzie promised to write from her training class, and she was shocked when she got there at how busy they kept her. They wore overalls that were too big for all of them, and had been made for men. The first thing the nurses had to do was alter them so they fit. It was a rigorous course, mostly to get them in better physical shape, and teach them army rules and protocols. They watched countless training films. Lizzie liked most of the women she met. Some of them were rougher than the women she was used to, but they all had nursing in common, and had chosen to be there. The four weeks flew by. At the end of it, Lizzie was given her orders. She was to report to the Presidio army base in San Francisco, and would work at Letterman Hospital there. It was said to be one of the best army posts in the country, and the women who had been assigned to less desirable locations envied her. The only thing Lizzie didn't like about it was that it was so far from Audrey, and she wouldn't get back often to see her. But other than that, she was excited to leave for San Francisco. She managed to spend one night in Annapolis with Audrey, then went home to Boston after that for a two-day leave, and showed up at her parents' home in uniform, which upset her mother. The uniform wasn't flattering, nor was the color, but she looked serious and official. She had chosen to wear the regulation trousers with it, which were easier to travel in, instead of the skirt, and her mother thought they looked awful. Her brothers were in the army by then too. Henry was in basic training at Fort Ord in Monterey, and Greg was in Alameda, waiting to be sent to the Pacific.

It was emotional for all three of them when she left her parents, but Lizzie loved San Francisco when she got there. It was a little gem of a city, next to a shimmering bay with strong winds and cool weather, and the new Golden Gate Bridge joined the city to the more rural Marin County. The hospital where she was going to work was efficient and modern. She was assigned to a dorm just for nurses, and there were always groups of women coming and going, or standing around having a smoke and a cup of coffee during their time off. The atmosphere was congenial and the nurses were quick to tell her the best places to visit on her days off.

Lizzie loved exploring the city, and the friendly attitude of the nurses she met there. Her letters to Audrey were full of enthusiasm, and she said she loved her job. The wounded were already returning from the Pacific by hospital ship, and the beds were full at the Presidio hospital. She felt that she was finally doing something useful and meaningful. The men being sent back from the Pacific were severely wounded, and many of them traumatized by what they'd been through. The fighting in the Pacific was savage. She spent many a night trying to comfort men suffering from shell shock and nightmares, in particular one who was barely older than she was. He had grown up on a farm in Alabama, and his wounds were severe enough to keep him in the hospital for quite some time, but not damaging enough to get him released from the army. She took care of him for a month, before they sent him back to active duty, still suffering from the trauma he'd experienced previously. The night before he left, he asked her to marry him, and she told him that she didn't want to marry. The man she'd loved had died at Pearl Harbor.

Her trauma patient was being sent to a base on the East Coast, and from there back into combat, this time in Europe. He was twenty-four years old, only a year older than she was, but he seemed like a child to her, as she tried to calm him the night before he left. It seemed cruel to her to send him back into battle, still so shattered by what he'd lived through before. He was leaving in the morning. He cried when he talked to her that night. Her heart ached for him. She had never seen anyone so ravaged and distraught, and it illustrated the cruelty of war so clearly to her.

"Don't make me go back into battle without telling me you love me," he begged her, and she felt sick listening to him. He needed someone to care about him when he left. It seemed like so little to give him. But she didn't want to mislead him, or encourage his romantic delusions about her.

"We don't know each other, Alfred," she said gently, trying to reason with him.

"Yes, we do. We've known each other for a month. People get married during wartime with less than that."

"They shouldn't," she said quietly, thinking of Will Parker. Their feelings for each other had taken off like wildfire, and that was before the war. But she had known him for two years before that.

"Will you write to me, if I write to you?" Alfred asked her, and she reluctantly nodded agreement. But what difference did it make, and what harm would it do? They'd never see each other again. "Could we say we're engaged?" he asked hopefully, and she drew the line there.

"No, we could not," she said firmly.

"When I come back, I'll make you fall in love with me," he said with determination, looking like an overgrown child.

She had other work to do. She went off duty at two A.M., and he was finally asleep. He left the hospital at eight that morning when she wasn't on duty. His letters to her started coming within days afterwards. Desperate, frightened, anguished pleas for love and support. He had grown up in foster homes in Alabama and had no family. She felt sorry for him, and wrote to him now and then to reassure him, trying to give him the strength to survive his return to the front. His handwriting was barely legible, and she felt sorry for him. She tried to encourage him without getting too deeply involved or too personal, but in each letter he poured out his love for her. All she hoped was that he'd survive the war and be able to make a decent life for himself when it was over, with what was left of his mind by then.

There were so many like him. She was careful not to encourage Alfred romantically, but he paid no attention to whatever she wrote and continued to declare his love for her, no matter what she said. She tried to taper off her letters, but he would beg for a response, and eventually she would feel sorry for him and send him a short note. The letters finally stopped and she assumed he'd been shipped off to Europe. It was a relief not to hear from him anymore. There was so little she could do for him and the others like him. She could heal their bodies better than their minds. There were so many broken souls returning from the war, men who would never be whole again. And there would be so many more before it was over.

When Alex finished her nurses' training, she was assigned to the Presidio in San Francisco. She stopped in New York for a night to see her parents, and flew out on a military flight the next day. Her father hoped that going to San Francisco didn't mean that she would be sent on to the Pacific. She was happy to be sent far from home. For the first time, she could pursue her own life without being told how peculiar and unlike her family she was, and how disappointed they were by her. San Francisco was a fresh start. She smiled broadly when she saw the city, as she rode into town on a military shuttle bus to the Presidio. She hopped on with her suitcase and her duffel bag, excited to be there. When she got off, it took her a little while to find the nurses' dormitory. There was a young female private in the office on the ground floor handing out room assignments to new arrivals. Alex made her way up the stairs to the room she'd been assigned. There were two beds in the room, and someone sound asleep in one of them. She assumed it was probably a nurse who'd been working all night. Alex tried to move around as quietly as she could, and put her things away in the narrow closet and an empty chest of drawers. The furniture in the room was old and battered. There were no frills or additional comforts, just the bare necessities. She didn't mind at all. It was a relief not to be burdened with the luxuries and trappings of her youth. She was like everyone else here. It was a melting pot of all kinds of people.

She found the communal bathroom at the far end of the hall, and when she got back, the girl in the bed was sitting on the edge of it smoking a cigarette. She looked like she'd had a rough night. She'd worked a double shift the day before, which was common.

"Hi, I'm Alex White," she said congenially, and the girl sitting on the bed smiled at her.

"I'm Lizzie Hatton. Welcome to Buckingham Palace. That's what they call it. They gave the nurses the best dormitory." Lizzie stood up and stretched when she said it. She was wearing pink satin pajamas with candy canes on them. "Sorry about the pajamas. My brother gave them to me for Christmas."

"My sister wanted to give me a straitjacket when I enlisted," Alex said and they both laughed.

"My family would have done the same," Lizzie said and showed Alex where everything was. The room looked as bare as any army barracks, but Lizzie had put a jar of flowers on the desk to cheer the place up. "Where are you from?" Lizzie asked her. She liked the look of her. She looked friendly and nice and happy to be there. All of the nurses had enlisted, so they were pleased with their choice and rarely, if ever, complained. It was a nice change from civilian life, where everyone at the hospital where she had worked groused about everything all the time. Life was harder in the army, but they didn't mind.

"I'm from New York," Alex said. "You?"

"Boston," Lizzie answered. "We lucked out with this post. It's supposed to be one of the best in the country. And it's three thousand miles from my parents, which is a definite plus."

"And mine." Alex grinned back at her, and sat down on her own bed, which she hadn't made up yet. She'd never made her own bed in her life until she joined the army. "What ward do you work on?" she asked, curious about her new roommate. She seemed like a very nice young woman.

"General. They move me around a lot. We get a lot of shell shock and trauma cases, along with the physical stuff." She thought of Alfred as she said it.

"I requested psychiatric, but I don't know my assignment yet. I'll be happy with whatever they give me."

"You'll love the city. It's beautiful," Lizzie said happily. There was something about Alex that suggested she was well brought up and well educated, but you never knew in the army, and met all kinds. They were all equal here.

Alex unpacked while they chatted, and then Lizzie went to shower and put on her uniform to go back on duty. By the time she left the room, she felt like she had a new friend. She liked the new arrival. Alex waved when she left, and Lizzie hurried down the stairs, and then walked the short distance to the hospital, thinking that she'd have to write to Audrey to tell her about her new roommate. Lizzie missed Audrey more than ever, but at least Alex seemed friendly and pleasant, and she had the feeling they'd get along. They had nursing in common and apparently parents who weren't happy when they enlisted in the army. It was a start.

The sun was shining and she had her workday ahead of her. It was never boring here, and so far she had met a lot of women she enjoyed working with and would never have met otherwise. It confirmed her belief that she had made the right decision enlisting in the army. As Alex watched her from the window, she was thinking the same thing. Becoming an army nurse had been the right answer for her too. Lizzie Hatton looked like she'd make a good friend. They were young, they were in a safe place. It was a plum assignment, compared to other bases. And despite the war, there were good people around them. The doctors were excellent, the nurses were happy to be there, and they were making a difference to the men they took care of, while serving their country. What more could they want? It was more than enough for Lizzie and Alex. And if they couldn't heal all the broken bodies and minds, they were doing all they could. Lizzie realized that maybe for the first time in her life, she felt fully alive. And for once, just being a nurse seemed like enough. This was her life now, and everything she wanted.

Chapter 6

While Lizzie and Alex explored the delights of San Francisco when they had days off together, Audrey was steadfastly caring for her mother. She loved hearing about their exploits in San Francisco, exotic dinners in Chinatown, walking on the beaches in Marin, although there were gun emplacements there now, and men assigned to watch for planes, after Pearl Harbor. An attack on the West Coast was always a possibility, but hadn't happened so far. The two young women had borrowed a car and driven as far south as Big Sur, and they reveled in its spectacular natural beauty. They drove north to Lake Tahoe in the mountains, where people skied in winter, and they had dinner in the restaurants of the Italian district in North Beach, in the city.

Audrey felt as though she had gotten to know Alex through Lizzie's descriptions of her. The nursing they did in the Presidio was demanding and exhausting, but also rewarding when they were able to help save a limb or a life. The men returning from the Pacific were badly damaged. Audrey knew that both of Lizzie's brothers were there now. Greg had enlisted in the army as a physician and was serving at a hospital in New Caledonia. It was a prefab building with a real structure, not a tent hospital, and he said it was very efficient, with running water and electricity. They treated the wounded from battle zones, and the men suffering from diseases like malaria. Henry was a medic south of the Solomon Islands. Both of them were a constant source of worry for Lizzie, and they all followed the news closely. The Hattons had all three children in the army now. Audrey knew her brother would have been there too, if he were still alive. He was one of the first casualties of the war.

By the fall of 1942, most of Europe had fallen into Hitler's hands, and the war was raging on. The German Luftwaffe had bombed England mercilessly, and there had been countless deaths during the Blitz in London: 43,000 civilians had died, and 140,000 were wounded. In November of 1942, British and American forces invaded North Africa.

Meanwhile, Audrey was waging her own war against her mother's illness, and slowly losing ground. A bad cold which turned into bronchitis nearly took Ellen's life on Christmas. Audrey sat up with her day and night, with visits from Mrs. Beavis to give her a break, until after Christmas. Miraculously her mother survived it, but Audrey knew then that they wouldn't be able to stop the inevitable for much longer. Ellen couldn't get out of bed by then, and hadn't in a long time. Audrey said little of it to Lizzie when she wrote to her. There was no point whining to her about it, and the reports would have been too depressing, so she soldiered on alone, with no break, no support, and only Mrs. Beavis to help her. She felt as though she were trapped on a desert island, shipwrecked, and help was no longer coming. She felt incredibly alone.

The life that Lizzie described, working at the hospital in the Presidio, sounded like heaven to her, no matter how injured her patients were. At least Lizzie and Alex had some chance to save them. Audrey knew that in the long run she had no chance at all to save her mother. She had always known that, but facing it now day by day, hour by hour, was a harsh dose of reality for her. Lizzie suspected it from what she didn't say, and admired her for her strength and courage. However different their lives were, she knew it would have been agony to watch her mother waste away with a debilitating illness. Ellen had been ill for seven years now, most of Audrey's adult life. She was twenty-two years old.

Alex was on regular duty in the psychiatric ward at the Presidio hospital by then, and loved the work, although it was challenging and often depressing. She brought a positive, cheerful attitude to it, and the men loved her, not just for her striking beauty, but for her compassion and how kind she was to them. She often achieved results with them that the doctors and other nurses couldn't. She had endless patience.

From little bits and snippets of things that slipped into Alex's conversation from time to time, Lizzie had begun to suspect that Alex's life at home was very different from the other nurses and people she lived with now. She accidentally admitted to Lizzie once, after a second glass of wine on a night out together, that she had been a debutante, and Lizzie shared with Audrey that she suspected Alex might be from a fancy family in New York, and that she had grown up in luxurious circumstances.

Compared to even Lizzie's very solid, educated, medical family in Boston, Alex seemed to have led a life that none of them even dreamed of, but she was careful not to talk about it, and never boasted or showed off. Alex was modest, simple, warm, and genuine in every way, and had loaned money to some of the other nurses occasionally, when they were short on cash before payday. Lizzie was sorry that Audrey still hadn't met her and hoped she would one day. Audrey was still her best friend, but she had grown very fond of Alex, and respected her.

In the early months of 1943, there were rumors that some of the medical personnel would be shipping out to the Pacific and to Europe, even the nurses. They needed more medical officers for the hospital ships: surgeons, doctors, nurses, corpsmen. The numbers of wounded were growing. Lizzie and Alex wondered if they would be among the nurses sent abroad in the coming months. They were both willing to go, and even liked the idea. After nearly a year of working in the Presidio, their work had begun to seem almost routine, and they were hungry for new challenges to conquer.

Audrey was taking longer and longer to respond to Lizzie's letters by then. The fight for her mother's life was all-consuming, and she rarely had the time to sit down and write to anyone, even Lizzie. Each day was a life-and-death battle, and in November, Ellen finally lost the war. Ellen was unconscious for the final days of her life, and quietly slipped away as Audrey sat and watched her. Audrey was alone in the house, in the deathly silence, as she closed her mother's eyes. Ellen had fought valiantly against her illness for a long time, and so had Audrey, and Ellen had earned her peace at last. Audrey kissed her cheek, and sat next to her for a long while, feeling her flesh cool rapidly. She realized as she looked at her mother that she was an orphan, alone in the world now. Both her parents, and her brother, were gone. She had no one. She wished that Lizzie could have been there with her. She felt excruciatingly alone. Audrey sent Lizzie a telegram in San Francisco telling Lizzie what had happened the day her mother died. Lizzie called her that night from the Presidio. Audrey had been crying when she answered.

"I'm so sorry, Aud," she said, and they both cried. It wasn't a surprise, but it was hard anyway. Caring for her mother had been her only life for two and a half years since she graduated from nursing school. The doctor had been amazed that Ellen had survived for as long as she had. It was mostly due to Audrey, and Ellen's own determination not to abandon her daughter. But the Fates had conspired against them, and the major losses Ellen had suffered had weakened her even further. "What are you going to do now?" Lizzie asked her, worried about her best friend, although she and Alex had formed a bond too. Working together in wartime brought people closer quickly, not just romances but also friendships. Alex had become a good friend, as they shared their experiences day by day, working in the hospital and rooming together.

"I have no idea. This is all I've known and done for years now." Since she was fifteen, when her father died and her mother got sick. "Maybe I should enlist, like you did." She had thought of it a few times, but there was no question of it while her mother was alive. "I have no one left, no family, nowhere I have to be. I was thinking of getting a job as a nurse. I need to take some classes to brush up. I've only been doing what Mom needed. I'm a little rusty on the rest."

"You can catch up in a month or two," Lizzie said. "I wish I could be sure we'd be stationed together." The armed forces kept fathers and sons and brothers together, when asked to do so, but friendships weren't always respected.

"Maybe I will anyway. I'll sign up for some classes. I need to do that anyway. I can't just sit here in an empty house and do nothing." She knew her mother had left her a little money, and she owned the house now, although she didn't want to live there alone. She was thinking about closing it up and getting a nursing job in Baltimore, or enlisting in the army. It was too soon to say. She hadn't even buried her mother yet.

"Let me know what you're doing," Lizzie said, and told her again how sorry she was. She would always have precious memories of Ellen and how kind she had been, and welcoming, when Audrey first brought her home from nursing school for Sunday dinners, which had become the mainstay of her student life, and a second family for her, warmer than her own.

The funeral was three days after Ellen died. Only Audrey, Mrs. Beavis, and two of their neighbors were there. Audrey arranged for burial in the naval cemetery at Annapolis, next to her father. The minister Audrey and her mother knew read from the Scriptures and spoke briefly about Ellen. Then her casket was lowered into the ground. It was a bleak November day, and Audrey went home alone. She started packing the next day. She didn't know where she was going. But she knew she couldn't stay long-term in the house that had become a hospital for her mother. It had served its purpose, but too many of its occupants were gone now. Audrey couldn't bear the thought of being there alone any longer than she had to.

She signed up for a refresher course at her old nursing school. It was scheduled to last for four weeks, and she was surprised how quickly the material came back to her. She hadn't forgotten as much as she had thought, even if she hadn't used it. She was halfway through the class on Thanksgiving weekend, still living at home in the silent house, when Lizzie called her. Audrey had decided to ignore the holiday. She had no one to spend it with and didn't want to celebrate. Lizzie sounded excited when Audrey answered.

"A whole group of us just signed up as flight nurses yesterday. They're sending us to Bowman Field in Kentucky. We're being reassigned as flight nurses with the Army Air Forces, and sent for Medical Air Evacuation Transport training for six weeks. We'll be learning field survival, ditching and crash procedures, parachutes, and some classroom hours related to flying. They need nurses and corpsmen to evacuate the wounded from the battlefields by air transport, in planes, and bring them back to hospitals. I knew a couple of girls who went to North Africa last year, as medical air evac flight nurses. I think they were the first to go. They didn't get much training. We don't know the details yet, but we're hoping we get sent to England. Another group got assigned to hospital ships in the Pacific. I like our assignment better. Alex got assigned to the same squadron I did. We start classes on January second, so I guess I'll be in Boston for Christmas. You can come up if you want. But I was thinking, if you enlist, you could volunteer for the Army Air Forces Flying Nurse Squadron and ask for Medical Air Evacuation Transport duty. Aud, I'd love to have you with us." Audrey thought about it as she listened. It sounded perfect to her, and just what she needed. It was exciting, and a real chance to do some serious nursing and help the boys at the front. And if she'd be with Lizzie, it felt like an answer to her prayers.

"Okay, Lieutenant, I'm in. I'll go to the recruiting station tomorrow." She wrote down everything she needed to know to volunteer for the right squadron if they let her. "I hope I don't flunk the physical or whatever they ask me, if they have an entrance exam." Audrey was so excited, she was shaking. It was a huge leap into an unknown future, but as she hung up the phone with a trembling hand, she knew her parents and her brother would have been proud of her.

Audrey went to the recruiting station in Annapolis the next day, and did what she had told Lizzie she would. She wrote down all the details of the training class she wanted to join. She had her physical a week later and passed with ease. She still didn't know if they would approve her for the training class she'd requested. It felt strangely appropriate that she had had the physical on the second anniversary of Pearl Harbor, two years after her brother's death.

She received her acceptance letter into the army on the fourteenth of December. Her request to volunteer for the Army Air Forces Flying Nurses had been approved, and they had granted her request for Medical Air Evacuation Transport (MAET) duty. She had been assigned to the same training class as Lizzie and Alex, and had to report to the base on the first of January, and start classes with the other nurses on the second. She let out a scream when she read the letter, and rushed to the phone to call Lizzie, who had just woken up in California.

"I got it! I got it!" Audrey shouted into the phone. "I'm in the same unit you are."

"Oh my God! That's fantastic!" They both spoke at once, and Audrey's mind was racing. She had two weeks to pack up her parents' house as much as she was going to. And she had to find someone to check it from time to time to make sure no pipes had burst or were frozen. She asked a neighbor, who was impressed that she had enlisted and agreed to visit the house periodically. She didn't even care about Christmas now, she had so much to do before she left. Lizzie invited her to Boston again for the holiday, but it was only ten days away. She wasn't sure she'd be finished by then, but said she'd try. All she could think of were all the things she was going to do and learn in the coming months, and the missions she would fly on, and that she would be back with her best friend. They were both hoping to be stationed in England. There was nothing to keep her in Annapolis now, or the States. She had something important to do for the war effort, and lives to save. Her life suddenly made sense again. She was going to be a lieutenant in the Army Air Forces, in a Medical Air Evacuation Transport unit. It was the most exciting thing that had ever happened to her. Her life had a purpose, other than just keeping her mother alive through the agonizing years of her illness. She was grateful she had gone to nursing school. It was going to serve her well with the men she would be assigned to care for.

All she could think about as she hung up the phone was how exciting her life had become, and this was just the beginning.

Two months from now, she'd be leaving for her assignment, wherever it was. She wondered how hard the classes would be, and she hoped she'd pass them. Lizzie had said that some of the training would be physically rigorous, from what she'd heard. But Audrey was ready to face anything. She knew she was on the right path now, and didn't doubt it for an instant, nor did Lizzie and Alex. The dangers and potential discomforts didn't even occur to them. They had a job to do, and could hardly wait to get started.

Audrey finished packing and closing her parents' house. She left Will's room untouched. Her mother had slept there, but left all of Will's belongings as he had had them. It still felt like a shrine to her, and she wanted to leave it that way until she came home. She wasn't ready to put his things away, even after two years. Her mother had never wanted to either.

She said goodbye to Mrs. Beavis, who was taking some time off before taking on a new patient. Ellen's death had hit her hard after so many years of caring for her, and Ellen had been such a sweet person.

Audrey took a train to Boston the morning of Christmas Eve, and Lizzie picked her up at the station. It had been twenty-one months since they'd seen each other, although it felt like only yesterday. Nothing had changed between them, and Lizzie felt like even more of a sister now that they would be army nurses together. On the way to the house, Lizzie said that she had told her parents the day before when she arrived, and they were upset that she was hoping to ship out to England, and was joining the air evac squadron. The war would be close at hand if they were sent to England, as they hoped, and the risks greater than being safely on American soil in San Francisco, as long as the Japanese didn't bomb them again. There was no sign of it so far.

"They never thought I'd get shipped out. I hope we will be. I told them you're coming too, and that just made my mother cry harder. I think my father is proud of me, but he won't say it in front of Mom, or she'd get angry at him. But all three of their children will be on the front lines now." It seemed like a lot to Audrey too, and she suspected her mother wouldn't have liked it either, but there was nothing to stop her now.

The holiday at the Hattons' was tense, with Lizzie's new assignment looming. She hoped she'd get a short leave to see them when she finished training, but she wasn't sure. She promised she'd come home to say goodbye if she could. The four of them spent Christmas Eve together, and went to midnight Mass. They spent a quiet Christmas Day.

Lizzie saw a few of her old friends, but all the boys she knew were in the army, many were in the Pacific, and some had been killed. She took Audrey with her when they visited. Dr. Hatton opened a bottle of champagne for them on New Year's Eve.

"Let's hope that 1944 is the year this terrible war ends," he said solemnly, and they toasted Greg and Henry, and "absent friends," which had new meaning now. Lizzie and Audrey added, "And Will."

The next morning, the two young nurses left the Hatton home, with Lizzie in uniform. Audrey didn't have hers yet. They were on their way to join their unit in Kentucky and begin their air evacuation classes the next day. They had much to learn.

Lizzie's parents stood on the platform waving at them, as the train pulled away. There was no stopping them now, or changing the world from the dangerous place it had become. But neither of the two young women, standing tall and straight, were afraid of what they were about to face. And they had each other, which made them both feel brave.

Alex's visit to her family in New York was no easier than Lizzie's in Boston. Her parents were in shock that she had joined a Medical Air Evacuation Transport unit, and would be shipping out afterwards. Charlotte had had her fourth daughter by then, and still thought her younger sister was insane.

"Can't you change your mind, and refuse to go?" Astrid White said plaintively. "I'm sure we can find a doctor to say you're not well enough," she said, glancing imploringly at her husband, expecting him to change their daughter's mind, or forbid her to go.

"I'm in the army, Mother. This isn't a volunteer job at the Red Cross. I'll be a deserter if I don't show up. And I *want* to go. They *need* nurses to bring the wounded back from the front lines."

"But you enlisted, didn't you?" her mother insisted. "You should never have done it. But that's like volunteering. Surely, you can quit."

"I can be released if I'm unfit for duty, for some valid reason," Alex said quietly. Her news had not been well received, and as usual, she felt like she was facing a firing squad at home.

"Does insanity count as valid?" Charlotte said snidely, sipping a glass of champagne at Christmas Eve dinner. As always, their parents had invited a wide circle of friends. They were twenty-four at their dining room table, with the women in evening gowns and the men in black tie. Her parents didn't hesitate to challenge Alex in front of all of them. Only her brother-in-law, Eustace Bosworth, whispered his support after dinner, but would never have dared say it out loud.

"Well done, Alex. Good on you. You're braver than I would be." He was 4-F due to his football injuries from Harvard, where he had had a serious knee injury and damaged his spleen as captain of the football team. He was sitting out the war at home, and thought Alex's enlisting as a nurse was impressive, although he was relieved that his wife didn't have the same patriotic ideas.

Alex's volunteering as an Army Air Forces medical evacuation nurse gave rise to considerable comment during dinner, but by dessert the conversation had moved on to the war in Europe, how difficult it was to buy a car these days with wartime production on, how sad that no one could travel to Europe, and a cousin of Astrid's said that her sister-in-law in San Francisco had lost all their Japanese domestic help and gardeners, when they were sent away to internment camps. Several of the men commented on how fortunate it was that Robert's wine cellar was so well stocked with French wine, and hoped it would last through the war, until France was liberated and he could stock up again.

At one point, Alex's father caught her eye during dinner and saw the look on her face. It was one of sad dismay, listening to the people she had grown up with and how insensitive they were to what the war really meant to the people suffering in Europe, and dying in the trenches. She felt as though she was constantly out of step with them, and she knew they considered her pathetically eccentric, and a rebel, to have enlisted to do whatever she could to help turn the tides. To these people she had known all her life, and no longer had any respect for, it was only about buying cars, French wine, and the unavailability of Japanese domestic help on the West Coast. She found it profoundly shocking and realized that she'd had nothing in common with them for years. Her parents had wanted her to select a husband among them, and she couldn't even remotely imagine it now. Even Eustace, who was a decent guy, only thought of himself and his spoiled self-indulgent wife. They had a house full of maids and nannies and a butler in Connecticut. Charlotte never lifted a finger for anyone but herself. She was beautiful, but Alex didn't think that was enough. She didn't care about her own looks, and never thought about it.

Alex had worn a black velvet evening gown to dinner, with a big white satin bow at the low-cut waist in the back, to please her mother. She looked lovely in it, but she was almost sorry she hadn't worn her uniform to remind them that there was a war on in the real world. They didn't live in the real world, and never had. They were trapped in another century. The only thing they had noticed was the unpleasantness of the stock market crash fourteen years before, which had removed some of their friends from their social circle when they lost their money. But they were quickly forgotten, and others with larger, more stable fortunes had taken their place.

Their values made Alex feel sick, and she couldn't imagine being married to any of them. It would have been her worst nightmare. She felt like a stranger in her own world, and even in her own home. She was sad to think that her four nieces would be brought up with her sister's superficial values, believing that only people in their own limited world had any merit, and a woman with a job, or an occupation of any kind, was to be treated as a pariah, ridiculed and shunned. Alex had every intention of continuing nursing after the war, and she knew that would be a battle with her parents too. Everything she did elicited their criticism. She could barely make it through dinner without speaking her mind and losing her temper, but she managed to slip away when everyone moved into the drawing room for coffee and brandy. The crowd was large enough that her absence wasn't noticed, and she sat peacefully in her own large pink satin bedroom, smoking a cigarette, and having a glass of champagne alone. This wasn't her idea of the spirit of Christmas, a night of showing off, snobbery, and insensitive bragging, but it was the way her family spent it, and her older sister fit in perfectly with all of their views and traditions. Alex never had, and now even less than ever.

She was startled when there was a knock at the door. She said, "Come in." It was her mother's maid, a small Frenchwoman who had worked for her family since Alex was a child.

"Yes, Brigitte?" She was surprised to see her, in her evening uniform of black dress with white lace apron and cap. Alex knew only too well that if any of her fellow nurses in the army had seen the trappings of her home life, they would have ridiculed and shunned her too. She was a misfit everywhere, and she had kept this side of her life well hidden from her colleagues in the army, even Lizzie, whom she considered her best friend. But there were some things she just couldn't share. They would never have understood.

"I just wanted to tell you that we, downstairs, are very proud of you. I am proud of you. My family is in Paris, living the Occupation. My nephew is in the Maquis, the Resistance, in the South. My brother has been in prison in Marseilles for three years for speaking against the Nazis and dropping leaflets in the streets. Some of our neighbors, Jews, have lost their homes and been sent to work camps, even children. The people in Europe need the Americans to help them get free again, and as a nurse, if they send you to Europe, you will help many. You're a brave woman. You were even as a little girl, and you know the right thing to do. Thank you," she said, bowed, and made a rapid exit before Alex could even react or comment, but there were tears in her eyes when she finished the glass of champagne. What Brigitte said had touched her profoundly. She had a feeling that conditions in Europe were even worse than they suspected, and she hoped that she would be part of the forces who were coming to help them. Brigitte was right. They needed American troops to free them. And those same troops needed Alex and the other nurses to keep them alive. Whatever her family believed, she was doing something important, and nothing was going to stop her. She didn't even care if it cost her her life in the process.

From everything Alex could see, she had nothing to come home to. The one thing she knew was that she could never return to this world after the war, or live this life again. She would rather die in Europe than waste her life in New York. All she could see around her was the shame of indolence, snobbery, and false values. She wanted to go to Europe with the Army Air Forces for Brigitte, her family and friends, and others like them. More than ever, it all made sense. And she was about to take her first step toward her goal with her flight training class in Kentucky.

Chapter 7

When the Japanese attacked Pearl Harbor in December 1941, Louise Jackson had already been a practicing registered nurse for a year and a half. She had graduated from nursing school in June of 1940 at twenty-one, and as a Black woman she had attended a segregated but very respected school for Black women. She had grown up in Raleigh, North Carolina, and got a job at a respected all-Black hospital, Saint Agnes, as an operating-room nurse. Her father was a cardiologist, and her mother was the superintendent of a segregated school. Aside from their focus on education, the Jacksons' origins were distinguished ones. Blanche Jackson's family was originally Ethiopian, and Louise had the exquisitely fine features of her maternal ancestors. Ted Jackson had been able to trace his ancestors' arrival on one of the original eighteenth-century slave ships that came to Virginia.

Louise was an only child, adored by both her parents, and the one thing they insisted on was that she studied hard, got a great education, and did well in school. Very little else mattered to them, and Louise had devoted herself to her studies accordingly. Her parents had had several requests to allow her to model in Paris from the time she was very young, since color was not an issue in France, as it was in the States. Her parents had declined every opportunity, which frustrated Louise in her teens, but by the time she entered nursing school at eighteen, modeling no longer interested her. She was a very beautiful young woman. She was twenty-one when she graduated from nursing school, and twenty-two when the Japanese bombed Pearl Harbor.

She had objected frequently, to her father, about hospital facilities being segregated, but it was something she had grown up with and was used to. It seemed profoundly wrong to her, but her parents said simply that the time had not yet come to change that. They hoped it would one day. North Carolina was their home and the place where Louise had grown up.

Louise profoundly shocked both her parents when she enlisted in the army as a nurse in January of 1942. Her father strenuously objected when she told them it was what she wanted to do. The United States Armed Forces were notoriously prejudiced and segregated, and he didn't want his daughter exposed to ignorant racial prejudice, slurs, and abuse. He did everything to convince her not to enlist, but Louise was a strong girl with a bright mind and her own opinions, and she refused to be deterred. She said if racial prejudice was going to change one day, then brave positions would have to be taken, and she was determined to serve her country like any other American man or woman.

She was an intelligent, nonbelligerent person, who expressed herself in a respectful way. She'd had her share of run-ins with her superiors at the hospital where she worked and officers in the military, but always handled them gracefully, and often convincingly. She was stationed in Chicago, rather than somewhere in the Deep South, which was a relief to her father. She was assigned to a unit of Negro nurses, and stayed within the parameters that were expected of her. She was one of the most capable nurses in her unit, when she volunteered as a nurse in the Army Air Forces Medical Air Evacuation Transport Squadron. One of the reasons she did so was to get transferred to Europe, and her application was immediately accepted. She was told that she was the only "colored" nurse who had been accepted in the squadron, or had even applied. The unit had not been designated as segregated so far, and they could hardly separate a single nurse from the others. The officer who went over the applications was progressive and decided to try it as an experiment. They would have to see how the other nurses reacted, and the governors of the RAF Unit with whom they'd be housed if they sent her to England.

Her father objected even more strenuously than he had when she enlisted in the army soon after war was declared. And this time his objection was that the missions she'd be flying as a nurse, bringing wounded men back from the front lines, would be dangerous. He didn't want to lose his only child. But nothing could ever stop Louise once she made up her mind, and this time was no different.

She arrived promptly at five P.M. on New Year's Day at Bowman Field, Kentucky. She was in proper uniform, suitcase in hand, ready for six weeks of intense training. The group was divided and assigned to twenty-bed barracks, and the sergeant in charge directed her to a bed on the far end. The sergeant was as startled as many of the nurses to see Louise appear, but she looked calm and confident as she changed into the overalls they'd been given to do an hour of push-ups before dinner. No one made a single comment to see a woman of her race in their midst. There were a few glances exchanged, but nothing was said.

She lined up behind Audrey and Lizzie in the mess tent, with Alex right behind her. Alex was groaning at the push-ups they'd just done, and Lizzie was making fun of her.

"What happened to map reading on the list of courses?" Alex complained. "I won't be able to walk tomorrow."

"Wait until 'simulated enemy attack' and parachute jumping," Lizzie added.

"I'm a nurse, not a stuntwoman," Alex said, and smiled at Louise. The overalls were too big for all of them, but there were none small enough for women, and they had to make do with what they were given. None of them had had time to make them fit.

"Did you all transfer in together?" Louise asked them. They seemed to know each other too well for the first day.

"Lizzie and I were stationed at the Presidio together, in San Francisco, and we just got transferred here," Alex explained. "Audrey and Lizzie went to nursing school together before the war, and Audrey just enlisted and finished basic nurses' training. And we all wound up here together. We requested it." They were at the front of the line by then, and Audrey turned to Louise with a warm smile.

"Do you want to join us for dinner?" She invited her and Louise was pleased.

"I'd love it. I just flew in from Chicago. I've been stationed there for two years. It's a great city."

The four of them helped themselves to a hearty but unappetizing meal, and were told as soon as they finished that their half of the unit was to report to the pool. They would be swimming forty laps immediately after dinner. The thought of it nearly made them feel sick.

"I get it," Alex complained again. "They're trying to kill us. Is this the simulated enemy attack? Death by cramps in the pool after dinner?"

"No, I think they do that by shooting at us," Lizzie answered her, and the others laughed. Louise had had a good time eating dinner with them. As they headed for the pool at a dead run after disposing of their trays, Louise wondered if anyone would object when she got into the pool. This was a new experience for her. Even in Chicago, which was a northern state, there were things she couldn't do, particularly in the military. Her unit in Chicago had been entirely composed of Black nurses, and the patients she ministered to were Black soldiers as well. She had never had a white patient, in nursing school or since. And as the only colored woman entering the pool, she expected someone to object, and was astonished when no one did. She paused for a moment at the edge of the pool, waiting for someone to say something unpleasant, and Alex noticed it.

"What are you waiting for? Oh God, I hope you can swim. I won't know how to save you, so please don't drown." The real reason for Louise's hesitation never occurred to Alex, which Louise realized too. As far as what she lived with on a daily basis, and had all her life, these women were innocents, and none of them were from the South, so the whole notion of segregation was foreign to them.

"No, just chicken," she answered Alex. "I figured I'd let you test how cold it is."

"Thanks a lot," Alex said and jumped in, and Louise dove in neatly beside her. They were all wearing extremely ugly army-issue bathing suits. And the water, they rapidly discovered, was freezing, intentionally.

After swimming forty laps, most of them could barely crawl out of the pool. While still soaking wet in January, they were ordered to run two miles before they could come back for a hot shower. By the time they did, they were all shivering and their legs were weak from the exertion. Their wet hair under their army-issue bathing caps made them even colder.

"Whose idea was this?" Lizzie said feeling miserable, looking at her three cohorts. "Take me back to San Francisco." Audrey had actually held up better than the others and surprised herself.

They were allowed to go back to their barracks after that, and were ordered to go to bed. They were told they'd have calisthenics the next morning at four A.M.

As Louise walked past the sergeant, the short, tough-looking woman spoke to her under her breath.

"You think you're special, don't you? Is your mama white?"

"No, she's Ethiopian," Louise said coolly.

"Smart-ass me, and you'll wind up in solitary."

"In the real world, Sergeant," Louise said quietly as the others listened, worried for her, "I outrank you."

"This isn't the real world. This is *my* world, and don't you forget it."

"Yes, Sergeant," Louise said, and walked to her bed. But she had said what she needed to, and the sergeant left a few minutes later.

"I think they're just trying to prepare us for combat," Lizzie said nervously. She hadn't run into anyone like the nasty little sergeant before.

"I'm used to it," Louise said softly. "I deal with that in some form every day." It shocked the others, who hadn't been exposed to it. But Louise looked undisturbed when they went to the bathroom together a few minutes later to brush their teeth, dry their hair with towels, and get ready for bed. It was the first time she had lived among white women.

"Why in God's name do we have to get up at four A.M.?" Alex complained as she got into bed.

"Just to prove they can make us do it," Audrey answered, and Lizzie agreed. "Eventually, we'll start classes, and it should get easier after that."

It didn't get easier for the nurses in the air evac training program for several weeks. The classes were fascinating and intense. The simulated enemy attack was terrifying, with blanks, which they were told were real bullets, whizzing past them and over their heads. The physical challenges were constant and exhausting. They learned field survival, ditching and crash procedures, how to use their parachutes, and what to do if they got lost behind enemy lines. They assumed that their medical skills were adequate for the job they had to do, but their military abilities had to be equally so, in the air and on the ground.

By the time they'd been there for a month, they had been prepared for almost every situation. And for the last two weeks of the course, they had to wear heavy combat airmen's flight gear everywhere, to get used to it and make things even more difficult.

All the women in the class felt as though they had been to hell and back, and they were proud of themselves for finishing the course. No one had dropped out or failed. At the end of the six weeks, they were as ready as they were ever going to be. They were told that they were leaving to ship out in five days. They had been given no time off during the training, which had been a relief to Louise, since she knew she would have run into rude comments and hostility by the locals in Kentucky, which was a Southern state.

They were being sent to England on a troop ship, which would be dangerous. And they were being given a three-day leave before they left. None of the four friends had boyfriends they were leaving behind, but Lizzie, Alex, and Louise had promised to visit their parents for a last time to say goodbye. Audrey declined Lizzie's offer to go to Boston with her and decided to stay on the base. She was going to rest and do some reading before they shipped out. She didn't want to intrude on Lizzie's last days with her parents.

The others left as soon as they were able. It was a short trip to New York for Alex, which she undertook with trepidation. Lizzie and Louise had farther to go. They were all dreading emotional farewells with their parents, which seemed inevitable. Audrey was one of the very few who stayed at the base. The others had men or families to go to, but she had neither, and was grateful for the downtime after the intense six-week course.

Alex's parents were at home having dinner when she walked into the apartment in her uniform and dropped her duffel bag in the front hall. She met them in the dining room and they were surprised to see her. She hadn't had time to call to tell them about her leave before she came.

"I'm not here for an argument," she warned them as she walked into the dining room. "I came to say goodbye. I'm shipping out in a few days." She wasn't supposed to say exactly when or to where. But she and the other nurses knew she was going to England to become one of the flying nurses in the Medical Air Evacuation Transport unit, rescuing injured men from the front.

She sat down to dinner with her parents and told them about the course she had just taken. Her father was deeply impressed. Alex had always seemed so feminine and graceful to him. He couldn't imagine her doing a tenth of what she described to them, or even doing it himself.

"It sounds like the course was designed for men," he said respectfully.

"Probably, but we have to be able to survive and get our patients back to the hospital at the base in any circumstances. Eighteen percent of the wounded are evacuated by air transport now, not ambulance. It's faster and saves lives. That's what we're there for." She didn't tell them that the Germans had been making a point of shooting down planes with a red cross on them, or any planes suspected of transporting wounded men, and sinking hospital ships, killing thousands more injured men.

"I'll be so happy when this war is over," her mother said, looking forlorn. "When President Roosevelt declared war, I was so grateful I didn't have any sons who would be drafted, and then you went and enlisted," she said in a plaintive tone.

"I'm sorry, Mother. I just couldn't see myself going to the cotillion as a spinster every year, until I died of old age. I'd rather do something useful for my country."

"You could roll bandages, like every other woman I know. Besides, you would have found a husband eventually. You'll be old now when the war ends."

"I'm turning twenty-four, not forty, Mom," Alex reminded her.

"At twenty-five, you'll be competing with eighteen-year-olds for a husband," her mother said, sounding discouraged.

"I'll just have to find someone who wants an old bag like me." Alex grinned at her, and clearly wasn't worried about it.

"Will you give up nursing after the war?" her father asked her.

"I hope not. I doubt it. I don't know what else I'd do. Somehow flower arranging and ladies' lunches don't appeal to me." He nodded and wasn't surprised.

"You could spend time with your sister in Greenwich, and help her with the children," her mother suggested, and Alex didn't comment. Jumping out of a plane with her parachute on, which had terrified her in evac training, sounded more appealing. She was a nurse, not a nanny.

"Do you know where you'll be stationed in England?" her father asked her.

"They haven't told us yet," she said vaguely, as she was supposed to, and gave nothing away. "But you can write to me just like you did when I was in San Francisco. It'll take longer, but I'll get it eventually."

"I wish they were sending you back there," her mother said mournfully. And shortly after, they left the dining room and retired to their rooms.

It was nice to be home, in the luxury of their apartment with all the comforts her parents provided for her, but there was a sense of unreality to it now too, as though all the bad things happening in the world beyond these walls didn't exist. Alex used her three-day leave to do errands and pick up things she'd need on the trip. She had the feeling that she might not have a chance like this again. She didn't know how much time off they would get once they were in England, or how close together their missions would be.

It felt odd walking around New York in her olive uniform and khaki blouse. She saw people looking at her, wondering what branch of the service she was in. There were little gold wings on her lapel, with a maroon "N" on them, which identified her as a flight nurse, which most people didn't recognize.

She had dinner with her parents on the last night and said good-bye to them after dinner. She would be leaving at six the next morning and didn't want to wake them. She had to report to the troop ship that would take them to England. It was hard to find the words to say goodbye, knowing that there was always the possibility that they might not see each other again. Her parents were acutely aware of it, and Alex tried not to be. On the whole, the three days had gone smoothly, and Charlotte had come to have dinner with them on the last night to say goodbye too. And for once, she was warm when she hugged Alex.

"I wish you weren't doing this," she said in an emotional tone.

"I wish I didn't have to. Hopefully, the war will end soon."

"Maybe I should have been nicer to you," she said, looking guilty. "Then you wouldn't have run away and joined the circus."

"I probably would have anyway. And the Army Air Forces needs nurses desperately."

"Just come home, Allie. I promise I'll be nicer when you do." Alex doubted that but appreciated her sister saying it.

"I'll be back soon, Char. Take care of your babies. Maybe you'll have a boy next time," Alex teased her, and Charlotte shook her head.

"Oh no, I'm done. Four girls are enough for me. I'll be ready to kill myself fifteen years from now with four teenage girls fighting with me."

"I admit, it's a frightening thought." Alex hugged her tight then, and Charlotte left shortly after, with tears running down her cheeks. Her parents hugged Alex again and went to bed. When she went to her room that night, Alex sat smoking quietly by the window and realized that, whatever their failings and no matter how different she was from them, her family loved her to the best of their limited abilities. It was a comforting thought as she prepared to leave them. For once, she was sad to leave, but she wasn't afraid of what lay ahead. She couldn't wait to get to England and start flying missions.

* * *

Lizzie had come to similar conclusions in Boston. Her parents were distressed that she was going overseas too, with both her brothers in the Pacific. But whatever their ideas, or their goals for her, and however little they understood the dreams she had, she never doubted that they loved her, and would always be there if she needed them. It was the best she could hope for, and all she needed to take with her.

Louise took the train from Kentucky to North Carolina, and she was grateful to have the time with her parents. Her father canceled his office hours for the day, and spent the time with her, and her mother joined them as soon as she could leave school.

She had always been close to them, and they had always encouraged her to follow her dreams and fight for what she believed in. She tried to live up to what they expected of her, and she set the bar high for herself. What she was doing now was no different. They were proud of her, and they stood tall on the station platform in the segregated section as they watched the train pull away when she left. She hung out the window waving at them, in her uniform. She could see the tears glistening on their cheeks, and she kept waving until she could no longer see them.

All three girls got to the ship punctually after their leave, and they were happy to see each other. It had been an emotional few days, saying goodbye to their families, and it had been a quiet reflective time for Audrey. All of them were excited about what lay ahead of them, who they would meet, what they would do. And they wondered if they would be equal to the tasks set before them.

Only Alex had ever been to England. The others had never been out of the country, and most of the girls they talked to in their unit hadn't either. It was going to be exciting too, working with the RAF and English nurses, and being housed with them. The army and the war were broadening their horizons and giving them new opportunities, which would change their lives forever.

All the nurses reported to the ship on time after their leaves. They headed to the SS *Henry Gibbons,* an army transport ship being used to carry troops between New York and Southampton. It had a capacity for over two thousand passengers. They were bunking six to a cabin, in triple bunks. Alex, Lizzie, Louise, and Audrey, and two other nurses had been assigned to the same cabin. There were eighty-two flight nurses traveling to England, and two thousand male troops on the ship. At six in the morning, the day after all of their leaves had ended and they boarded the ship, and a full twenty-four hours before they had all been told they were sailing, an alarm sounded and the troop ship they were traveling on left the dock on the tides with no further warning. Alex woke up with a start, but most of the others slept through it. They were leaving a day earlier than they'd been told, for wartime security. They would travel as swiftly as possible, sailing both day and night, hoping to avoid U-boats and German fighter planes spotting them. They were to dock in Southampton, and the nurses would travel in buses for two hours to Down Ampney in Gloucestershire, the RAF base where they would be stationed. They'd been told it was two and a half hours from London.

The nurses tended to stick together on the journey, standing at the rail and talking about where they'd been, where they came from, where they had been assigned in England. They would be briefed by the RAF about their procedures when they got there.

And as they stood at the rail in the morning sunshine, on a crystal clear cold day, they looked at the sea of men below them on the lower decks, and Lizzie wondered how many of them they would be transporting one day, after they were injured. It was a sobering thought. They were all traveling in uniform. A mass of thousands of khaki uniforms. The nurses were the only females on board.

A few of the nurses mingled secretly with the enlisted men, which was not allowed. It didn't seem worth the risk to Audrey and the others, just to flirt with the men, so they stayed with the other nurses.

"And here, my mom was worried I'd never find a husband," Alex commented, and the others laughed, as they stared at the soldiers below them. "Somehow I never counted on meeting a man while I'm in the army." But others did, and found them, for a night, or longer.

"I don't want to meet a guy," Lizzie said. She hadn't gotten over Will yet, even two years later. Every man she met paled in comparison to him.

"Maybe a nice English boy," Audrey said. She hadn't had a date, or time for one, while her mother was sick. She liked the idea of meeting a nice man one day, but she hadn't had the opportunity in years.

"I'd rather wait til the war is over," Louise said soberly, and her situation was more complicated.

None of them were desperate to find boyfriends. They had too much else on their minds.

The two nurses they were sharing their cabin with had looked startled when they saw Louise, but made no comment after a quick glance at each other. The others seemed nice enough, and they decided to ignore her.

The days on the ship dragged by and there were some tense moments, when the ship slowed, and they all suspected the lookouts had spotted something or the captain had been warned. Then their speed would pick up again. The captain was pushing the ship hard to get to England in a hurry. Ships just like theirs had been torpedoed and sunk by U-boats or attacked by the German Luftwaffe, but day followed day without incident. And finally, five days later, land came into sight. More than two thousand cheers rose from the ship as they all stood on deck. They had made the journey safely, and their next adventures awaited them.

Chapter 8

When war was declared in Europe in September 1939, although they were older, Prudence Pommery's parents were among the first to offer their home to house as many children as they could manage during the evacuation of children from London. They had three grown children of their own. Maximillian was twenty-two, Prudence was twenty, and Phillip was nineteen. Both their sons enlisted in the RAF immediately. A month after war was declared, Prudence signed on for an accelerated two-and-a-half-year nursing course at the local college, near their Yorkshire manor.

The Pommerys turned nearly all the guest rooms into dormitories and hired local girls to help take care of the children. The government urged all parents to send their children out of the cities, on relocation programs to keep them safe from the bombing. Many children had already been killed. Families in the countryside all over England were volunteering to take them in and house them. Few people took as many as the Pommerys, but they had an enormous home. They had twenty-four children staying with them, and four village girls to help them. Prudence pitched in whenever she wasn't at her nursing classes. The operation ran surprisingly smoothly. Lord and Lady Pommery called them their adopted grandchildren and faced the situation with kindness and good humor. Four and a half years later, in the spring of 1944, nearly half the children had lost their parents, either in combat or during the bombing of London. They would be placed in adoptive homes after the war. But in the meantime, they remained with the Pommerys in Yorkshire. In some cases, brothers and sisters had been placed with them, but in many cases, siblings had been separated. The youngest child they had there was nearly six now, and the oldest had just turned eighteen and was about to enlist in the army. Running the house and supervising the children was a full-time job for Lady Pommery. The children attended the village school, and the Pommerys had acquired their own school bus. Lord and Lady Pommery took turns driving the bus to school, and thoroughly enjoyed it, almost as much as Prudence had enjoyed her nursing classes. She had graduated in February 1942, and was a volunteer nurse at the local hospital for a year after she graduated. Then she decided to enlist in the RAF Nursing Corps and went to London.

She had been there for a year when she volunteered for the Medical Air Evacuation Transport Squadron. She had been there for three months, in a combined unit with American air forces flight nurses, and some British and Australians. They flew on Douglas C-47 Skytrain cargo planes, heavy, dependable two-engine planes perfectly suited to short flights and heavy cargo. They carried up to twenty-four litter patients, and sometimes the walking wounded.

The patients were tended to by a nurse and two medical corpsmen on each flight. A flight surgeon and senior nurse oversaw the squadrons from the ground. The planes flew into areas of heavy fighting and brought out as many wounded as they could, those who could be saved and would survive the journey. They had to do rapid triage when they picked up the wounded, and there were sometimes terrible decisions to make. But they saved many lives by removing the wounded by plane instead of ambulance, which was slow going and often over rough terrain. They lost far fewer patients transporting them by air. The planes faced all the perils of battle themselves, at risk of being shot down by the enemy. And with men and cargo on board, the army was not allowed to mark the planes with the red cross and were considered legitimate military targets. They were given fighter plane coverage when possible, which wasn't always the case.

Prudence had been part of the Medical Air Evacuation Transport Squadron bringing the wounded back to the hospital at the airbase for over a year now, and she loved every minute of it. She was twenty-five years old. She was considered senior and very skilled among the air evacuation nurses because she was fully trained and very competent. Many of the others weren't experienced and had minimum training. Many of them were in fact civilians in uniform, but without official rank. Pru was a proper nurse in the RAF.

Her brothers had flown countless missions over Germany in the RAF. Her younger brother, Phillip, was the more daring of the two at twenty-four, maybe the best pilot, and willing to take more chances. Max was twenty-seven, and more cautious by nature. Both were superb pilots. They teased their sister for her work on the flying ambulances, and said she did it to pick up men. But both were well aware of the risks the crews of the air evac transports took, and were secretly very proud of her. She had also been a courageous young girl, who tried to compete with her brothers as a child, on foot or on horseback, racing her bicycle down a lane, or climbing a tree higher than they did. And no matter how badly battered she was, she never cried when she got hurt. It was something Max had always admired about her. He readily admitted now that he had cried more often than she did. Phillip was the terror of the threesome, a daredevil who would stop at nothing and seemed to have nine lives. He had used several of them since he started flying for the RAF. He was famous for the many times he had extricated himself from what looked like disaster.

When Pru came back from her mission that afternoon, she was told that there were American flight nurses arriving the next day. She was excited to hear it. She had worked with American flight nurses before, and she found them efficient, brave, well trained, and a pleasure to work with. They never complained, and adapted to every situation, no matter how hard. And she had fun spending time with them after hours. They enjoyed a good time as much as she and the other RAF nurses did.

Her brothers were legends in the RAF, and extremely popular with her women friends. It was no secret who her parents were, although no one made a fuss about it. The children of many aristocrats, in fact most of them, had enlisted in the RAF, the navy, and the army, and were defending their country valiantly. Pru was greatly respected as a nurse on the medical air evac transports. She was said to be fearless, which she insisted wasn't true. But she was modest to the point of humble, unassuming, and tireless, and one of the best nurses in the squadron. She was well liked by every corpsman who ever worked with her, and good fun at the pub afterwards, they claimed. She could drink them under the table and show up fresh as a daisy the next day.

"I have brothers," she said with a wink whenever they commented on her fearless behavior and ability to drink without showing any sign of it, and show up on time the next day in good humor.

"I would hate her if I didn't love her so damn much," Ed Murphy, the corpsman who worked with her most often said about her. "I swear, you could run her over with a bus, and she'd pop up, hop on the plane, and work for twenty hours without complaining. She's not human." No one who worked with her had ever met anyone who didn't like her. She never pulled rank without a good reason to do so, and even then, only in extremis. She was never unfair in her decisions, and never traded on her aristocratic lineage. She got the job done, did everything humanly possible to save her patients, and was ready to take off again the next day—on every mission they were assigned, on two hours' sleep if she had to, and sometimes with no sleep at all.

All in all, Prudence Pommery came from a lovely family of caring, responsible, compassionate people, and Pru had a heart of gold.

The night the American flight nurses arrived, she came back from the airstrip after seeing all her patients put into ambulances. She had filled out her reports and sent all the paperwork to the hospital with Ed Murphy. The dormitory was exploding at the seams with the new arrivals when she came in. She stopped at the front office to inquire about them.

"Are the Yanks in?" It sounded like there was a party going on upstairs, or several of them. She could hear voices and laughing, and girls calling to each other in the halls as they settled in.

"They arrived this afternoon," the private at the desk confirmed.

"Sounds like fun up there." Pru smiled. She was tired, but it didn't show. They had almost lost one of their patients, but some heroic measures on her part, with Ed's help, had saved him. She was going to check on the patient at the hospital later that night, but wanted to shower and grab something to eat first. She hadn't had time to eat all day. And they had been chased by a German fighter plane, which their own fighter escort shot down. Her dark brown hair was disheveled, and there was dried blood on her flight suit. She was tall and slim, with warm brown eyes, dark brown hair, and a ready smile.

She headed up the stairs, and saw half a dozen women sitting on some beds through an open door, and she stuck her head in. "Welcome to jolly England, and air evac, ladies. We've been waiting for you. We need you desperately. There's a fine Irish pub down the road, with a fish and chips shop next door. I'll take you down there tomorrow. I've got to stop in at the hospital tonight, to check on some of my boys. I'm Pru Pommery, by the way," she said with a broad, welcoming smile, as she walked into the room. Alex, Lizzie, and Louise turned and smiled at her. Audrey was in the shower at the end of the hall.

"Did you just fly in?" Alex asked her. Pru looked like a lively, fun person, with a broad smile that lit up her eyes.

"Just back. My room's just down the hall, by the way, if you need anything. I'm sort of the house mother on this floor, aspirin, safety pins, steri strips, kirby grips—oh booby pins, I think you call them, for your hair." The three of them laughed.

"*Bobby* pins," Lizzie corrected her, "but I think I like booby pins better. Most days, I get a booby prize for my hair." She always complained that her blond curls were uncontrollable.

"I have mine done every day at four," Pru said, patting her mop of hair that looked an absolute mess after the arduous flight and the stress of saving a man from bleeding to death. They all laughed again, as Audrey walked in, wearing a terrycloth robe with her hair soaking wet, and introduced herself.

"You'll all start classes tomorrow, it's really an orientation to tell you how the RAF does everything. Protocols and all that. It's a total waste of time. You'll do just fine without it. They just want to impress you with how efficient we are." Pru went to take a shower herself then, and soon came back to see them in a clean flight suit, as they were leaving for the mess hall. Pru was postponing dinner to check on her patient. "I'm off to see one of my boys," she explained. "He gave us a bit of a fright today. You'll each be flying with one of us for the first few flights, and then you'll be on your own. I hope I get a chance to fly with you," Pru said, and walked down the stairs with them, and then walked swiftly to the hospital. The soldier they'd saved that afternoon was still alive, but in critical condition. There was a good chance that her corpsman had saved his leg. She sat next to the boy who had nearly died and talked to him quietly until he drifted off to sleep. He'd been happy to see her again, and she told him how well he was doing and how brave he was.

She hitched a ride to the pub on the way back to tell Ed what a good job he'd done. He was a strapping, handsome blond Irishman who'd been a pharmacist's assistant before the war, and had trained as a medic in the army. He dreamed of becoming a doctor, but probably never would. He had too many relatives who needed his help in Ireland. His father had died when he was a boy and he had worked all the odd jobs he could to help his mother support his seven younger brothers and sisters.

"You did a good job, Ed," Pru said and patted him on the back. "If he lives, the surgeons think he'll keep the leg." Ed had applied a tourniquet so perfectly, he had kept the patient from bleeding to death, but not so tightly that he'd lose the leg. The soldier was nineteen years old, barely more than a boy. The war was devouring boys like him every day, and killing most of them. It broke Pru's heart when she lost one of them. She did everything she could to save them, including threatening the life of Reggie, her pilot, if he didn't get them back fast enough. It was a race against time on every flight every day. "We got a load of new nurses in today," she told Ed as he handed her a pint she didn't want, but she took a sip anyway. "Americans." Ed was a ladies' man, and he could never resist a pretty nurse. He had the charm of the Irish, and many of the nurses found him irresistible. Aside from being good-looking, he was an incredibly nice guy, a great corpsman, and a talented medic.

"Music to my ears." He smiled at her.

"I shouldn't drink the beer," she said, smiling back at him. "I haven't eaten. I just want to go to bed."

"Shall I get you some fish and chips next door?"

"I'm too tired to eat," she admitted. "We've got a four A.M. start time tomorrow. I'm heading to bed."

"Me too," he said, glancing around the room. "I just haven't figured out with who yet." She laughed and knew he wasn't as indiscriminate as he liked people to think. It was more of a game he played. He loved to flirt. Women loved him. And men admired him.

"Save yourself for the Americans. There were about six beauties in the room, or maybe it was four, when I stopped in to say hello to them."

"Are any of them flying with us?"

"Not tomorrow, but probably soon. We have to brief them first. They don't really need it. They'll figure it out as they go along, like the rest of us. Well, I'm off," she said, handing him her beer to finish.

"I'll drive you back," he volunteered, setting the beer down. "You look done in. You're asleep on your feet."

"Not quite, but getting there." She smiled at him.

She followed him outside, and they chatted on the short drive back to her barracks. The nurses' dormitory was one of the biggest buildings on the base.

"See you in the morning," he said and waved as he drove away. He was thinking about the American nurses who had just arrived and wondered if they were as good-looking as Pru said. He could hardly wait to see for himself.

Emma Jones was already sound asleep in her bed when Pru walked into the dimly lit room they shared, and undressed. They had been roommates for a year, and after a stormy beginning, had become fast friends. Pru had heard that Emma had had a rough flight that day and lost a patient, which was rare for her. Of all of them, she had been a nurse for the longest time before the war. Emma had grown up in the slums in the East End of London. Her father had died at the end of the Great War shortly before she was born. Her mother had died of drink when Emma was fifteen. She'd spent three years in a Catholic home for orphans after that, and had somehow resisted the usual temptations of prostitution and minor crime to survive. She had no family, had grown up dirt poor, and had all the toughness and the accent of the East End that went with it when she and Pru met in the RAF.

She had been determined to make something of herself as a young girl, and to not wind up like her mother and too many women she knew like her. By sheer grit and determination, she had gotten a scholarship to a state nursing school before the war, became a nurse and then a midwife, and had worked as a midwife in Poplar in the East End. She had remained faithful to her roots. When the bombing of London started, she had joined the army and later the Medical Air Evacuation Transport Squadron as soon as it was formed. She had had a boyfriend when the war started. He'd been shot down and killed over Germany in 1941. She hadn't loved another man since, and didn't want to. She concentrated on her work.

She was twenty-six years old, although she was so small she looked like a child at times. But she was all woman and all heart, and fought like a cat, or the street fighter she was, any time she felt she needed to defend someone or something she cared about. She fought for her patients' lives harder than any nurse Pru had ever known.

They'd had their share of run-ins at first. Emma had a profound distrust of anyone from the upper classes, and she got into arguments with Pru constantly until she finally realized that Pru wasn't snobbish and didn't give a damn where Emma had grown up, or that she was from the East End. They had been best friends ever since. She teased Pru at times about where she came from, and Pru returned the favor by calling her an "East End guttersnipe." The insults they cheerfully exchanged horrified anyone who heard them, only to realize later that the two women loved each other and would have died defending each other. Emma had punched a soldier in a pub once when she thought he had insulted Pru, and a bar fight had broken out all around them. The two women had escaped before the police arrived, and they laughed all the way back to their barracks.

Pru felt bad about the boy she'd heard Emma had lost that day. She knew how hard Emma took her losses and that she always considered it a failure on her part. But no matter how hard they tried, they couldn't save them all. They tried to, but sometimes the damage was so great that even extreme measures didn't make a difference. The worst part of their jobs was the men they lost, although the time saved by airlifting them out of the battle zones and flying them back to the hospital saved many of them. It was a new fight for the nurses and the corpsmen every day.

Emma stirred as Pru changed into her nightgown and slipped into her bed across from Emma's. Emma popped her head up, with her short bright red hair sticking up like a pixie's. She was half asleep.

"Is that you?" Emma asked sleepily.

"No, it's Claudette Colbert," Pru said with a grin.

"Oh shut up, did you eat?" she asked, lying down again. They took care of each other since no one else did. They were combat buddies in the best sense of the word.

"No, I went to the hospital to check on one of our boys. We almost lost him on the way back."

"I lost one today," Emma said sadly, wide-awake now, when she thought of it. "We tried everything. Terrible chest wound. He died halfway back. We should have taken off sooner, but we didn't have a full load yet, and they took too long to bring the others on."

"You can't guess at that, Em. He might have died anyway. I lost one like that last month. It happens."

"He was twenty years old, just a kid."

"They're all kids. There are no old men on the battlefields. They're all boys, who should never have to be there." Emma nodded and didn't speak for a minute.

"A load of Americans arrived today. I saw them when I came in. They talk and laugh a lot," Emma commented, and Pru smiled.

"That'll liven the place up. I met a few of them on my way in. They were nice." The Australians were usually jolly too, and good fun.

"I guess so." Emma was slower to warm up to people than Pru was, and she was always a little suspicious of new faces in their midst.

"We should try to get to meet them. We'll be flying with them soon," Pru commented.

"I hope they're good," Emma said seriously.

"I'm sure they will be. And in the end, we all figure it out as we go." Emma nodded agreement and closed her eyes again. "Get some sleep. You look knackered," Pru told her.

"I am. I have to be up at three-thirty. We fly at four tomorrow."

"Me too."

"Wake me, if I don't get up," Emma said, as she turned on her side, and was already half asleep again.

"Night, Em. Sleep tight," Pru whispered and closed her eyes, trying to forget the images of the day. She didn't know how she'd survive it sometimes, if it weren't for her friends, like Emma and Ed. They gave each other the strength to do it all again every day. She wondered if any of the Americans who had arrived would turn out to be good friends too. Time would tell.

The alarm Emma had set the night before went off at three-thirty, which gave them both just enough time to roll out of bed and into their flight clothes, head down the hall to brush their teeth, wash their faces, and comb their hair, and then run down the stairs, and grab a cup of coffee, rush out to a car and head to the tarmac less than a mile away. Or if there was no car, they ran there. They had the time calculated down to the last second, without a minute to spare, to get every last second of sleep they could before facing another day.

The wartime coffee was bitter, and sugar was rationed, but tea was hard to come by. Neither Emma nor Prudence took the time to eat breakfast. Their corpsmen would bring them something from the mess hall, even if it was a single piece of toast and an apple, or a paper cup of porridge. It was enough to start the day.

Their planes were side by side on the tarmac, and their pilots were already there, checking the engines. Ed drove up minutes after Pru got there. He looked fresh and alert, and he smiled when he saw her. Emma had already climbed the ladder into her own C-47 and was checking the supplies. They had used a lot the day before, and her corpsmen had restocked them. Ten minutes later, they were ready to go. Pru glanced at the empty beds on her plane. They were ready for twenty-four men to be brought back to the base.

"Where are we headed?" she asked the pilot. He had the flight plan and the map. She put her parachute on as they taxied down the runway a few minutes later. They went where the battles were hottest, and where they'd been radioed in code that the need was greatest. They would have the wounded ready for them on litters when they arrived.

"We got a call an hour ago. Luftwaffe hit about eighty miles from here. They have thirty-nine men injured. It won't take us long to get there. They've got the boys ready to load, we can take twenty-four and another transport will pick up the fifteen or sixteen walking wounded after us," he said matter-of-factly, in the jargon that was familiar to her now.

Emma's flight took off first, and they were right behind her. Pru saw them take off in the opposite direction. The Luftwaffe had been busy the night before. It was an ugly thought, but she hoped that their own boys had done just as much damage in Germany that night. She was so tired of the war. They all were.

The heavy C-47 took off in a velvet sky filled with stars. They would land at their destination before the dawn, and bring the boys back to the base, restock supplies, and take off again. They would spend the day ferrying broken bodies and bleeding men back with them, twenty-four of them on every flight, a never-ending stream of wounded after four and a half years of war. The cities were in rubble. Almost every family had lost a son, or several, and children had lost parents. Prudence sat in her jump seat looking at the night sky. It looked so peaceful. It was hard to believe that they kept killing people every day.

"Beautiful up here, isn't it?" Ed said softly, sitting just behind her, and he handed her an apple. She nodded in answer and took a bite. "We'll miss this one day."

"No, we won't. How can you say that?" She turned to look at him.

"It gives our lives purpose, and meaning. We know why we're here. We have a mission, and we fulfill it many times. We have a chance to win again every day, and save lives."

"And when we don't, it hurts like hell." She thought of Emma the night before, and the sadness in her eyes over the boy they had lost. She didn't know him, they never did. It didn't matter. The boy's life was precious. They all were. Pru thought sometimes that she'd never want children after this. She had already lost too many. She didn't know how their parents, or the parents who had lost little children in the bombings in London, survived it. She couldn't have borne it, and never wanted to be this brave again. She longed for peacetime. She had grown up with war. It had gone on for too long. The plane took a sharp turn then, and they dropped altitude sharply. She looked at Reggie, the pilot. He was watching the sky intently.

"I saw something." A moment later they saw a fighter plane heading toward a target, with two more behind it, and they dropped lower. No one spoke as Reggie maneuvered, waiting for the fighter planes to come after them and attack. They saw the sky light up when the bombs hit the ground in the distance. Death had come early in the day to the people below them. They took another sharp turn and stayed well below the fighter planes that kept heading into the distance. They didn't bother to come after the big cargo plane. They had completed their mission and headed back to Germany. Prudence and her crew had been lucky this time. The fighter planes could have come after them, but they didn't. Pru and Ed and the pilot watched the fires grow beneath them as the bombs did their damage, and they headed toward their mission to pick up twenty-four men who might get lucky that day. Some lived and some died, some would be saved, and some couldn't be. It was all in a day's work for Pru and the men she flew with.

"Ten minutes," the pilot said a little while later. The copilot took out a map and confirmed that they were almost at their destination, while Pru and Ed, and Charlie, the other corpsman, got everything set for their pickup. Her heart was pounding as they got ready to land and start another day. The sky was slowly turning purple with pink streaks starting across it. The pilot brought down the landing gear as they descended, and Ed smiled at Pru.

"It'll be a good day," he predicted, and as they touched down on an old rutted runway, with the loaded litters lying on the grass beside it, she hoped he was right.

Chapter 9

Pru's and Emma's last flights came in right behind each other that night. They'd been flying missions for fourteen hours, and were both more tired than they were willing to admit. Ground crews got the wounded to where the transports could land, and the planes either came back for another load of wounded or moved on to another destination. It was a continuing process. They had changed pilots once several hours before, but the medical crew remained the same until their day's work was done. Lifting the litters and sometimes carrying the men, moving them, dealing with their severe injuries was backbreaking work and emotionally draining. Whenever possible, they talked to the wounded to reassure them and keep them alive. Some were unconscious, or heavily drugged, but many were awake, frightened, and in pain. It required constant concentration and rapid decisions that could cost or save their lives. There were no hard-and-fast rules. Pru and her crew, and the others, were willing to try anything to save the boys.

When they went into particularly dangerous areas, they were assigned fighter planes to go with them and protect them. But often they flew alone. They were a legitimate target for the enemy since the C-47s bore no red cross to indicate their medical mission. Since they carried both cargo and men, they were fair game for the enemy. There were no polite rules in this war, no gentlemen's agreements or humanity or compassion. Hitler's armies and his allies had one primary goal: to destroy them and in addition, to sink morale.

When they left the airstrip after a halfway decent day, Pru walked along next to Emma with a tired smile. Neither of them had lost a patient, so far, which made it a successful day for them. It was all they cared about.

Ed had manually held an eighteen-year-old soldier's entrails in place for one of their flights that day and saved his life, while talking to him about Ireland when he was a boy, just to keep the soldier's mind on something else. The ambulance drivers and medics took over once they landed back at Down Ampney, their home base. With the last man off both their flights, Emma and Pru were free for the night, until the next day when it would all begin again. They had to have tremendous fortitude to face it every day, but that was what they were here for. And neither of them, nor their fellow flight nurses, would have wanted any other job. This was why they had enlisted, not to sit at a desk or walk down a hospital corridor. They had come for the rough work, and there was plenty of it.

"Are you up to stopping in to see the Americans I met last night?" Pru suggested. Emma hesitated and then nodded. She was bone-tired but wanted to be a good sport. She didn't know where Pru got her energy from. She was game to go anytime, even after a fourteen-hour day with critically ill men depending on her. If anything, it seemed to energize her and give her superhuman strength, except when they lost one, and then the bottom fell out of her world. It was true for all of them. They took the losses very personally. They remembered all the boys they lost, and always met afterwards to discuss whether the situation could have been handled differently, for a better result next time.

"Yeah, why not?" Emma said, matching Pru's long strides with her shorter ones. "They looked nice enough."

"It's a good thing the Americans are sending us their nurses," Pru commented, and Emma bristled.

"We're just as well trained as they are," she said, and Prudence smiled.

"Yeah, but they haven't been in it as long. They're fresher. We've been at it for four and a half years. They've been at it for two, and they're only training them as flight nurses now. It's a whole new game for them."

"True," Emma said. She couldn't deny it. She felt as though she had grown up here, or maybe just grown old. It was hard to feel young with what they saw every day, so much tragedy and loss of life, such a waste of human beings, lives that were cut short, and dreams that ended with a single bullet or a bomb.

They walked to the nurses' barracks since they weren't in a hurry, and it was nice to get fresh air after a day with the smell of blood, burned and torn flesh, vomit, and disinfectant all around them. They both took deep breaths of the evening air and the smell of the earth.

There were clusters of women in uniform outside the dormitory, and as they walked past them, Pru and Emma could hear American accents mixed with English ones, from all walks of life. There were a group of Australian nurses banded together, laughing at something. And as they walked into the building, Pru spotted the women she had met the day before. They had notebooks in their hands and had just come in from their day in the classroom. Pru stopped to talk to Alex, and then introduced Emma to all the girls she'd met.

"So did you learn all about the RAF today?" Pru asked them with a wry grin. "Tell them to hurry the hell up. We need you in the air with us, and you won't need all those protocols once you get up there. You know as much as we do, or you wouldn't be here. And I hear your air evac training is hell on wheels." They all laughed and agreed with her.

"It almost killed me," Lizzie said, and Audrey nodded.

"Can we talk you into dinner at the pub, or are you in love with the fine cuisine in our mess hall?"

"It's no worse than ours," Alex answered generously, although they had all agreed after the night before that it quite possibly was worse, due to the rigors of rationing and food in short supply. The whole country was hungry and being short rationed.

"The pub sounds like a nice change," Louise said politely, and Emma smiled.

"It's all we've got if we don't want the slop they serve here," she said, and the others laughed. The six of them headed toward the pub a few minutes later. They were all happy to order a pint of ale or a glass of wine, and they ordered sausages and beans, and a wartime version of shepherd's pie, which bore little resemblance to what it used to taste like before the war. But it was food, and the beer and wine raised their spirits after a long day.

"When do you start flying with us?" Emma asked them. She liked Lizzie and Louise and had talked to both of them. Audrey and Alex were talking to Pru. Emma decided Pru was right. They were nice women. She hoped they were good nurses too.

"They said next week," Louise answered. "Or the others will. They're assigning me to the hospital at first, and I have to do a rotation with the injured German POWs they have in a locked ward on the base."

"Oh that." Pru glanced at Emma knowingly, who nodded, and then Pru spoke to Louise to give her the straight scoop, in case no one had. "We don't have segregation in our army the way you do in yours, but there are some 'special assignments' reserved for colored nurses, British nurses too, not just Americans. The German POWs are one of them. Just about all their nurses are colored, and they do a rotation at the hospital before they fly the transports with us. There's no segregation in the dorms, you can room with whoever you want. And you can date whoever you want, but you get stuck with German POWs. I have no idea why. I guess no one else wants to manage them."

"It's still better than what happens at home. My father didn't want me to enlist because the army is notorious for how segregated it is. And there's not a single Black nurse in the navy. So whatever happens here is an improvement. I'm glad they let me enlist in the air evac training, and I was the only woman of color in it. I don't think they accept many."

"You're probably a damn good nurse, and they knew it," Pru said fairly, and the others nodded. Louise was smart and dedicated. She had been a wonderful addition to their group, but they were well aware that in certain parts of the United States she would have been in an all-Black unit, and wouldn't have been allowed to treat white patients. She was better off in England, from what Pru was saying. She hadn't met any odd stares since they'd landed. And she could tell from the way men on the base had looked at her that they didn't have the same taboos and prejudices here. They looked at her as they would have any other woman, not as an object of hatred, unbridled lust, or disdain. She felt like an ordinary person here, she could already tell. Although POW duty didn't sound enticing, particularly caring for their enemies, and it wasn't why she had come to England. She had come to fly on the air evacuation teams, but it sounded like she would get there eventually. She just had to go through some extra steps, which was still a better deal than she would have gotten in the States, where she would have been treated like a second-class citizen, or even subhuman, by some ignorant whites.

"Okay, so let's get down to the important stuff," Pru said after they ordered their second round of wine and ale. "Who has a boyfriend and who doesn't?" They all laughed at the question.

"We're a sorry lot," Alex answered for them. "I don't. I enlisted in order to avoid being married off to any dreary banker my parents considered socially desirable in New York. I bolted and went to nursing school, enlisted in the army after Pearl Harbor, and haven't had a date since, or not one I cared about. My mother assures me that men hate women in ugly uniforms or with jobs. She says khaki's not my color, and I look like hell in pants." Pru and Emma laughed heartily at her blunt honesty, which was Alex's usual style.

Audrey went next. "No boyfriend for me either. My father died when I was fifteen, nine years ago, and my mother got seriously ill after that. I went to nursing school so I could take better care of her. She passed away a few months ago, and I had been taking care of her until then. I enlisted when she died, this is my first assignment. I was always afraid to leave her at night, and taking care of her, I never had a chance to meet any boys. I've never had a real date or fallen in love. Maybe it will happen here." She blushed as she said it. It wasn't her primary goal, but a possibility for all of them.

"I certainly hope so," Pru said.

Lizzie went next and kept it brief. "I was in love with Audrey's brother for two years before he noticed me. Audrey and I went to nursing school together," she explained. "He was in the navy, stationed in Honolulu, and we went to visit him as a graduation present from Audrey's mom. He finally noticed me. We fell in love." Her eyes filled with tears then. "He was the greatest guy I'll ever know. Three weeks later, they bombed Pearl Harbor, and he was killed. That was a little more than two years ago. I haven't had a date since and don't care. I came here to work, that's all I want." She smiled and brushed the tears off her cheeks, and Emma patted her hand.

"Me too. I had a great boyfriend at the beginning of the war. A gunner in the RAF, of course. He was a terrific bloke. He got shot down and killed over Germany three years ago, so that was it for me. No dates since, no interest. I'm a nurse, that's all I want. Besides, the posh ones don't want me with my East End London accent, and I don't want them." She smiled at her new American friends then. "Those are the worst slums in England, by the way, my home turf. The dumb ones are too much trouble and they bore me. And the guys where I grew up work on the docks or drive lorries, drink too much, and beat their wives. I'm just fine on my own," she said, and sat up a little straighter. Their answers to Pru's question were very telling about each of them, where they came from and who they were.

"You've all had more interesting lives than I have," Pru told them. "I grew up in Yorkshire, in the country, riding horses and climbing trees with my brothers. I've known all the men in my area since I was born, and they're not very interesting. I suppose I'm expected to marry one of them one day. I went to nursing school and joined the RAF. My brothers are in the RAF too. I've had some dates, no one I cared about, and this seems like such an unsettled time. I don't want to fall in love and then lose the guy, so I'm just trotting on. For now, my work is enough, and my friends." She smiled at them.

"Me too," Louise said quietly. "All my parents care about is education. My father is a doctor, my mom is the head of a school. I had to be a good student, top of my class, and I always was. Now I want to be a good nurse and do a good job here. And dating is complicated in the States if you're my color. We live in the South, in North Carolina, and I'm just keeping to myself for now."

"What a ridiculously virtuous group we are," Pru said, with a look of disgust, when they had made the round of all six. "There's not a slut among us, no loose morals, no shocking affairs we regret. I am *so* disappointed in all of us, and I sincerely hope that the next time I ask the question, you'll have much more exciting answers for us, even if you have to lie!" They all laughed. What it showed was that they were decent girls, dedicated to their work, and two out of the six of them had already lost men they loved to the war. And Audrey had lost a brother. Further conversation as they talked and smoked and opened up to each other revealed that collectively they had four brothers in the army, Lizzie had two and so did Pru. They all had a lot at stake in the war, and what Pru had said wasn't wrong. It seemed so risky to fall in love and take a chance on get- ting one's heart broken and dreams shattered if the men were killed. They felt safer doing their jobs and spending time with their friends. Camaraderie seemed more important to them than ro- mance. There were plenty of girls who felt differently than they did. And for lustful soldiers, there were always women who were only too happy to play with them. But the stakes were high, and as a former midwife, Emma commented about how many illegitimate babies would be born, or already had been, spawned by soldiers who were killed, or who moved on without marrying those babies' mothers.

"I saw a lot of that in Poplar, when I was growing up," she said. "I never wanted to be one of those girls. And I was damn careful with my guy before he was shot down," she admitted, not claiming to be a saint. Several of the others were still virgins, but she was a few years older than they were, and came from a rougher world, with no family to support or protect her. They all admired her for what she'd shared. It seemed, from what she'd said, that she had had the roughest start, but had done well in spite of it.

By the time they all wandered back to the dormitory together, a little worse for wear but in good spirits, new friendships had been formed, based on mutual respect.

A week later, after their brief transition class to introduce them to the rules, traditions, and expectations of the RAF, the American nurses were assigned to fly on transports with their British counterparts, at least for a few missions, until they felt comfortable taking charge of a flight on their own.

Louise went to work at the hospital, caring for men of color in the British army, and she spent three days a week with the German POWs. She didn't like it, but found that several of them were officers and spoke fluent English. And she found their conversations interesting and intelligent while she dressed their wounds. She didn't like what they stood for or what their countrymen were doing, but she found that many of them were very content to spend the rest of the war in England and to be relieved of the miseries and hardships of war, which existed on their side too. She was eager to start flying like the other nurses, but the brief detour wasn't as unpleasant as she had feared.

She told Emma about it one night, and Emma warned her, "Now don't go falling for a German. You could never take him home. And they're still Nazis, however educated and charming they are." Louise had had a conversation with an officer only that day about Goethe and Thomas Mann. She couldn't imagine having that same conversation with any American soldier she knew, Black or white. The German POWs, particularly the officers, seemed very intellectual and intelligent. It was a refreshing change, but she knew Emma was right, and getting too friendly with any of them was a bad idea. She missed the kind of cultural exchanges she'd had with her parents growing up, but that would just have to wait until she got home.

When the others started flying, Lizzie was assigned to fly with Pru and her crew, Alex with Emma, and Audrey with an Australian nurse she'd met, and liked, from their dorm. Emma was a little hesitant about Alex at first, and mentioned it to Pru.

"I wish they'd have given me one of the others. Alex should be flying with you."

"Why?" She looked surprised by what Emma had said.

"Because you both hide it very politely, but you're both posh girls. She's from a fancy family, it's written all over her, and you heard what she said at the pub that night. You'd know what to talk to her about, I won't."

"Well for one thing, all you'll be talking about is the soldier who got his leg shot off and you're trying to stop from bleeding to death before you land, or the one who lost an arm, or can't see, or will never walk again. You don't need to discuss literature and ballet," she said in her usual direct way, and Emma laughed. "And she's American, so she won't hear your East End accent. Neither do I, nor do I care. And you never have trouble talking to me."

"That's because I know you."

"We're all the same here, Emma. That's what the uniform is about, especially for us. We're all nurses, trying to keep these guys alive. It doesn't matter where we came from, or why we joined up.

We're here to save their lives. It's a rotten business, and we're all in it together. And she may be 'posh,' as you put it, but she's not thinking about that when one of those boys bleeds all over her or throws up on her, or she has his guts in her hands, or he dies in her arms. Who gives a damn about posh then? I'm sure she doesn't."

"Maybe you're right," Emma conceded. "I always expect people to think less of me because I'm from Poplar and they can hear it. And people are such snobs sometimes."

"Not here, and anyone worth a damn as a human being won't care. I know this is a ridiculously snobbish country, but let's hope the war changes that. You're every bit as good as I am, and possibly a better nurse. These girls are American. They didn't grow up with all that crap that you and I did, which tries to keep everyone in their place, and has for centuries. You're much smarter and far more educated than all the posh girls I've ever known. All they had were dancing lessons, how to do watercolors, and they were taught French. Most of them are so dumb, they bore me to sobs and I can't sit through lunch with them. It didn't sound like Alex was too enchanted with her world either before she enlisted and came out here. That way of life just doesn't make a lot of sense anymore, not to me, and maybe not to her either. Give her a chance." Emma nodded and made her peace with it. Pru always made so much sense, and she was so fair.

The first day that Lizzie went out with Pru and her corpsmen, her knees were shaking as they climbed the ladder to the plane. She had heard so much about their missions by then that she wondered if she would be equal to the nursing requirements, or even if their plane would be shot down. It happened. Several of the flight nurses and air evac crews had been killed. It didn't happen often, but it did happen. But she was more worried about doing the right things as a nurse than getting killed herself.

Pru could see how nervous she was, and tried to reassure her, as they checked supplies and made sure that all their beds were ready.

"Don't worry, we'll take good care of you." Pru smiled at her.

"I'm more worried that I won't know what to do for the men in an emergency. This is my first combat mission."

"You'll be fine, Liz," Pru said confidently, and remembered what Lizzie had said about Audrey's brother. It was a sad story, but there were so many like it, in England too. She felt sorry for Audrey too. Pru could only imagine how she would feel if one of her brothers died. She worried about them all the time, particularly Phillip, who was a daredevil. Her older brother, Max, was only a few years older than Phillip, but had always been more cautious, even when they were children. "You just have to treat each case individually. The corpsmen do triage as soon as the men come on, and they tell us who to take care of first. They do a lot of the initial work for us. Some of the soldiers just need to be made comfortable for the flight. And when needed, we give them morphine if they're in too much pain, so they sleep. There's only so much we can do up here. We can't fix them. We're kind of a medicalized taxi service, and now and then we have to deal with a real medical emergency. But most of it is fairly straightforward, and obvious when they come on. We know what we've got on the flight, and some of them are ambulatory. They're not all at death's door. Some are, and then you just do what you can, and pray they hang on till we get back to the base. Stay close to me or Ed, and you'll find your feet very quickly." Pru had confidence in her as a nurse, more than Lizzie had in herself.

She introduced Lizzie to both corpsmen, and then the pilots a few minutes later. Their second corpsman was Charlie Burns, a lively Scotsman and an excellent medic. Ed Murphy was the best corpsman Pru had ever worked with, and he knew far more than most corpsmen did. His medical knowledge was impressive.

"He should have been a doctor," Pru said to Lizzie as they took their jump seats for takeoff and strapped in.

"I wanted to go to medical school," Lizzie said conversationally as they taxied down the runway. "My father wouldn't let me. He's a cardiologist and my mother is a nurse, or was until she had children. My brother is an orthopedist now, and my younger brother left medical school to enlist after Pearl Harbor. My father thinks being a doctor is too much for a woman, and they should get married, stay home, and have kids. So I went to nursing school, which was what my parents wanted. But I wanted to be a doctor, not a nurse."

"Maybe you can do that after the war," Pru suggested.

"Do what?" Ed entered the conversation. He'd been talking to Charlie Burns about going up to London on the weekend. Someone had told him about a jazz club that was a great place to meet women, and he wanted Charlie to come too.

"We're talking about medical school," Pru filled him in, and he looked immediately interested.

"I couldn't afford to go before the war, but there should be educational opportunities for veterans after the war. My mom needed my help with my brothers and sisters, so I took a lot of jobs to help her out. But they'll all be old enough to work by the end of the war. I still have my dream about becoming a doctor."

"You're lucky," Lizzie said quietly. "My father wouldn't let me go."

"Why?"

"Because I'm a woman."

"So? How many women do you know willing to jump out of an airplane with a parachute or take on a job like this?" he asked, and she smiled.

"No one I can think of who would be crazy enough."

"Exactly. So I think you could handle being a doctor. That's pretty tame, if you can stand the years of studying. Were you a good student?"

"Good enough," she answered. She liked him. He was direct and easy to talk to, and he thought the same thing about her. He didn't know anything about her history, but he thought she was a very pretty woman.

"Where are you from?" he asked as they leveled off, heading for the battle lines on the border of France.

"Boston," she said, and he smiled.

"I have a cousin there, a crazy guy, he owns a fish restaurant. He's been there for years, and he's 4-F, so he's still there, doing a booming business while we're here risking our asses with the damn Germans. Why are you here, by the way?"

"It made sense. I was stationed in San Francisco before this, and I didn't feel like I was doing enough, so I signed up for air evac transport in the air forces."

"Good girl." He nodded as his eyes searched the sky for oncoming fighter planes. "I had the same idea. I lost my fiancée in the first year they bombed London. Driving an ambulance didn't seem good enough after that."

"I lost someone too," she said softly, "at Pearl Harbor." He nodded, and neither of them spoke for a few minutes after that. The pilot had just warned them that they were ten minutes from their destination. Both corpsmen left their seats and checked the beds and supplies again. They were ready. They started their descent a few minutes later, and the pilot warned them that getting in might be tricky, and getting out even more so. They were close to the German lines.

"I'm not in the mood to become a POW with the goddamn Jerries today, Reggie, so make it good. I want to be back at the pub tonight, not at a beer garden."

"Yeah, yeah, I know," the pilot said, expertly handling the big plane, and they touched down on another old, abandoned runway a few minutes later. Ed and Charlie threw open the doors and lowered the ladder as Pru and Lizzie watched, at the ready. Soldiers on the ground ran toward them and handed the litters up to them. Ed and Charlie both had powerful arms, and the copilot helped them, while Reggie stayed in his seat, ready for a fast takeoff. In less than ten minutes, they had all twenty-four patients strapped in, in their litters. Pru slammed the doors and locked them, ran to her seat in the front, and they took off again. Miraculously no one followed them. They could see the German battle line from the air, and Pru left her seat immediately after takeoff to check on the men. Ed filled her in quickly, standing in a little bay where they could talk.

"We've got two critical chest wounds, and a serious head wound. The head wound is unconscious, dosed on morphine at the field hospital. One of the chest wounds is having trouble breathing, it could be the altitude. We have a gangrenous leg and an amputated arm." He went down the list, including severe burns and a soldier who had lost his eyes in an explosion. There was every possible kind of serious injury, and listening to them, Lizzie stepped into the exchange.

"What can I do? I'll check the chest wounds if you like. I can sit with the one who's having trouble breathing and keep an eye on him."

"That would be a help," Ed told her as Pru went to check the man with the gangrenous leg and the soldier with the amputated arm. The one with the leg needed an amputation too, but they hadn't felt prepared to deal with his other complications at the field hospital, and wanted it done at the base.

All four of them were busy for the rest of the flight, dealing with the wounded men they were transporting. The boy with the worst chest wound started gasping for air halfway through the flight and his heartbeat was irregular. Charlie administered a shot of Adrenalin with Pru's permission. Lizzie watched him closely, and then moved among the other men, taking vital signs where necessary, and administering a dose of morphine IV to the boy who'd lost his arm. It was touch and go for several of them, and they had to follow a circuitous route on the way back, which took longer. By the time they reached the ground an hour and a half later, none of them had died or were worse than they had been when they were put on the plane. The ambulances were waiting for them on arrival, and in fifteen minutes, all the patients were on their way to the hospital, and the boy with the open chest wound was doing better. He was going straight into surgery when he got to the hospital. They were ready for him.

After flying her first mission with them, Lizzie could see what a difference the flying transport made. Many of the men wouldn't have survived being moved by ambulances or military transport trucks. The planes got them to critical help faster and into operating rooms they couldn't provide at field hospitals, for complicated surgeries.

"You guys do an incredible job," Lizzie said, in awe of what she'd seen. And Pru was right, Ed had more advanced skills than an ordinary corpsman or medic. He had the skills of a doctor in several areas.

The pilot walked past them then. They'd just called him on the radio. "We're going out again in twenty minutes. I'm going to refuel, and then we'll go. You have time for a cup of coffee," he said, and climbed down the ladder to see about refueling. Pru and Lizzie and the two corpsmen headed into the hangar to grab a cup of coffee before they took off again.

They did five flights that day, and Lizzie was deeply impressed by the variety of injuries they dealt with, and how expertly they handled each case. She followed them on their rounds among the litters and did what she could for the patients they assigned to her. By the end of the first day, she felt like part of a well-oiled machine, and a highly efficient team, and Ed looked at her with admiration.

"You'll do," he said to her, smiling slowly. "You're going to do fine when you're in charge, after you fly a few times with me and Pru. All you need are two good corpsmen, and we have some damn good ones here. And you're a fine nurse, Lieutenant."

"Thank you." She smiled back at him. And as she left the plane with Pru to go back to their barracks, she knew she had made a friend. She hoped he did make it to medical school one day. She knew she never would, but he had everything it took to be an excellent doctor. With luck, maybe one day he could afford to go to medical school. As he left the plane with Charlie after they set up the beds for the next flight and restocked the supplies, he thought exactly the same thing about her.

Chapter 10

Emma wasn't entirely convinced that she and Alex would get along when they started flying together in order to familiarize Alex with their procedures. Emma could see that Alex was a competent nurse from her reactions to the men and her assessments of their injuries, but she expected Alex to have an attitude with her, and was braced for her to express it when they were alone or working together. She was sure Alex would make some snide, snobbish comment, but much to Emma's surprise, she never did. Instead, she was easygoing and respectful, and grateful for any advice Emma could give her about how to do the job better while they were in the air.

At the end of the first day, after their patients had all been removed to ambulances, Emma looked at Alex with surprise when Alex thanked her profusely for what an incredible day it had been. They had saved more than one life working together. And Emma had two very capable corpsmen to support her.

"You know, you're so different than I thought you'd be," Emma told Alex as they walked back to the barracks.

"In what way?" Alex asked her, surprised.

"You're very modest, and open to advice, you're a terrific team player, and a great nurse."

"Wow! Thank you." Alex was touched. "So are you. I loved working with you today. I hope they let me ride with you for a while. I have a lot to learn."

"Less than you think. You would have done fine without me in any of those situations today, and the boys are very good." The corpsmen she worked with were excellent.

"You're all very good. Better than that, you're amazing. All of you nurses here are like flying angels. Half of those boys wouldn't be alive if they had tried to bring them back on the ground. The air evac really makes a difference. I can see that now. I was worried about there not being a doctor on the flight. But you don't need one. Your knowledge and experience are way more advanced than that of most nurses." Emma laughed in response.

"My experience," Emma reminded her, "is as a midwife. And I'm probably losing my touch at that. I haven't delivered a baby since I enlisted."

"You're doing something far more important here," Alex said, deeply impressed.

"I thought you'd give me a hard time," Emma said, looking embarrassed.

"Why would I do that?" Alex looked startled when she said it.

"Because you come from a much fancier background than I do. I grew up in the slums, in a rat-infested tenement. Anyone English knows exactly what I come from by the way I speak. And you obviously had a much more posh background than anyone here. I felt that way about Pru in the beginning too. British aristocrats are such snobs. I thought she would be too, and she's the sweetest, simplest, most humble woman I know. And I think you are too."

"Thank you, Emma." Alex smiled and almost wanted to hug her for the compliment, but she didn't dare. Emma was a little bristly and took time to warm up, but she'd been warm and kind all day. "Fancy doesn't necessarily mean good. I'm not too impressed by anyone in my family. They've never accomplished a damn thing, except my father in business maybe. They're spoiled rotten, lazy, self-centered. I have a sister who's convinced she's the queen of the universe, and she never thinks of anyone but herself, or of doing anything for anyone else. All I knew when I was growing up was that I didn't want to be like them. I still don't. I don't respect them, and I don't want to lead the lives they do. I'm pretty sure I'll wind up alone. No one I grew up with would put up with me or has the same ideas. My sister's husband is a decent guy, but their values horrify me. I hate to think of their children growing up as spoiled and selfish as they are."

"You're not like that," Emma said in an admiring tone.

"No, I'm not. But I'm a lone voice in what I consider a very dark world."

"I don't think Pru feels that way about her family, her parents sound like nice people. They took in a huge number of children who had been evacuated from London, many of whom are orphans now. Her people just bore her, although I've never liked the idea of aristocrats. But she's the only one I've ever actually met, and she's a lovely person." Emma sounded sincere as she said it, and deeply affectionate toward Pru. Everyone loved Pru. She was what aristocrats should be, and often weren't, and an example to others.

"My family disgusts me," Alex said bluntly. "I'm ashamed to be one of them."

"Maybe you can do things differently when you go back. People think that the war will change things here, in the social system, and it might. Although I don't have much hope for it. We British are so steeped in our traditions, and part of that is keeping the lower classes down and not giving them a chance to make something of themselves. Whatever you're born is what you stay here, forever. I'll always be a poor, low-class girl from the slums here. America is the land of opportunity. It's different there. And things will probably change there. Women have joined the workforce, even here. They've managed everything—family businesses, children, jobs—while their husbands were at war. They can't just shut women away and ignore them again when the war ends. We have a voice now. And that should be true in your world too. You should be able to do what you want and be what you want when you go back to America."

"I don't think my family believes that," Alex said seriously, impressed by what Emma had said to her, and even more so by what she had overcome to survive poverty, go to nursing school and become a midwife, and now what she was doing in the RAF with the air evacuation transports. She had really made something of herself, no matter what class she had started out in. "You know, you've really defied the class system yourself," Alex reminded her.

"Pru says that too, but I doubt that any other aristocrat would admit that or give me credit for it. Pru is a very special woman, and a very caring human being. Most of them aren't."

"Her parents sound like they are, with all those children and orphans they took in. Not many people would do that. My family certainly wouldn't," Alex said thoughtfully.

"Maybe you can teach them a new way," Emma said gently. "You have to try when you go home. We all have to make things different. It's the only reward for having been through this. It has to change all of us, and make this a better world, for everyone." What Emma said was very moving, but idealistic too. In a perfect world she was right. But Alex knew that the world was far from perfect. It was broken now, and would take years to repair. And not everyone would want to come out of the war and make it a better place for others. Alex wished it, but she had trouble believing it would happen and imagining her family in that role. They would just complain about how hard it was to find servants, or how much things cost, or that the hotels that they liked in the South of France were still closed. They wouldn't care about the reasons for it, or what they could do to change it. Emma had a profound visceral distrust of the British upper classes and aristocracy. But who knew, maybe the class system would alter slightly and the world would change after all. And in the meantime, Emma was grateful for people like Pru and Alex, who didn't give a fig about it and accepted her as she was, East End accent and all.

They had dinner with the others that night, and Alex talked about how impressive their missions had been. All of the nurses felt that. The air evacuation program was accomplishing what it was meant to, and they were saving a significant number of lives. The War Office was very pleased with it.

Ed showed up at the pub that night and stopped by to talk to them. Lizzie was with her friends, and Emma and Alex were deep in conversation. Pru wasn't at the pub with them. He sat next to Lizzie for a few minutes. He was enjoying working with her.

"Where's Pru?" he asked.

"She had a headache and went to bed," Lizzie said, and slid over on the banquette in a booth to make room for him. He perched next to her to chat for a few minutes. He liked talking to her in the times when they weren't busy with patients during the flights. Sometimes it was insanely hectic, and then quieter at other times, between missions.

"I thought about what you said on the first transport we flew together, about losing your man at Pearl Harbor. It's hard to get past something like that. It happened to me with Belinda. By now, most of us have lost someone we cared about, or loved, or wanted to marry, or were married to, or a sibling, or a friend. No one escapes it entirely, but you can't let it stop you from living. Their destiny happened the way it was meant to, but we still have ours to live. We're all young. One day the war will be over, and we'll have our futures back, if we live through it. Don't spend the rest of your life or too many years mourning, Liz. It's not my place to say that to you, but I say it as a friend. I've been through it too. I finally realized that Belinda wouldn't have wanted me to mourn her forever.

She wasn't that kind of person. She was full of life. Maybe your man was too."

"He was," she confirmed, thinking about Will.

"Then you have to go on and live fully. What happened to them wasn't fair. But one day someone will come along who was meant to be with you, and you'll start over again." She still couldn't imagine it, even more than two years later. But she knew Ed meant well. She smiled. She loved listening to his soft Irish brogue. He sounded so gentle when he comforted the patients, and now he was comforting her.

He left the pub a few minutes later, and the other girls questioned her about him.

"He's got a crush on you," Louise said to her, and Lizzie denied it.

"No he doesn't. He's just friendly."

They hooted at her, and she blushed. "I swear to you, he's not after me. Pru and her other corpsman say he has a million girlfriends."

"Until he finds the right one," Alex said, grinning at her. Emma laughed too.

"Where I come from, any girl with eyes in her head would grab a guy who looks like that and hold on to him," Emma said. Pru had tried to get Emma interested in Ed, but she said she still wasn't over the boyfriend she had lost in the first year of the war. She didn't want to get hooked on another guy who might die, and Ed flew dangerous missions. They all did. There were no safe jobs in the war, even for civilians. The building you were in could be bombed at any time, or even the home where you slept at night. They were all at constant risk, and even more so in the RAF, doing what they did. They were all fully aware that they could die on any day, and they were willing to take that risk, for the good of the men they rescued.

After he left the bar, Ed thought about what he had said to her, about opening her heart again, and he realized that it wasn't entirely without motive. He hadn't been as attracted to any woman since Belinda had died, and the speech he had made to her was somewhat self-serving.

They flew together the next day, and he tried to stay professional. Pru wasn't feeling well, but had come to work anyway, and she let Lizzie do most of the work. It was good practice for her, and she was entirely equal to the task. And it threw Lizzie and Ed together more than it would have otherwise. And at one point, without thinking, he gently touched her arm, and she looked up at him, surprised. He took his hand away quickly and moved away from her, on the pretext of taking a patient's vital signs, but he had just wanted to touch her and connect with her in some deeper way. He was still thinking about it after work that night. He didn't want to frighten her away, but he was suddenly thinking about her all the time. Pru had noticed it too: how close he stood to her, how often he spoke to her, how gentle he was when he helped her with a patient, or helped her down the ladder at the end of the day. Lizzie took his breath away when he was close to her.

"You're falling for her, aren't you?" Pru said to him in the supply closet one day after a flight, and he didn't know what to say. He just nodded, and their eyes met. "That's dangerous here," Pru reminded him. "Any of us could die any day. You'll get your heart broken again if that happens." It was something they had to be aware of, and remember every day. And she knew he was more sensitive than he looked. Dating lots of women kept him from getting attached to one.

"You can't think that way, Pru. Or I can't. Yes, I got hurt and lost someone I loved. But life doesn't end there. It can't. We're all young, and for most of us, there will be a future. We have to believe in that, or life isn't worth living."

"She's a good woman," Pru vouched for her.

"I know. I can tell. She should go to medical school. She'd make a terrific doctor. She has great judgment, good hands, and she's a great diagnostician."

"You should go to medical school too." Pru had said it to him before, and he wished he could. But for now, he had to be content with being a corpsman, and maybe an ambulance driver after the war, which was as far as he could get.

They flew a number of tough missions that week, and Pru told Lizzie she thought her breaking-in period should be over, although she enjoyed flying with her. She was going to sign off on her and officially approve her to fly on her own, without supervision.

That night, Lizzie went back to her room, and she and Audrey chatted for a few minutes before she went to sleep. Audrey had gone out to dinner with an RAF fighter pilot, and she told Lizzie about him. They felt like two girls in high school, and Lizzie laughed about it before she went to sleep.

She was already in a deep sleep when Audrey shook her awake two hours later. She'd had a long day and was so tired she didn't remember where she was for a minute when she woke up. She saw Audrey's face close to hers and remembered. She wondered if it was an air raid, but it was silent outside when she sat up in bed.

"What's up?" Lizzie asked her, confused.

"There's someone downstairs to see you," Audrey said. "The night warden just knocked on the door to tell us."

"At this hour?" Audrey nodded, not wanting to frighten Lizzie, but it reminded her of when they had come to tell her mother about Will. "Do I have to get dressed?" She put on her bathrobe, and Audrey shook her head.

"I don't see why at this time of night." Audrey hoped it was good news, but she had a premonition it wouldn't be. Good news didn't knock on the door at midnight.

Lizzie hurried down the stairs in her bathrobe and slippers, looking fresh-faced and young with her blond hair cascading down her back, when she saw two officers waiting for her in the sitting area reserved for the nurses. Men were allowed to visit them there, but they could go no farther. Both men were in uniform, and it suddenly struck her that they were American. One was an Army Air Forces captain, and the other was a second lieutenant. There were American officers on the base to coordinate their troops with the RAF on their joint missions, using personnel from both armies.

They stood up when she walked into the room and she saluted them, but then didn't know what to say.

"Lieutenant Hatton," the captain said cautiously, "I'm sorry to come by at this hour, but your unit commander says you start your missions sometimes at four and five A.M., and I thought it was best to see you tonight." He pointed to the chair and she sat down, afraid of what would come next. Maybe she was being sent home, or had committed some unpardonable mistake.

"Is something wrong?" He glanced at the second lieutenant and went on.

"I'm afraid we don't have good news. Your brother, Lieutenant Gregory Hatton, died in a surprise attack on the hospital where he was working in New Caledonia earlier today. They were strafed by Japanese planes and there were a number of casualties, your brother among them while trying to protect his patients. We wanted to make you aware as soon as possible. Unfortunately, under the circumstances, and with the risk of shipping you back to the States, we can't give you compassionate leave to go home. Of course, you may take as many days off as you feel you'll need, but you have to stay here." She nodded, unable to speak, trying to absorb what they had said. It didn't seem possible. It couldn't be true. Greg was always going to be there. He was a doctor. He had finished medical school. He was her big brother. He couldn't be dead.

"Would you like a glass of water, Lieutenant?" the second lieutenant asked her, and she shook her head. What difference would water make? Her brother was dead. "Would you like us to call someone? One of the nurses in your unit?" They were clearly worried about her. They had woken her in the middle of the night to drop a bomb on her.

"Do my parents know?" was all she could think of to say.

"Yes, they were advised several hours ago."

"Can I call them?"

"That can be arranged," the captain said quietly, as he watched the force of his words sink in. He had done this too often in recent months. "You could call them now, if you like. It's just after seven P.M. in Boston."

"Yes, I'd like that," she said in a small voice, and he went to the barracks office to arrange it. They had her parents' number. They were listed as her next of kin too. The captain came back five minutes later.

"We're going to put the call through now. You can have the office to yourself for as long as you need it."

"Thank you," she said in barely more than a whisper, and followed him to the barracks office. The captain spoke into the phone, they connected the line, and he handed her the phone and left the room. Her father had answered the phone and he was crying.

"Daddy? Daddy? Are you and Mom okay? They just told me . . . oh I'm so sorry . . . I'm so sorry . . . and I can't even come home to be with you. They said it's too dangerous right now."

"We don't want you to come home. We don't want anything to happen to you too." The devastation in his voice was so complete that it made her stronger to try and help him. Her mother sounded even worse when she got on. They talked for twenty minutes and the three of them sobbed the whole time. He had been trying to help get patients to safety after the first planes attacked. It was unthinkable. Lizzie couldn't imagine a world without Greg in it, nor could her parents.

When they finally hung up, and she left the office, she saw that both officers were still waiting for her. She thanked them, and they told her again how sorry they were, then she went upstairs in a daze, her head throbbing after crying so hard. Audrey was still awake, waiting for her, when Lizzie got back to their room. And she knew the minute she saw Lizzie's face. They sat on Lizzie's bed. Audrey took Lizzie in her arms and held her as Lizzie rocked back and forth. Lizzie couldn't even find words for what she was feeling, but Audrey knew. It was how she had felt when Will was killed at Pearl Harbor. And now Lizzie had lost her big brother too. It was one more tie to bind them, and such a terrible one.

Lizzie cried until she had no more tears and then lay down on her bed. Audrey made a cup of tea for her and handed it to her, and Lizzie sipped it. It was two in the morning by then, and Lizzie kept thinking of her parents, and how heartbroken they were. She had never heard her father cry before, and he had cried like a child.

"Now what do I do?" Lizzie asked Audrey as she looked at her. "I don't know what to do. I can't even go to his funeral. The captain said it's too dangerous, and Dad said they don't want me to. I have to stay here. They said I could take time off, but what'll I do? I'd rather go to work." Then she could pretend it hadn't happened, but it had. It was all too real. She wished she could talk to Henry too, but he was in the Solomon Islands and she had no way to reach him. He was in the jungle somewhere. She knew he would be devastated too.

She lay there wide-awake for two more hours, and Audrey stayed awake with her. Then Lizzie got up and started to dress in her flight suit.

"You don't need to go to work," Audrey told her gently. Lizzie looked disheveled and confused, but she seemed lucid.

"I can't stay in bed all day. I'll go crazy thinking of him, and my dad crying. If I go to work, I'll have to keep it together. Maybe that's better."

"Whatever feels right to you," Audrey told her.

"Nothing feels right. My brother is dead. I'll never see him again."

"I know," Audrey said sadly. She'd been through it with her own brother: the shock, the void, the agony, the missing him for months, and even years. "Are you sure you want to fly today?"

"I don't know what else to do. Maybe I can help someone else." Audrey had to fly that morning too. They both got dressed, and Audrey did whatever she could to help her friend. She almost dressed Lizzie. Lizzie had put on her flight overalls, and her hair didn't look as tidy as usual, but it was less noticeable under her cap. She laced up her combat boots, and she and Audrey left a few minutes later. Audrey stayed with her until she had to report for her own flight, and she watched Lizzie head up the ladder of the C-47 Skytrain with a heavy heart.

Pru, Charlie, and Ed were already on board when she got there, and both pilots were in the cockpit. Reggie had already started the engines, but they had another twenty minutes to spare before they left. Lizzie didn't speak to anyone and sat down quietly in her usual jump seat. Ed looked at Pru with a question in his eyes, and she shook her head. A few minutes later, he spoke to Pru in a whisper.

"Is she okay? She looks sick, or like she's been on a three-week drunk."

"As far as I know." Lizzie was usually chatty when she came on board and inquired about their mission. But her eyes looked dead when she got up, and she stood alone in the supply closet for a minute to compose herself. Ed couldn't help himself. He followed her, slipped in, and looked down at her with a worried expression.

"Are you okay, Liz? You don't have to fly today if you're feeling under the weather." He didn't want to pry, and she didn't answer him at first when her eyes met his.

"I need to fly today. We have a job to do." Her voice didn't sound like her.

"If you're sure . . ." he said and was about to leave when her words stopped him in his tracks.

"My brother Greg died yesterday. They came to tell me at midnight last night. He was a doctor. The hospital where he was working was strafed by Japanese fighter pilots and he was killed." She stood still like a statue, for a minute, and without saying a word, he took her in his arms and held her as she shook with silent sobs, and he clung to her as tightly as he could. There was nothing he could say to her. They had all been through it before, or most of them had. All he could do was be there. She clutched him as though she would drown if she didn't.

"I'm sorry, Lizzie . . . so sorry. Do you want to go back to the barracks?" he whispered. "I can have someone drive you back." She shook her head vehemently and looked up at him.

"I want to be with you, and I need to work." She knew it was the only thing that would keep her sane, and she realized that she wanted to be with him. She knew he understood, just as Audrey did. He brought her a cloth dipped in cool water and she put it on her face and held it there for a minute. Then she dropped it in a bucket and nodded at him, and he gently led her back to her seat where she strapped herself in. Pru looked at him questioningly when he took his own seat, and he shook his head almost imperceptibly and she understood. It was a look that they all understood, one that said the worst had happened. She didn't know who, but she could guess what. Lizzie's world had been blown to bits for the second time in less than two and a half years. It was a cruel turn of fate. The cruelest.

Ed kept a close eye on her for the rest of the day, to make sure she was careful and alert during their brief landing. He didn't want anything to happen to her. She managed to tend to the men she needed to. Pru put a gentle hand on her shoulder and gave her a hug once the men were loaded.

They flew four missions that day, and Lizzie looked like she'd been beaten when their last patients of the day had left in ambulances with the medics. Ed walked her back to her barracks then, and held her again for a moment before he walked her inside. Audrey was waiting for her in the hall. She had told the others, so they all knew what had happened.

Lizzie looked at Ed before she left him.

"Thank you," were the only words she could find to say to him. She could never have gotten through the day without him. He gently touched her cheek and nodded.

"I'm here if you need me. Send for me if I can do anything to help." But they both knew he couldn't. There was nothing any of them could do now. Greg was dead and nothing would change that.

Audrey walked her up the stairs to their room, with her arm around her, and gently lay Lizzie on the bed in her flight suit. Lizzie lay there and sobbed until she finally fell asleep. Audrey covered her with a blanket and turned off the light. It was all anyone could do for her.

Chapter 11

In the weeks after Greg died, Ed followed Lizzie like a shadow, and was always nearby when she wanted him. His attention wasn't oppressive. His gentle compassion and kindness, and Audrey's, and that of the other nurses were what kept her going, and able to function at all. Ed got her to take a few days off, and she called her parents on the day of Greg's funeral. There was no body. There was nothing to bury after the explosion that killed him. They had a service at St. Leonard's church in Boston, and were going to put a headstone in the Hatton family plot at the cemetery. Her parents were trying valiantly to be brave, but every day was filled with terror for them, worrying that either Henry or Lizzie would be killed too.

When Lizzie felt strong enough to do so, she began flying missions on her own, as the nurse in charge. It forced her to focus. She missed flying with Ed, Pru, Charlie, and Reggie, but she was proud to have a crew of her own. She met up with Ed every day after work, and they either had dinner at the pub or the fish and chips shop. She needed him now just as she needed to breathe air. He infused her with his own strength. They were walking home from the pub one balmy night in late May, and when he kissed her, it seemed like the most natural thing in the world. It felt to both of them as though it had happened before, and their being together was their destiny now. It didn't surprise their friends either. From the moment Greg had died, Ed had become Lizzie's source of strength and her protector.

They were walking back from the airstrip a few days later when he turned to her to make a suggestion. The idea had been gnawing at him for weeks, and he had talked to Pru about it. She liked the idea too, and told him to tell Lizzie. They talked about everything now: the future, the past, the present, their dreams, their worst fears. Without meaning to or trying, she had found her soulmate.

Audrey was happy for her. She was still dating the RAF pilot she had met a few months before. They weren't in love with each other, and it wasn't passionate or even physical, but they enjoyed each other's company enough to have dinner or go to a movie every few weeks, when he had time off and she wasn't busy. The other nurses teased her about it, but she didn't mind. She would have liked to feel for Geoff what Lizzie did for Ed, but she didn't. She and Geoff both wanted to see what life had in store for them when the war ended, and not get into anything too deeply before that. But they always had a nice time and good laugh when they went out. He had kissed her a few times after the movies, but bells hadn't gone off in her head, and her heart didn't pound.

"Maybe we're just meant to be friends," she said. He said it was a possibility. Neither of them wanted to make plans for the future, or stop seeing each other. What they had from time to time was enough for now, for both of them. It wasn't romantic, but it was still fun. Lizzie was disappointed for her, and hoped she'd meet someone else.

The suggestion Ed made to Lizzie the month after Greg died took her by surprise.

"If we both survive this mess," he said calmly, "why don't we both go to medical school, together. I have no idea how I'd pay for it. But my mom seems to be doing okay. She has a decent job now since the war started, and all my brothers and sisters are out of the house now and have jobs." Two of his brothers were medically disqualified from military service, and young male employees were in high demand. His other three brothers were in the army, but all had survived thus far. One of his sisters had married the son of the local butcher when he was home on leave, and her husband's family could provide good jobs for both of them, and his other sister was a nun, so suddenly Ed's burdens were going to be lighter after the war. "There's talk about veterans' loans when this is all over. And educational opportunities. I could drive an ambulance with the training I've had, but if I survive this godforsaken war, maybe there's a reason for it, other than the fact that I love you and we found each other. And if you don't go to medical school, Lizzie, it will be nothing short of a crime. You've got more medical talent than any doctor I know."

"So do you," she said, smiling at him. They were both reluctant to make plans. There were too many unknowns in their lives, and they were afraid to tempt fate. "And then what? Practice medicine together?" She loved the idea, but it seemed a long way off. "Where would we go to school? We'd have to practice in the country where we go to medical school," she said practically. And she had to go back to Boston for her parents.

"Don't forget, I have a cousin in Boston," he teased her. She knew she'd have to go home to Boston after the war, since the family lost Greg. "What specialty would you want, or just general practice?" he asked her.

She thought about it for a minute before she answered. "Maybe pediatrics. It seems like a nice, happy practice after all this. You?"

"I've thought about it. I like the idea of obstetrics for the same reason. If I never see another bleeding male body, torn to bits and broken beyond repair, it will suit me just fine."

Suddenly the idea of medical school didn't seem like it would cause such a battle with her father. She had the feeling that he might not fight her on it so vehemently after the war. But they all had to stay alive and get home first. They couldn't make plans yet.

There were rumors that a big invasion was being planned on the coast of France, but it was top secret and no one knew anything for sure. Their C-47s were too awkward and cumbersome to land on the beaches, so they wouldn't be able to pick up the wounded. The air evac unit would have to come in by ship from France, or from hospital ships off the coast of England. There were rumors that two or three ships would be coming soon, but they hadn't seen any so far.

Five days after their casual conversation about medical school, which was just something to talk about, Audrey and Lizzie were sound asleep in their beds in the dorm when the night duty officer went floor to floor pounding on the doors and an alarm bell sounded. Within minutes, everyone was up and in the halls. A hospital ship was lying off the coast at anchor. It had come in during the night, and the Germans had bombed it. It was sinking, and the nurses were needed on land and sea to help rescue the injured men who would otherwise go down with the ship. The C-47s were going to try to land on the coast as close as they could to fly the wounded in as quickly as possible. The officers who ordered them to their posts said the ship was burning and would go down soon. The Luftwaffe had clearly known about the ship and had bombed it mercilessly despite the visible red cross. A second hospital ship had been sunk at sea, heading for Southampton.

As soon as they jumped into their flight suits, Lizzie took off at a dead run for the airstrip with dozens of nurses. She saw Pru run past her and wondered if the men would already be there. Emma and Audrey were with them, and all the familiar faces. Every available nurse was heading for the hospital or the airstrip, ambulances were taking off at full speed. Lizzie's crew got to their plane seconds after she did, and C-47s lined up on the airstrip for takeoff one after the other. They flew low and reached the coast quickly. They saw the hospital ship, and hundreds of men in the water. There were said to be fifteen hundred wounded on board with crew. It was pandemonium and the ship was listing badly as the German fighter planes returned to strafe them again and killed many of the

men on deck and in the water. It was a scene of total carnage. Reggie tried to stay out of sight until the fighter planes left again, and
then landed in a field as close as he dared get to the water. Ambulance crews and trucks of personnel grabbed litters and headed to
the shore, where navy rescue boats were circling the ship, trying to
grab men out of the water, and pull others from lifeboats.

The ship continued to explode from the fuel they had on board,
and the scene on the shore was one of organized chaos. Ambulances were coming and going, rescue boats were circling. Rescuers
and severely injured men and dead bodies were in the water. The
rescuers worked steadily until dawn as best they could to save any
survivors. There weren't many. In the end, three hundred and
ninety souls were saved. Fourteen hundred men had died. The ship
sank before the sun came up, and steam continued to rise from it
for hours. The rescuers were filthy and exhausted when it was over,
and the hospital on the base was bursting at the seams. Their fleet
of C-47s had to be used to transport hundreds of wounded to other
bases and hospitals. Lizzie flew a hundred of them in four trips to
the hospitals equipped to take them, and she lost several patients
before they got there. Many were burned beyond recognition.

She saw Ed at the main mess hall for the base when she and her
crew went there for something to eat when they were finished. It
had been a hard night's work and a tragedy of epic proportions, and
a huge victory for the German air force. They had sunk two ships
that night, and there had been only eighty-four survivors from the
ship they sank en route to Southampton. The rescue crews were
tired and angry over the merciless murder of so many men. Ed and

Bertie, Reggie's copilot, came to sit at her table when they saw her, and Pru joined them a little while later.

"Are you okay?" Ed asked Lizzie, and she nodded. Disheartened and sad, she kept thinking of the parents who would receive visits that day from officers, and telegrams for those of lesser rank, and all the broken hearts over their lost sons. She understood it only too well now.

"I've never seen anything like it," Ed said with a savage look.

"I hope I never do again," Bertie muttered under his breath. It was war at its worst and most cruel.

They all had the afternoon off. They were too tired to fly any more missions, and couldn't get to the men at the front that day. The nurses sat in small groups talking about it, and all had double shifts at the hospital. Lizzie volunteered to help them. Ed went back to his barracks to sleep for a few hours. They were all exhausted.

Exactly a week later, to the day, the top secret invasion of Normandy began, and the wounded had to come in by ship to the British coastline, where the air evac planes picked them up and distributed them to hospitals. Every base was bulging with wounded. The army, air force, and navy were all collaborating, handling different aspects of the invasion. The ultimate goal was to recapture France, break the back of the German Occupation, and ultimately reach Paris. In the meantime, men were dying like flies in the sea and on the beaches. They were treating the wounded wherever they could find a safe place to minister to them on the beaches, as the landing craft continued to arrive, bringing more men to the battle and taking the wounded back to England. They pounded the

German fortifications relentlessly as destroyers, cruisers, and battleships sat in the sea just offshore.

As soon as the landing craft arrived with fresh troops, the boats were loaded up with wounded men to send them back to the ships for treatment, and to eventually get them to where the air evac planes could pick them up and bring them back to the base. It was a giant operation, bigger than anything they'd ever seen before. They had specially equipped landing craft, where as many as a hundred and forty-seven litters could be stacked in tiers to bring them back to the ships offshore for emergency treatment. Because it was a water landing, with all the action on the beaches and in the water, there were no nurses involved in the operation, only physicians and corpsmen. The naval base hospital near Southampton was giving emergency treatment and triaging the injured to other base hospitals in England. The physicians and corpsmen were being killed and injured almost as frequently as the soldiers. It was a highly dangerous mission. There were injured men being evacuated from the beaches for seventeen days after the initial invasion.

For weeks afterwards, the nurses of the air evac transports were doing double duty: flying their usual missions by day, to bring back wounded men from the front lines, and working extra shifts at night to care for the extreme number of wounded at the base hospital. There were men on litters and gurneys in the hallways, with nowhere else to put them. The nurses ministered to them where they found them. Corpsmen never stopped running, and there were injured men everywhere. The hospital was teeming with nurses, doctors, corpsmen, and orderlies dealing with a staggering number of wounded men. Louise was pulled off her regular shifts with the prisoners of war and assigned to the hospital with the other nurses. For the first time since she'd gotten there, she was treating Allied soldiers of all races. It was a breakthrough for her.

Alex was running frantically from one bed to the next, stopping every few feet for men begging for help or pain relief, with bandaged eyes and burned bodies and faces, amputated limbs, and shrapnel-riddled bodies. The invasion had been a success, but the number of wounded was staggering. Alex hadn't stopped for hours, when a tall man on a gurney with his legs hanging off reached out and grabbed her as she flew by, hurrying to a man farther down the hall who was begging for morphine. The man on the gurney had a craggy masculine face and a deep voice as he held fast to her arm.

"I'll be back in one minute, I promise," she said to him. "I've got to give that man a shot, he's been waiting for hours."

"You're American," he said with a smile and a look of surprise. "I thought everyone here was British." He was American too.

"Not everyone." She freed her arm from his firm grip, hurried to administer the morphine, and returned as promised a few minutes later.

"What are you doing here?" he asked. He had dark hair and warm brown eyes. His leg was broken and in a cast, and he had burns on his arms and shoulders.

"I'm a nurse." She smiled at him, anxious to make the rounds to check on her patients. She had thirty assigned to her, several of them severely wounded and waiting for transfer back to the States, but they'd lost two hospital ships the month before. The men they were caring for were all U.S. Navy and marines.

"Why are you in England?" She could see he wanted to talk, and she didn't have time. He looked desperately uncomfortable on the gurney that was too short for his long legs, with one of them broken, but he wasn't complaining.

"I'm U.S. Army Air Forces, attached to an RAF Medical Air Evacuation Transport Squadron," she told him. "And now I'm taking care of you brave men after your brief visit to Normandy." She smiled at him again.

"Do you have a smoke?" he asked her, and she shook her head.

"Not on me. You're not really supposed to smoke here in the halls. Fire hazard."

"Do you suppose you can find me one, and wheel me somewhere where I can?" he asked with a look of mischief. There was something rough about him, but he wasn't rude to her, and he wasn't complaining about the pain he was in, which impressed her. She'd been dealing with crying men all night, and some screaming in agony. There was too little she could do for them with their extreme injuries, and some had terrible burns.

She thought about it for a minute before she answered him. "I've got a break in an hour, if I get my medication rounds done. I'll see what I can do then. I wish I could find you a longer gurney."

"It's better than where I was lying on the beach when they found me and dragged me into the landing craft. I nearly got run over by two tanks and a bulldozer."

"That would have been unpleasant." She winced at the thought.

Others had been hurt, and some even killed, by the vehicles on the beach, as the injured and dying littered their path.

"Where are you from?" he asked her. He seemed lonely and hungry to talk after all he'd been through.

"New York."

"That's a pretty fancy accent you've got," he said, and she looked uncomfortable. No one in England recognized it, and even the American nurses never paid much attention. It was a problem Pru had with the British too, like with Emma when they first met and she instantly heard Pru's upper-class diction and hated her for it. Emma had a chip on her shoulder about the aristocracy.

"I don't think so," she said vaguely, itching to get back to her med rounds for her patients.

"What's your name?"

"Lieutenant White," she said formally, and he laughed.

"I'm Petty Officer Third Class Dan Stanley from Pittsburgh." He seemed to want her to know who he was, as though he needed to be more than just an anonymous injured soldier, a broken body with no name.

"Hello, Officer." She smiled at him. "I've got to get back to work, or I'm going to have thirty very angry patients without pain meds."

"Do you have a first name?" he asked her boldly, but he wasn't fresh, just persistent. He needed a friend and someone to talk to.

"Alex," she said. "Are any of the men in your unit here, do you know?" She wondered if she could have him moved, so he'd have someone to chat with. He was wide-awake and wanted company.

"They got sent to another hospital. I got separated from them on the beach when I broke my leg. And I got sent here from the ship that picked me up. It might have been my lucky day," he said with a glint in his eye.

"I'll come back with a smoke if I find one," she said, and hurried away before he trapped her into further conversation.

It took her an hour and a half to make her rounds and hand out all the meds she was supposed to. She remembered the petty officer who wanted the smoke then, and asked one of the corpsmen if he had a spare cigarette.

"Can you smoke on duty?" He looked surprised, and she laughed.

"I'm overdue for my break and it's for my patient."

He smiled in answer and handed her one with a book of matches, and she made her way back to the hallway where the navy officer was lying on the gurney, staring at the ceiling and still awake. He smiled broadly as soon as he saw her.

"You're back."

"And I'm taking you for your dressing change," she said officially, and he looked disappointed.

"They changed them earlier," he said, as she carefully moved him away from the wall and pushed him slowly down the hallway. She made a somewhat perilous left turn, took him down another hall, and stopped there. There were no treatment rooms, and no patients on gurneys, as she reached into her pocket and pulled out the cigarette and the matches. He laughed as soon as he saw it.

"You're a sharp one," he said as he put the cigarette to his lips gratefully, and tried to light it from a prone position, which looked awkward and dangerous. He already had burns. He didn't need more. She took the matches from him and lit the cigarette, then handed him back the book of matches.

"If you set yourself on fire, I'll be court-martialed and sent home, and I like my job here. Most of the time, when I'm flying."

"Thank you for the cigarette. I figured you'd forget about me." It would have been hard to do, he had a definite personality, and she could see he had a sense of humor, despite his injuries. They had been through hell on the beach, but he seemed in surprisingly good spirits, and grateful to be alive. "What do you do in real life, Alex, when you're not here?" He wanted to know her, and he wanted someone to know him, and remember him, as though to prove he was still alive, which he very much seemed to be, in spite of what he'd been through.

"I go to parties and fight with my mother," she said with a grin. "Actually, I'm a nurse in 'real life' too, which is how I wound up here. I was stationed in San Francisco with the army for a while, and then volunteered to come here for the air evac transport unit, which is kind of a flying ambulance that brings men back from the front lines."

"That's dangerous," he said, visibly impressed.

"Sometimes," she admitted. "I've been lucky."

"Me too. Especially tonight, when I met you." He had finished the cigarette, and she took it from him, stubbed it out on the sole of her shoe, and slipped the butt in her apron pocket. Then she carefully maneuvered the gurney again to take him back to his original location. "Thanks for the smoke," he said, smiling happily.

"Now you should try and get some rest. I'll check on you again before I leave," she promised as she put him back where he started and set the brake so he didn't roll away.

"When is that?"

"I'm off at midnight, and no, you can't go to the pub for a drink and a smoke," she said sternly, and he laughed. She didn't know why, but she liked him. He was something of a rough diamond, but he seemed like a nice guy.

"Don't work too hard," he said as she waved and hurried off. She had some critically ill patients to check on before her shift was over.

She wandered by to check on him before she left, and he was lying flat on his back and snoring. She smiled and signed out at the nurses' desk. He had been the bright spot in the night. One of her patients had died of his injuries, and most of them were suffering from their wounds. She suspected that he'd be shipped back to the States soon, but at least the war would be over for him, and he could go home. For some, they would be there for months, and had numerous surgeries to look forward to, and a severely altered life, or permanent disfigurement. Petty Officer Stanley was right, she decided. He'd been lucky.

She walked the short distance to her barracks. It was a beautiful June night, and she could easily have been fooled into believing that all was well with the world. But her patients, and the nurses who cared for them, knew better, which made it hard to believe that the world would ever be whole again.

Chapter 12

Just to keep his spirits up, Alex stopped by to check on Petty Officer Stanley the next day on the way in for her night shift, after she flew her regular missions with her crew during the day. They had all been working double and triple time since the invasion of Normandy, but slowly the less seriously injured men were leaving to go back to their ships, and the critically injured to be sent home once they were well enough to move. There were navy officers in and out of the hospital constantly to check on the status of their men and categorize them with their own triage system, some of which shocked the nurses and doctors. Some of the men the navy was returning to serve were in no condition to face combat again, but they sent them anyway. They needed them too badly to send them all home.

When Alex checked on Petty Officer Stanley, she found that he'd been moved to a ward. She went to see him and found him in a proper bed. He had showered and shaved, with assistance, since he couldn't get his cast wet.

"You've changed address," she said when she saw him, greeted him with a smile, and slipped him a cigarette. He smiled broadly when she did.

"Thanks for that." He tucked it into the pocket of the pajama top provided by the hospital.

"How are you feeling today?" she asked him, and he smiled.

"Better now that I've seen you. I had bad news this morning. Whenever I'm back on my feet, they're sending me back to the front, wherever it is at the time." Alex was surprised.

"They're not sending you home with third degree burns and a broken leg?" She was shocked.

"It takes more than that to impress the navy. They figure I'll be up and back on my feet in a matter of weeks. That is not good news to me. I've been here for two and a half years. That's a long time. I'm ready for this war to end."

"We all are," Alex added. "You'll be with us for a while. You'll be in that cast for six weeks at least." So he'd be at the hospital until mid- or late July.

"I'll be ready to go back into combat by then. I want to kill a German or two before I go home. They've given us enough grief."

The Allies' goal was to liberate Paris, but advancing through the French countryside, town by town, was going slowly. The Resistance was doing all they could to help.

"At least I'll have a chance to see more of you before I leave," he said, gazing at her longingly. He looked at her intently when he spoke to her, as though he wanted to see into her soul. It made her uncomfortable, but at the same time, his gaze was so piercing that she found she couldn't resist. She was attracted to him, but she didn't know why. He wasn't handsome. He was powerful-looking, but there was a gentle side to him too. He made her laugh when she stopped to talk to him. And he made it very clear that he was attracted to her. None of the men she knew and had grown up with had ever been so direct.

"What does your father do?" he asked her one day, curious about her. She seemed intelligent and well bred.

"He's a banker," she said, feeling suddenly shy with him. He asked real questions and wanted real answers.

"Do you have a boyfriend here? Or one at home?" She thought the question much too personal, but answered it too.

"No, I don't. They keep us too busy to have time for romance." Although some of her fellow nurses managed it, like Lizzie. She and Ed had become a couple now in everyone's mind.

"Why not?" Dan Stanley pursued his question. "You're a beautiful girl, you must have men running after you all the time." She smiled at that.

"I'm a nurse, Officer, not a movie star. I fly air evac missions all day and bring twenty-four injured men back from the front with every load. And now I do a night shift here. I'm exhausted by the time I go home. But we won't be doing the extra shifts forever."

"My family is in the commercial meat business," he volunteered. "We provide meat, mainly beef, for high-end restaurants and hotels. It's not glamorous, but it's a lucrative business. Our family lives well on it. My father owns the business and I run it for him. We have the finest top-quality butcher shop in Philadelphia, and a booming wholesale business in Pittsburgh. That must sound vulgar to you," he said, and hit the nail on the head. She had been thinking just that, and felt like her mother when she did. She hated her mother's snobbism and was ashamed to realize that she was thinking something her mother would have. What difference did it make how he made his money? She tried to envision him at one of her parents' parties and almost laughed out loud. "Was I right when I said you have a fancy accent? Something tells me there is some very blue blood in those veins." He waved vaguely at her arms.

"Why does it matter?" she asked seriously.

"It doesn't," he said simply. "Except maybe to you or your parents." He pegged that squarely too, about her parents.

"It doesn't matter to me. That stuff is just an excuse for a lot of snobbery, antiquated traditions, and bad behavior, none of which appeals to me."

"You're a rebel, then, or a modern woman."

"Maybe a little of both." Though she'd never thought of it that way before.

"Is that why you enlisted? To prove to yourself that you're not like your parents?"

"Maybe some of that too. But I mostly enlisted to serve my country."

"That's admirable," he said. "You didn't have to do that. You could have stayed home and paid lip service to it, and gone to parties like your mother."

"I'm not that kind of woman. I stand up for what I believe in. I just don't believe in my parents' value system. Other things are more important to me, like winning this war. And I'm doing everything I can to help that." Then she looked at him strangely. "Why am I telling you all this?"

"Because I asked you, and you're an honest person. I'm fascinated by you, Alex. I was from the first minute I saw you. And you're a woman of your word. You came back with that first cigarette, and you came to see me every time you said you would."

"It must be hard for you, being so far from home, and injured. What happened in Normandy sounds terrifying. You must be a very brave man," she said gently.

"Not really," he said, honest again. "You do what you're called on to do, to the best of your abilities. The rest always takes care of itself."

"I like to believe that too. There's a lot of luck involved in having a good life. My parents are very fortunate people. They have a very nice life, and so does my sister. They don't realize it, they aren't grateful for anything. I'm grateful every morning when I wake up."

"I had a feeling like that about you when I first met you."

"Well, I'm going to have a very bad life, if I don't do my med rounds, my patients won't have pain relief, if my supervisor catches me at it."

"I like it when you stop by to see me," he said with a shy smile. "I've been thinking about you a lot. I don't care what you come from, or who you are. I like you. I wanted you to know that. I like teasing you about your fancy accent. But it doesn't matter to me. I'm a butcher from Pittsburgh. I'm nobody. Just a guy in a hospital, with a broken leg." She didn't care where he came from either. There was something wonderfully masculine about him. He was like a big teddy bear. Her parents would have hated him if they'd met him, but she didn't care about that either. This was another world. And it was real.

She stopped to see him every night on the way in, and she came to chat with him during her break. She dropped by to say good night when she left. It became a comfortable habit, and she liked talking to him.

When they took his cast off, she was startled by how tall he was. He was just a hair under six-five, and he looked more like a teddy bear than ever. He invited her to lunch on her day off, and they had a lively conversation about baseball, which he was passionate about. They talked about her work with the air evac unit, and her going back to nursing after the war. He had an older brother he had no respect for, who never worked and had lived off the family business all his life. She could tell Dan worked hard when he talked about their business.

"When we get to Paris, and we will, and kick those damn Nazis back to Germany where they belong, can I come back here to see you?"

"If I'm still here," she said cautiously. She liked him more than she had expected to, as a person and a man. He was someone she could respect, without pretension or artifice. She liked how hardworking he was. He had explained to her all about his business. He was thirty-three years old. She was twenty-four, but the war had aged them all.

"Maybe you could come to Paris, before we all ship back to the States. And I could visit you in New York." She smiled at the thought of it. Her mother would have a heart attack if she saw him. Dan Stanley, a wholesale butcher from Pittsburgh, but she thought he was the most attractive man she'd met in years. He was a man's man, and there was nothing phony about him. He was real.

"You won't like my family," she said.

"And they won't like me either. Will that matter to you, Alex?"

"I don't think so. I don't think they like me much either. They've disapproved of me all my life. They think I'm weird."

"Do they have any idea what you do here?" he asked her. "I've asked around about what your unit does. They call you the Flying Angels, and it sounds to me like that's exactly what you are. I've never seen you in action. But you were an angel to me while I was here. Omaha Beach was pretty damn rough. I figured I was dying there, and then I woke up here in the hospital, and I met you, and I felt like maybe I was meant to be here, so I could meet you. I've never met a woman I was serious about. I was too busy building the family business into something we could all be proud of, and I am. And now you show up. The women I've met all wanted something. They had an agenda, a plan. You don't want a damn thing from me. You're just who you are, an angel in a flight suit. I don't want to lose sight of you. I want to see you again when we're back home. I'll come to New York and take you to a Yankees game, and then take you out for a decent dinner. Some of our best customers are in New York. The Plaza Hotel, the Pierre. The Twenty-One Club." She realized then just how major his business was. They were some of the best restaurants in New York. He hadn't wanted to try to impress her before. He just wanted to meet her as a man and a woman, as a nurse and a butcher, not a debutante and a successful businessman.

She came to see him off when he left to rejoin his unit. They were on the Cotentin Peninsula by then and had captured the port of Cherbourg. Allied bombers had caused extensive damage to the city of Caen, the Germans retreated, and Caen was liberated. They'd made some progress while he was in the hospital, and so had he and Alex.

"Take care of yourself. I'm expecting to see you in Paris one day, or New York. And be good to that leg," she warned him.

"You too," he said gently. "Watch out for those Krauts when you're flying your missions." She nodded, and he bent down, pulled her into his powerful arms, and kissed her. She smiled up at him afterwards. It felt perfect. "Stay safe, Alex. We have a lot to look forward to when we go home." She waved as the bus that was taking him back to his unit with four other men who had been released from the hospital pulled away. She walked back to her barracks with a smile on her face. She felt young, and alive, and like a girl for the first time in a long time. She hoped they'd both make it through the war and come out safely at the other end. She had something to look forward to now, instead of dreading going home. No matter what her parents thought of him when they met him, she knew Dan Stanley was just the man for her. She hoped that he would survive and she'd see him again.

After Dan left at the end of July, almost two months after the navy's invasion of Normandy, the Germans were pummeling the British even harder than before. British cities took a beating, and even the countryside was being hit hard. There were bombings in Yorkshire, near Pru's parents' home, which worried her. So far they'd been lucky. Her brothers hadn't been wounded, and her parents were well.

Due to the increased activity of the Luftwaffe, they sometimes put two nurses on a flight, and they gave them a fighter escort for some of their missions. It was somewhat reassuring, but their missions had become more dangerous with more intense fighting on the ground. Emma was assigned to one of Pru's missions, and they enjoyed working together.

They were on their way to their pickup location, on their second mission of the day, with two fighter escorts, when there was a strange staccato sound from the engine. Reggie checked his dials carefully, and looked first at his copilot, then at Pru. Ed had a day off, which was rare for him, but he and Lizzie had synchronized their days off to be together, and Pru had two new corpsmen with her.

"What's up?" she asked Reggie, and he looked at her in dismay. "We've got an engine failure in the right engine." And two minutes later, he turned to her. "We're going down, Pru. Put your parachutes on," he told the crew. He radioed their position in code, and he knew the fighter pilots would communicate it to the base. He showed a hand signal to one of the fighter pilots, and the plane started going down fast. Pru looked at Emma, and she looked scared. They both had their chutes on, and Pru grabbed a backpack of supplies for an emergency like this one, with a limited amount of food, a thermos of water, and a gun. The corpsmen did the same, and Reggie shouted at them. There was no controlling the plane. The copilot had opened the rear door and Reggie ordered them all to jump. Pru let Emma go first and followed her as closely as she could. She thought the corpsmen were right behind them, so they'd land near enough to each other. What they had to avoid now was getting caught by a German patrol, when they landed in the vicinity of battle lines.

Emma took a long time to pull her rip cord, but she finally did and the chute opened sharply, then she drifted gently down clear of the tree line. This was the part she had hated most in their training, but she made a smooth landing and got rid of her chute quickly, under a thicket of bushes. There was no sound of gunshots nearby, although they could hear heavy artillery in the distance. And another C-47 was going to have to pick up the wounded Pru's flight wouldn't reach now. She made a sharper landing than Emma but got rid of her chute swiftly too. They headed into the trees as silently as they could. Pru put a finger to her lips and Emma nodded. They started walking away from the German front toward where they believed the British line was, near the French border. But technically, they were behind enemy lines now. The plane had come down hard in a field, and damaged a wing, but there was no explosion. The crew had made a smooth getaway too, in the opposite direction. They knew to spread out rapidly. Pru and Emma had no idea where they were and didn't see them again after they landed.

They walked steadily until nightfall, but didn't see any houses or farms. They wouldn't have approached them anyway, since they were in occupied territory on the frontier of France.

They had no idea where they were by the time it was fully dark, and they hadn't stopped to eat all day. They finally sat down and ate some of their meager supplies, then sipped some of the water.

Pru figured they had a long walk ahead of them the next day. They weren't far from a road, and heard a German patrol go by that night.

By then, everyone on the base knew what had happened, from the fighter pilots who had seen it all, and reported to the base immediately, to the commander of the evac unit. The nurses were worried about them. They hadn't had a plane go down in months, but at least their fighter escort said there had been no sound of ground fire after everyone bailed out of the plane. It was a tense night while everyone waited for the two nurses and their crew to show up somewhere and make contact.

By midmorning the next day, the pilot, copilot, and corpsmen had made it to a safe house on the border. They had been picked up and were back safely by that night. But Emma and Pru still hadn't turned up. Lizzie, Audrey, Alex, and Louise were worried sick about them, as were the other nurses in their squadron. Two days later, three since they'd bailed out of the plane, they were officially listed as missing in action by the War Office, and Pru's parents were notified. Two more days, and their squadron leader was fairly sure they'd been picked up by a German patrol or there would have been some sign of them along the way. They used a reconnaissance plane, and the other C-47s were keeping an eye out for them. They were the first women who would have been picked up by the Germans. By six days after bailout, it seemed fairly certain that they were either dead or in a German prison camp by then, and had probably been moved deeper into Germany.

Lizzie felt sick every time she thought about it, and Ed was suffering from extreme guilt for having taken a day off. He and Lizzie had found a small inn near the base, where they could rent a room and spend a few hours together, enjoy the pleasures of the flesh, and give wings to their love.

A week after Pru and Emma had bailed, it seemed certain that they were either prisoners or dead. In either case, their whole squadron was deeply shocked and mourning two women who were so greatly appreciated and beloved by their colleagues.

Ed and Lizzie were coming back from the mess hall on the eighth day, looking ravaged, when a farmer's truck drove onto the base carrying bales of hay, and two bedraggled figures hopped off the truck. Ed stared at them and gave a shout. He screamed to anyone who could hear him.

"They're back!!! They're back!!" People came running. Lizzie threw her arms around them, and within minutes, nurses poured out of the barracks. Emma and Pru reported to their commanding officer, looking as though they had been shipwrecked, and smelling of dead fish. They had walked across a good part of France and been smuggled across the channel in a small fishing boat by a boy and his father. The farmer had given them a ride to the base from the coast.

"What happened?" Everyone wanted to know.

"We had a few disagreements about the map," Pru said with a grin, glancing at Emma, who looked sheepish. "Don't ever bail out of a plane with a girl from the East End. She's never been out of the city."

"I'm a midwife, not a bloody explorer," Emma said defensively, but they had made it back to the base safely, with no harm done.

They were hungry, tired, and filthy, with scratches on their faces and hands from the bushes they had walked through and hidden under. Someone brought them each a plate of food, and they were ravenous. They went back to their barracks afterwards to shower, as the two women looked at each other and grinned, and their friends hovered around them.

"I thought we were as good as dead for a while there," Pru admitted. "There were more German patrols out than taxis in Leicester Square, but the gods must have been with us, because they never saw us. We spent a lot of time lying under bushes and sitting in thickets, but we made it." They hadn't eaten in two days, but they knew enough not to overeat when they first got back. They both slept for fourteen hours after everyone left them in their room to recover from their ordeal. And Ed had cried in Lizzie's arms, in relief that they'd made it back safely.

It was one of those experiences both women knew they would never forget. It had been terrifying, but Pru had never lost her head, nor had Emma. They just kept on plugging away and walking until they got to the coast, and then got on the fishing boat. Until then, they both expected to be shot at any moment.

They were as calm as though nothing had happened when they both reported for their missions the next day.

Ed beamed when he saw them. They were scheduled to fly together, and they had a fighter escort again.

"What are we waiting for? Let's get on with it," Pru said matter-of-factly as Reggie grinned and shook his head. They locked the doors, strapped in, and taxied down the runway. They had twenty-four injured men to pick up, and everything went smoothly. Pru grinned at Emma after they landed safely back on base with their precious cargo.

"Better flight than last time, eh, Em?" she asked her, and Emma shrugged coolly.

"It was good enough. The last one wasn't bad either." They both laughed and walked into the hangar arm in arm for a cup of coffee before their next mission. They had a busy day ahead.

Chapter 13

As though to prove they were in control, or to regain it, the Germans increased the bombings in August, with severe damage to the cities and industrial areas, and intense hand-to-hand combat with fixed bayonets in rural areas on the ground. As a result, the flight nurses were flying with full loads of wounded, and sometimes took on more men than they had beds for. They couldn't bear to leave anyone behind, and came back for second and third loads whenever they could.

Pru had flown six missions that day, with only enough time to refuel between them, when she walked into the barracks on a warm summer evening. Her overalls were covered with dirt and blood, and all she wanted was a shower and to lie down for a few minutes. The house officer pointed to the nurses' battered sitting room when she walked by. There was a tall, thin, serious-looking officer waiting for her. She hesitated before walking in, steeled herself, and saluted him, and he invited her to sit down. She knew what that meant and braced herself for whatever he was waiting to tell her. He delivered the bad news swiftly, like a saber run through her heart.

Her younger brother Phillip's plane had been shot down the night before on a massive bombing raid against the Falaise pocket, where the German army was fighting fiercely. Eighteen bombers had gone down the night before. Phillip had been one of the daring fighter escorts, and he had been shot down too. They had had confirmation that afternoon that he and his crew were all dead. They had become another statistic in the war that was devouring brothers and fathers, lovers and husbands and sons. Pru was one of the bereaved now. Her family had been lucky until then. The officer extended his condolences and left as quietly as he had come. He was the angel of death visiting the survivors, leaving tragedy in his wake.

She walked up the stairs slowly and was surrounded by her friends when she got to her room. The officer had told her that she had been cleared for a three-day leave to go home to Yorkshire, to see her parents. They had heard the news by then. She didn't have the heart to call them. All she wanted was to go home. Her mind was a blank and Emma and the others helped her pack. Trains were scarce and were running off schedule, and all nonessential travel was discouraged. But she knew that if she waited long enough, she could catch a train north that night. She had priority as an officer. And all she had to do was hope that the train or the tracks didn't get bombed while she was aboard.

She left the barracks in a blur an hour later, after all the girls hugged her. Someone with a car drove her to the train station—she couldn't even remember who afterwards. All she knew was that her baby brother was dead. He had been flying daring missions for al-most exactly five years, as her older brother, Max, had too. She had been told that they would not be able to recover his body. The plane had exploded in midair after the first volley of shots. She hoped it had been quick, and she was sure he would have been mad as hell when they went down. She hadn't called her parents because she had no idea what to say. She saw men die every day, but she didn't have to face their mothers and fathers or any of the people who had loved them.

She caught a freight train out at eight o'clock that night, and sat staring blindly out the window, remembering what a terror he had been as a little boy, how he had taunted her into climbing the tallest trees, and blamed her for everything he'd done. She had hated him for a while. Her older brother, Max, was always the sensible one. Then she had come to love Phillip more than ever before as they grew up. And now he was gone.

The train left her at the station in York at one in the morning. She hadn't told anyone she was coming, and with her suitcase in hand, she walked the five miles from the station in the silent dark-ness, grateful to be alone to gather her thoughts. She would have to face her parents in the morning. She wondered if Max had gotten leave to come home too. She hoped so. They hadn't seen him in months, and she needed his solid comfort now. He would be devas-tated too.

Emma had helped her put on her uniform after she heard the news. She had dressed her as she would a child. Pru saw that there were still dim lights behind the blackout shades at her home, when she got there after two in the morning. The faint trace of light was coming from her parents' room. When she opened the front door, which was never locked in the big rambling manor house, she could hear them talking in the back parlor. There was a fire dying in the grate. The house was always drafty, even in the summer. Her mother turned to look at her in the dying light of the embers. Max was sitting with her, and their father was dozing in a chair by the fire, his chin on his chest. Even in the half darkness, they suddenly looked so much older to her. Everyone did now, a whole nation of people who had aged from hunger, heartache, and grief for five years of war. Max stood up, walked toward her, and put his arms around her. He looked just like their father when he was younger, which was comforting in an odd way. There was a sense of continuity to it.

"I was hoping you'd come," she said softly, her words muffled by his jacket as he held her. "How are they?" she whispered about their parents, but she could see for herself when she went to kiss their mother. She held tightly to Pru's hand as Pru sat down next to her, and her eyes looked ravaged. But she was as they always were: strong, quiet, determined to prevail no matter what it cost them, brave in the face of sorrow. They were the people she could count on, whatever happened, just as they could count on her. She hugged her mother close, and they both cried for a moment, and then her mother sat up straighter and Max watched them both. They were the two women he most admired. He always thought of them as brave and strong, and now was no different.

"I've spoken to Reverend Alsop. We'll hold a service for Phillip in two days, before you and Max have to leave," she said quietly. Pru wondered how many more of these services they could endure going to. There were so many. So many boys from the farms had been killed, and from the great houses. All the boys she had grown up with and found so boring before the war. They weren't boring now. Most of them were gone, had been killed in the last five years in battles with names she would always remember, in Europe, North Africa, in places she had never been to.

Her mother gently woke her father, and they all stood up and walked upstairs together.

"You've come home, then," was all her father said to her. He hadn't doubted that she would, or that Max would. They had always faced everything together, and they would face this too. Pru kissed her mother when they said good night. The door to her parents' room closed softly, and Max walked Pru to her own room.

"Will you be all right?" he asked, with eyes filled with loss and sorrow too.

"We always are, aren't we?" Pru said quietly, and he nodded. "I can't imagine him not being here when the war is over." Max nodded agreement, gently stroked her long brown hair, and then walked to his own room to grieve in silence.

After she put her nightgown on and turned out the light, Pru stood looking out over their land in the moonlight. It had always been such a peaceful place, where she felt safe, until the war started. And now nothing was safe, nothing was sacred, nothing was certain, and she never knew who would be gone tomorrow. She longed to come back here, and just be with Max and her parents. But who knew what would happen by then, who else they would lose, how much more sorrow and loss they would have to endure, or how strong they would have to be, how many times. A cloud crossed the moon as she thought of Phillip. In his own room, Max was looking out the window, with silent tears running down his face, thinking how hard it must be to be a woman, always having to be strong and comfort others, and how lonely it was to be a man.

Constance, Pru's mother, was already in the dining room the next morning when Pru came down to breakfast. The table was set impeccably, as it always had been, although her mother did it now. There were hardly any servants left. The young ones had gone, and only very old ones were left. Their butler had died of pneumonia in the first year of the war. But her mother saw to it that everything looked the same.

"How's Father?" Pru asked her, wondering why it was always the men they worried about. They seemed to be much more frail in hard times somehow.

"He's all right." It had been a terrible shock to both of them, but now they were no different than their neighbors. Everyone in the village and all their friends in London had lost someone. They no longer went there in the war, and preferred to stay in Yorkshire. Constance had the children they were housing to think about. They would keep her busy now, which she viewed as a blessing not a burden. The young women who took care of them had already given them breakfast in the old servants' dining room that no one used now, and had taken them outside to help with the gardening and then take a walk to the lake that Pru and her brothers had loved as children. Their old governess had always been afraid they would drown, and scolded them when they went there alone, which they did as frequently as possible.

Max came into the dining room then, poured himself a cup of coffee, and sat down with a careful look at their mother. She seemed all right, which didn't surprise him. He expected nothing less of her.

"Father?" His concern was in the single word. His father wasn't young, nor was his mother, but she showed her age less, with her long stride and straight back, and a healthy glow from the outdoors year-round. Today was different. She could have let her guard down, her strong protective shield, but she never did.

"He'll be all right. It's a terrible shock, but we're the last ones we know to go through it." All of their friends had lost at least one son in the last five years. And now they were no different, no matter how painful it was, or what a golden child Phillip had been. No one was exempt. "One wonders if it will ever be over."

"We'll never give up the fight, if that's what you mean, Mother," Max said staunchly. "We'll fight on, whatever it takes. Churchill estimates it will take another year."

"I hope not," Constance said with an exhausted look.

"How are your missions going?" Max asked Pru as he sipped his coffee. He didn't ask his mother for sugar, since it was rationed and he knew how hard it was to come by. "The Flying Angels, isn't that what you call yourselves?" There was a teasing look in his eyes, which was comfortably familiar and reassured her that some things hadn't changed despite the enormous loss they had just suffered. Max would have to do all the teasing now, since Phillip wouldn't be there to do his share. They loved teasing Pru, even at their age.

"That's what the others call us," Pru said quietly. "We're just nurses."

"And doing a damn fine job, from what I hear. Two of my friends have passed through your hands, or your colleagues', and spoke well of you. One of them claims the Flying Angels saved his life. He was delirious, I suspect. Flying Devils, more like, if you're part of it," he said and smiled at her as their father walked into the room, and Max stood up in respect. Thomas Pommery looked like he'd been through the wars himself, but his back was straight as he took his place at the head of the table, and they ate in silence. Constance served him toast with the jam she made from the fruit in their orchards. There was no butter, and he hated the taste of the margarine. They were both rationed, and there was little enough of that too.

After breakfast, their parents went for a walk to discuss the service for Phillip, and they walked to the cemetery on their property to decide where they would put the monument to him. Pru and Max sat in the sunshine in the garden. It was peaceful there, in spite of what had happened. It felt good to be home, together, whatever the reason. Max was stationed at a base not far from where she was, but he never had time to visit.

They took a walk down to the lake on the path that was so full of memories for both of them. Pru looked up at the trees she had climbed to escape her brothers or taunt them. She'd jumped into the lake more than once in all her clothes.

"You were always braver than we were, you know." Max smiled at her. "We just pretended. You really were brave. Phillip said that to me once, and I never realized it before, but he was right."

"I don't know that I was. I don't know how brave I am now. You just do what you have to do to get the job done. I took a bit of a walking tour behind enemy lines in France a few weeks ago. We lost an engine and went down. We were MIA for a while, but we got back all right. It took eight days." It didn't surprise him, nor the cool way she said it, but it worried him anyway.

"You and your crew?"

"One of the nurses and me. Hell of a plucky girl. We've been working together for quite some time. She's rubbish at reading a map, but a hell of a nurse, and made of strong stuff. She's a bit of a firebrand, bright ginger hair to go with it." She smiled, thinking of Emma and their eight days on the run.

"One of your Flying Devils, I assume," he said with a laugh, and Pru grinned. It felt strange to smile now, with Phillip gone. It almost made her feel guilty.

"Of course. Good person to get lost with, behind enemy lines. I have no idea how we did it, but we slipped by all the German patrols, and they never caught us. We got picked up by a fishing boat on the French coast and came back smelling like a year of dead fish."

"Sounds delightful." He was sure there was much she wasn't telling him, like all the dangers and risks they encountered. "Were you involved in the business in Normandy?" he asked. Neither of them knew much about the other's missions. They weren't supposed to. She shook her head in answer to his question, which was safe to ask her now.

"Nowhere for us to land. They took the wounded off by boat and brought them to us. It was an ugly business. The hospitals were full to the gills, and still are, two months later."

"We lost some men there. But it will turn the tides, so it was worth it." She wondered who decided what was worth it, and how many men one had to sacrifice to turn the tides.

"I hope so," was all she said, and they walked back to the house and ran into their parents coming back from the family cemetery. They both looked like they'd been crying.

The service the next day was predictably painful, and just what it ought to have been: solemn, respectful, tender, poignant, and no longer than it had to be. Their neighbors had come, friends of their parents' generation. It was beautiful in a simple way for a greatly loved son who had given his life for his king and country, and would be long remembered as a man and a boy by those who loved him.

Max drove her back to the base when he left, since he had borrowed a car to come. It was easier than waiting for another unscheduled freight train, which was dangerous now anyway. The Germans blew them up whenever they could. They rode in silence much of the time, thinking of their brother, and then chatted for a while. She asked Max if he had a girlfriend, and he said he didn't.

"It wouldn't be fair, really. You never know what's going to happen." She felt the same way for herself.

"Do you think Phillip did?" she asked, curious. They never spoke of such things, but he might have to Max.

"A hundred of them." He laughed. "I never knew him to spend more than a week or two with any girl. He tired of them easily, and loved them all." It sounded about right to her too, knowing her younger brother. It was sad to think that was all over now. A young life ended all too quickly, but he had had fun too, and made every-one who knew him happy. It was something to remember him for.

Max drove her to her dormitory when they got to the base and promised to come and visit her soon.

"You won't," she said with a smile. "There's never time, is there?" She knew he was busy too. "We should try and get up to see Mum and Dad, though, when we can. They're brave, but they need us now."

He was quiet for a moment. "We need each other too. You're a good sister, you know, even if I don't say it often. Take care of your-self, Pru. Don't do anything too mad with your Flying Devils, or take too many walking tours behind enemy lines." He hadn't liked that story, although she made light of it so he wouldn't worry, which was so much her style, and part of the bravery he had referred to and respected so much about her.

"You too," she said quietly. "You don't need to be a hero. Just get out of this alive. Our parents need us now, more than they did be-fore." There was a crack in their armor now, and time wasn't on their side.

"You remember that too," he said seriously. "Take care of your-self, Pru. I'll be up to see you soon, to check on you. It's what big brothers are supposed to do." She hugged him and he kissed her cheek and drove away a few minutes later, thinking how lucky he was to have her as a sister. She was a noble girl with a heart of gold and more courage than anyone he'd ever known, man or woman. He wished he were more like her. She was an example to them all, and never made a fuss about anything. She just got on with it and did what she knew was right every time.

*   *   *

As the Allies approached Paris in late August, the Germans fought harder, and the Resistance fought back with everything they had. There were more Resistance fighters being killed by the Germans than there had been for a while, and more desperate acts committed by the freedom fighters, blowing up arms factories, munitions dumps, railways, and doing everything they could to hurt the Germans. The Allies were doing all they could to help the Resistance, and the British had sent forces in to rescue Resistance units when it was possible. The Germans wanted all the members of the Resistance dead if the Nazis had to leave France.

There was a midnight call in the nurses' barracks for nurses needed for a delicate mission. And with the final push toward Paris, the air evac nurses were being pulled in all directions.

Louise Jackson was one of the nurses called on for the highly sensitive mission, which she accepted, and in the circumstances, no one objected to her color. They needed topflight nurses to rescue nine Resistance fighters behind enemy lines. The Germans were closing in on the fighters to kill them, and the British had promised to help. One of the Resistance fighters the Germans were after was the most dangerous agent of the Resistance in all of France. The German High Command wanted him, dead or alive. He was known only as Tristan. The British had been notified that he was gravely injured.

Louise was on the tarmac at one A.M., wide-awake, prepared and ready to do whatever was necessary. She was fearless, and one of their best nurses. They sent two other nurses in with her, one of the

Australian girls and a British nurse she had worked with before. They were briefed on their mission by an officer on the tarmac. They were going to be parachuted in with two corpsmen, and it was made clear to them how dangerous the mission was. She didn't hesitate to accept it nonetheless. They headed toward France once they took off. The pilot flew low and made the drop successfully, and all three nurses and the two corpsmen headed immediately toward the agreed-upon meeting point, which was a farmhouse in the Maritime Alps. It took them three hours walking over rough terrain to get there. Louise and the others were quiet along the way. They were carrying nothing that could identify them as British military, and they all knew that they would be shot as spies if they got caught. Only Louise and the Australian nurse and one of the corpsmen spoke French, but none of them well enough to pass as natives.

Louise could feel her heart pound as the farmhouse came into view. It was an old stone house with a barn in the back. There were sheep and goats in the front yard, and a dog barked as they approached. The two corpsmen walked ahead of the nurses, and a youngish man in overalls came out of the house smoking a cigarette and carrying a shovel, which identified him as their contact.

"We're here to see your grandfather," the corpsman said in French. They looked like visitors, and each of them was wearing a small backpack with the medical supplies they needed. The nine Resistance fighters they were coming to see had been injured in an explosion when they blew up a train carrying German troops two days earlier. Many of the German soldiers had been killed, along with several officers. Two of the Resistance fighters were gravely injured. They had been supplying vital information to the British, and had to be gotten out of France as quickly as possible, but several of them were too damaged to transport, and would surely be tortured and killed if left behind. Their leader was critically wounded, and he couldn't be moved.

The young man led the way to a shed behind the barn as the visitors threaded their way through the livestock in the front yard. All of them were on the alert for any unexpected, suspicious movements, but there were none as they walked into the dark, dusty shed, cluttered with rusting farm equipment. The young Frenchman was quick to push away the dirt on the floor, and a trapdoor appeared. The two corpsmen silently helped him, and all of them disappeared below it. The men put the trapdoor back in place over their heads, then descended a staircase down a narrow tunnel, and they found themselves in a well-lit room filled with men. There was another room beyond it. The air was stale and heavy with cigarette smoke and sweat. A generator was keeping the room lit, and there were air vents above them, concealed by bushes on the farm. It was a serious operation, and looked astonishingly efficient. It had been a command post of the Resistance for the southern region for most of the war, and the Germans had never found it, although they had tried.

There were a dozen men in the room, and two women, and one of the women explained in better than adequate English that the most injured men were in the room beyond, and one of them had been unconscious since that morning. They had to be in good enough condition to move on by the next day. Six of the men in the main room and one of the two women were identified as the victims of the explosion. The nurses examined them immediately and found them all to be suffering from severe burns under their clothing—burns that hadn't been cleaned or tended to, for lack of anything to dress them with. None of them complained as the two nurses and one corpsman treated them. One of the men had lost a finger, which was an ugly wound.

Louise headed quickly into the back room with the other corpsman. There was a man lying unconscious on an old mattress, and a teenage boy lying on a blanket with a nasty abdominal wound. He had been close to the explosion. His wound was infected and he had a raging fever. Louise understood immediately that they were at the heart of the Resistance and the unconscious man on the mattress was their leader. She wondered if he would even survive long enough to worry about the Germans capturing him. But whatever happened, the Nazis would surely kill the others.

She knelt beside the unconscious man and opened the bag she had brought with her. The corpsman was dealing with the boy, who moaned when his wound was dressed, and then the corpsman left the room to join the others. The boy looked a little better by then.

Louise opened the leader's clothes and saw that there was shrapnel embedded in his chest and arms. While he slept, she removed it with the instruments she'd brought, taking advantage of the fact that he was unconscious. She cleaned the wounds and dressed them, and put antibiotic powder in the wounds. She gave him two injections to help fight the infection, and she started an IV of antibiotics. She examined the rest of his body, and found a bullet wound in his calf, which she dressed as well. The soles of his shoes were bare, and his clothes were tattered from the explosion. He had minor burns as well. Carefully, she cleaned him up, bandaged what she could, and sat silently beside him and waited for him to wake up. One of the men from the Resistance came in to check on him several times and was satisfied with what Louise was doing. She seemed like a very competent nurse and had wasted no time treating him.

"What's his name?" she whispered to the Frenchman who watched her.

He hesitated before he answered. "He answers to 'Tristan.'" She didn't challenge him, but she wanted something more.

"It's important," she said.

And after hesitating again, he whispered, "Gonzague."

She nodded, and began speaking to her patient softly, as though he could hear her. The young Frenchman left and she was alone with her patient. She bathed his brow with cool water. He had a heavy brown beard, and she gently stroked his face and one un-damaged arm, and then rubbed his hands to increase the circulation. An hour later, he moaned, and slowly opened his eyes.

"You're safe, Gonzague. You're going to be all right," she said in French. He tried to move the leg where he'd been shot, and he moaned again. The bullet had been dug out by someone else before she got there. They'd done a rough job.

"Who are you?" he said in a voice that was more of a groan. His voice was hoarse.

"We came to help you. You're at Gaston's farm," she said, using the code name for the location. "Uncle George sent us," she added, which meant they'd been sent by the British. He tried to get up and found he couldn't. Every part of him felt heavy and his wounds like they were on fire. "Try not to move. We'll get you up later. You'll be leaving tomorrow, you need to get your strength back tonight." He nodded and went back to sleep for a while. She gave him another shot for pain, and he woke up two hours later. She offered him a sip of water, and he looked at her and frowned.

"They sent you?" She nodded. "You shouldn't be here."

"Neither should you." She smiled at him. "I'm a nurse."

"It's dangerous for you to be here, and to help me." She nodded. He had spoken to her in English that time.

"I know. You needed help, badly. Your friends want you to live, and to get you out." He shrugged as though it didn't matter and was part of his job. He had been injured many times before, jailed by the Germans, and escaped. He had been underground for two years, moving around France.

"You're not afraid?" He was intrigued by her as he lay on the mattress and looked up at her. She was very beautiful, and exotic-looking. She shook her head in answer to his question and he could see that she wasn't afraid. She was very calm as she watched him. She checked his bandages and took his pulse from time to time. "They'll kill you if they find you with me. You must be very careful when you leave here. You came alone?" She shook her head.

"There are five of us. The others are taking care of your men, and one of the women." The young boy had been moved to the other room hours before, and he was doing better. The corpsman who came to check on her said that he was eating a meal, which was a good sign.

"How will you leave here?" He was concerned about her, and restless, as she sat beside him and gave him another drink.

"The same way we came. You don't need to worry about it."

He smiled as he looked at her. "You're an angel, dropped from the skies to help us."

"You have friends far away." He nodded. He knew who they were. He had done many things for the British intelligence services, not just for those who remained faithful to France. He was a legend in the Resistance.

He slept again for a while, and she could see that he was better when he woke again. The fever was gone, and he sat up on the mattress and looked at her intently. She hadn't eaten a meal all day because she hadn't wanted to leave him for an instant, in case he took a turn for the worse. Some of the French boys had brought a crust of bread, some grapes, and a peach, and she had eaten them gratefully and nothing else.

"Are you a doctor?" he asked, intrigued by her. She had told him before but he'd forgotten.

"No, I'm a nurse, with a special unit." He didn't ask which unit, and they both knew it was better if he didn't know.

"Were you assigned to this mission?" She nodded.

"Yes."

He smiled and looked very handsome when he did. She could see that when he wasn't injured, dirty, and sick, he was probably a good-looking man, and younger than he appeared. He seemed ten or twenty years older than he was.

"What's your name?" He could know that at least.

"Louise. Louise Jackson."

"You're American?" She nodded. "You must be stationed in England. They came then." He looked pleased, and then focused on her again. "I will find you one day, Louise Jackson, and come to thank you myself. If you save me now, you will save my country. What you're doing is important to many people, and to France. There are many of us left, not so many as before, but France will rise again. I will come to you after that." It sounded grandiose to her and she thought he was delusional from the pain and infection. He didn't say it, but he thought she was the most beautiful woman he had ever seen, and the gentlest. "You're in the army?" he asked, still curious, and lucid enough to ask questions. He was a strong man, even though seriously wounded.

"Air Forces," she conceded.

"You don't look like a soldier."

"Looks can be deceiving." She smiled at him. "Do you think you can stand up?" She wanted to get him as steady on his feet as she could before he left. It might save his life when they moved on. She helped him to his feet and he nearly fell. He was weak from loss of blood and his injuries. She made him walk across the room with her help. "This isn't my usual nursing protocol in a case like this," she apologized, "but we need to get you mobile fast, Gonzague."

"No one has called me that in years." He smiled at her. "Count Gonzague Antoine de Lafayette." He attempted to bow and nearly fell over.

"Stop showing off. We have work to do. I'd rather you be a walking peasant than a falling count when you leave here." She was unimpressed by the title he claimed he had, but she was intrigued by him. She walked him back and forth across the room several times and then let him sit down. "I'll give you a shot of morphine before you go. It will help."

"You are an angel, aren't you?" She let him lie down again then. It was nearly dawn, although they couldn't see it from underground.

"Close your eyes and rest. Don't talk. Save your strength. You're going to need it." His survival was going to depend on it. She leaned her back against the damp well as she sat with him. One of his men came to check on him and saw that they were both asleep. He was satisfied that their leader was doing better. He had heard Gonzague talking to the nurse for hours, and one of the others had seen him on his feet and walking with her help.

They came to warn Louise that he'd be leaving in an hour. She nodded, got up, and checked Gonzague's dressings and his leg wound again while he slept. Half an hour later, when she woke him, she gave him a shot of morphine and a shot of a local anesthetic for the leg.

"You'll be able to walk better with that. You won't look so suspicious. They'll be looking for someone who is having trouble walking. Try to look strong and confident. You can lean on one of your men," she said.

"I wish I could take you with me," he said, and looked as though he meant it. She would have liked that too. He was the most interesting man she had ever met, and he had eyes that mesmerized her. They were piercing and bright blue. "You think that you won't see me again, Louise. But I promise you that you will. I'll find you. If I'm alive at the end of this nightmare, I'll find you wherever you are. And whether I live or die, I owe you a debt. I won't forget it, if they don't kill me."

"Don't let them kill you," she said softly. "Many people depend on you." She could tell that from the way his men looked out for him, and what the British were doing for him. "I want to see you again," she said, and meant every word. It had been the strangest night of her life, trying to save him so he could escape. He leaned forward then, and his hands were strong but gentle as he pulled her toward him and kissed her in a way she knew she would never forget if she lived a hundred years. Her eyes were full of tears when he stopped. She wanted him to live so she could see him again. Or maybe he would just be a fantasy forever. She was a young Black air forces nurse from Raleigh, North Carolina. If what he said was true, he was a French count. She guessed him to be about ten years older than she was. He was a white French nobleman, a powerful agent of the Resistance whom every German in the area wanted to put in front of a firing squad. The chances of her ever seeing him again were slim to none. In her mind, she knew it, but in her heart she wished it could be otherwise. There was a fairy-tale quality to meeting him that she wanted to remember in every detail.

One of his men came to walk him into the next room when it was time to leave. They cheered when they saw him on his feet, and the shots Louise had given him helped him to move more freely than he should. He might pay for it in pain later, but for now, he looked like a healthy man again, which might save his life. She quietly joined her team and watched him from across the room. He and his men and the two women went up the ladder. Louise and her team were to wait an hour, and then two members of the Resistance would lead them back the way they'd come. They would be picked up that night at a designated location by a British transport plane. And Gonzague would be on his way over the mountains by then, in a truck headed north to the Swiss border.

He was the last one of his group to leave the subterranean room, and he turned with one hand on the ladder. His piercing sky-blue eyes found her again. He said nothing, but she remembered his lips on hers. He nodded, thinking the same thing, silently reminding her of his promise to find her, and then he was gone.

Chapter 14

Louise's team returned safely to the base after an arduous journey. The plane picking them up had trouble landing and there were German fighter planes in the area, but they eventually were picked up after the pilot made several passes at it and then flew them home.

Five days later, Paris was liberated. Five hundred Resistance fighters were killed in the fight for Paris. Louise and her crew had saved nine of them, one of them being the most important Resistance leader of the war.

Even after the liberation of Paris, which was a jubilant event, people's nerves were frayed. They were tired of the war. It had gone on for too long. Five years since it all started in Europe. And three for the Americans, who were fighting alongside their Allies in Europe and the Pacific, even if not on home turf, as the Europeans were. They kept hearing promises that it would be over soon, but it never was. Another devastating battle would happen, another border would be crossed, and for every victory there were costly defeats and heavy losses.

It had been two months since Pru's brother had been killed in August, and she wanted to go back to Yorkshire to see her parents, but hadn't had a day off since. She knew Max hadn't had leave since then either. He hadn't had time to visit her. They all worked constantly. Pru wrote to her mother regularly, and her mother's letters sounded valiant, but there was an undercurrent of sadness now beneath the surface of the brave words.

Pru had just mailed her a letter the day before she took off on a flight to pick up men in the Argonne Forest, from a field near the American 12th Evacuation Hospital. Ed was supposed to fly with her, but Lizzie had somehow gotten a day off, and he put in a request for a day off so he could be with her. He apologized to Pru the night before. She said she didn't mind.

"Someone should have some fun around here." She hadn't in a long time. She was still sad about her brother but tried not to let it show. Everyone had their losses to deal with and her stock-in-trade was her cheerful, positive demeanor. She thought it was important for a nurse. And she didn't begrudge Ed the time off. He and Lizzie were so much in love that it made everyone around them happy to see it, and she told him to have fun and forget their missions for a day.

Reggie got the flight off smoothly the next morning despite some fog low to the ground. Autumn weather had set in, but they rose through the clouds into blue skies above. As soon as they did, they saw two fighter planes head toward them. Reggie tried to outrun them. They hadn't picked up their wounded yet, and Reggie played tag in and out of the cloud cover with the planes. He thought he had outflown them when a third one appeared just above and opened fire. The others flew close, and they could see Reggie in the pilot seat when they too opened fire on them. The three fighter planes shot through their fuselage and peppered the plane with hits. The C-47 plummeted with a trail of smoke behind it, and hit the ground with a massive explosion from a full tank of fuel. The copilot had radioed back to the base while they were under attack, before they killed him. Reggie was already dead, and one of the corpsmen had taken a direct hit, and he said the nurse in charge was down too. He went off the airwaves after that.

A reconnaissance team went out looking for the wreckage later that day and saw where it had gone down. There was a blackened crater where the plane had exploded close to the location the co-pilot had given them. There was some debris in the area, and nothing else left. The crew of five had died when the plane crashed, and some before. There had been no other passengers, no wounded aboard.

The crew of the reconnaissance plane was silent on the way back. The successful Luftwaffe kill was confirmed when they reached the base, and the names of those who had died were reported to the commanding officer and the War Office. Their names were listed on a bulletin board in the mess hall, and in the nurses' dormitory. Word of mouth spread like wildfire, as it always did. Emma sat in her room that night, crying, surrounded by her friends. It was the first of their air evac transport planes that had been shot down in months. Morale plummeted when that happened. Everyone in the squadron had known Pru and loved her.

Emma could only imagine how her parents felt, having lost a son only two months before. And Max had lost both his siblings now. She sobbed in the arms of her fellow nurses. Her American counterparts had come to love Pru as much as she did.

"She was the only person of her kind who never cared that I grew up in the East End. She didn't have a snobbish bone in her body," Emma said, crying. "All she had was that huge heart of hers." The matron on their floor asked Emma to pack Pru's things to send home to her family. Emma was wracked by sobs when she did, and in the bottom drawer of the dresser Pru had used, she found a dog-eared red leather journal that she had seen Pru write in occasionally, though not very often. She never had time. Emma put it aside and decided to read it. She would send it to Pru's family after she did. They wouldn't miss it. They didn't know it existed. And when she sat down with it that night, a handful of photographs fell out, all of Emma and their other friends at various times, from fun moments they had shared, birthday parties and dinners out, plus a photograph of Ed and one of Reggie in the cockpit. He was gone now too. She thought the journal might mean more to Max, since it was mostly about her time in the air force, and some of it might make him laugh. Emma felt sorry for him too, but had never met him or Pru's parents, so she felt awkward just sending it to him.

Ed was as devastated as Emma, even more so because he was guilt-ridden for having taken the day off. The same thing had happened when their crew's plane lost an engine and Pru and Emma were MIA for eight days. But this time the entire crew had died, and he hadn't, and he couldn't forgive himself. He sobbed in Lizzie's arms when he found out, and he got blind drunk that night. Why hadn't he died with her? Why had he been spared? The questions kept going around in his mind, and Emma was the first to absolve him.

"We don't decide these things," Emma said, trying to get through to him in the abyss of guilt where he was drowning. "They happen. We're in the wrong place, or the right one, on any given day. God decides. We don't."

"She was twenty-five years old. She didn't deserve to die. She was the best person I knew, always kind to everyone, always generous, always forgiving. Why Pru?" he sobbed.

"It was her destiny. It could be you or me tomorrow. None of us knows." Her brother, Phillip, had been twenty-four.

"It should have been me instead of her," he said angrily.

"And what good would that do? What about Lizzie? She needs you too. How would she feel now if you'd been on that plane? She's already lost a brother, she doesn't need to lose you too." He nodded, hearing reason finally. But Pru's parents had lost two children now. It made Emma think of the journal again. She wanted to finish reading it and send it to them. She read more of it that night and fell asleep with it in her hand. There were several entries in it about Emma that made her laugh and cry. Pru talked about how much fun they had, what a terrific girl Emma was and how much she liked her. The entries touched her and, in some ways, made Pru's death seem even worse. She talked about how much she loved her family too. Emma realized again how much the journal would mean to them as soon as she finished reading it. She meant to send it as soon as she could, but she was so tired, she fell asleep at night with it in her hand, and never seemed to get through it.

The clothes and personal possessions she had boxed up for Pru's family had been sent to them by the RAF, but Emma still had the journal she knew they should have too.

Everyone kept saying that the war would end soon, that the Allies were turning it around. Having the Americans on the ground since the invasion of Normandy in June was helpful. Paris had been liberated, and the Germans had lost some ground around Europe, but not enough, and the Luftwaffe was relentless. The Germans still hadn't surrendered.

Emma said afterwards that the Fates seemed to have saved the worst for last for them. Three weeks after Pru's plane was shot down with her crew, Audrey went out on a mission in November, and her plane was shot down too. Everyone on the flight was lost, this time with twenty-four wounded men on board that they had just picked up. The plane exploded midair. Twenty-nine souls were lost. Lizzie floated around the dormitory like a ghost, unable to believe what had happened. This time, Ed consoled her, as she had him three weeks before when Pru died. And ironically, it happened on Thanksgiving Day. She had lost her older brother, the man she loved, and her best friend to the war by then. It was a crushing blow. The whole unit mourned both women. Like Pru, Audrey was such a good person, always giving to others and doing for them. Her whole life had been a gift to someone else, first to her mother, then her patients, to Lizzie as a friend, and to her fellow nurses.

Unlike Pru, who had a family, Audrey had no one to mourn her. She had no family left. Her parents were gone, her brother had been killed in the war. There were only her friends and the nurses she had worked with. They hadn't had a recent casualty in the Women's Flying Corps until Pru and Audrey so close together, just weeks apart. Their deaths had cost the unit, and everyone who knew and loved them, dearly.

There was some talk about a commemorative headstone in the cemetery they used on the base, since there were no remains. With Ed's encouragement, Lizzie went to see their commanding officer to explain Audrey's heritage, and that her parents and brother and grandfather were buried at the cemetery of the Naval Academy in Annapolis, and Audrey should have a headstone there. The air forces agreed to undertake the arrangements, and pay for it if necessary, and to notify the cemetery in Annapolis, since she was from a distinguished naval family, and Audrey had distinguished herself in combat.

Speaking to the commanding officer made Lizzie wonder what Audrey's financial situation had been. She had never thought of it before, but she knew she had kept her parents' house and it had stood empty and closed up since she'd enlisted in the Army Air Forces. She had no idea what would happen to the house in a case like this. She spoke to Ed about it, and he didn't know either. He smiled gently at Lizzie, who was glad she'd told the CO about the cemetery in Annapolis. The CO had told her that Audrey would be awarded a medal for distinguished service posthumously. It could be put on display at the cemetery or incorporated in the headstone. The ceremony and the medal would come later, and she was sure the Americans would give Audrey a medal as well. It was small consolation but it was something. Audrey's service to her country should never be forgotten. Lizzie knew she would love and remember her forever. It saddened Lizzie to realize that Audrey's whole family was gone now, and Audrey too.

When she talked to Ed about Audrey's house in Maryland, and what would happen to it now with no one left, he smiled wryly. "I'm not the one to consult about that. No one in my family has ever inherited money, or anything, or had a penny. I don't know what happens in a case like that."

A month later, a few days before Christmas, Lizzie found out. She was packing a few more of Audrey's things that she'd found in the bottom drawer of a chest in their room, and came upon an envelope that said only "To Whom It May Concern" on it in Audrey's handwriting. She hesitated, and then opened it, since there was no one to send it to. It was a handwritten will Audrey had written when they came to England and started flying missions. She acknowledged that it was wartime, and her job as an air evac transport nurse was dangerous. She referred to a bank account at a bank in Maryland and her family house in Annapolis, which were all she had of some value. Lizzie's eyes widened as she read the letter. She had left it all to her beloved friend Elizabeth Hatton, whom she said was like a sister to her, and whom she wanted to have whatever her worldly possessions were at the time of her death. The house would have considerable value. It was in a solid residential neighborhood, and the money was what her mother had left Audrey when she died. She had spent none of it. She had told Lizzie that she didn't want to move back to Annapolis after the war. It would make her too sad with everyone gone. She had talked about moving to New York, or Boston if Lizzie returned there. But the value of what she had left would make a difference to Lizzie now, and to Ed.

There was a footnote on the letter, which said that she had sent a copy of her will to her bank, to handle everything in the event of her death.

Lizzie put on a warm jacket and hurried to Ed's barracks. He had just come in from the pub with a few of his friends, and he came downstairs to talk to Lizzie.

"Is something wrong?"

She showed him the letter and he read it and looked at her. "Wow, Liz, that's amazing. Generous to the end. She loved you." He had never doubted it, and he was glad for Lizzie. It sounded like a nice nest egg, from what Lizzie described of the house.

"Do you realize what this is?"

"Yes, a house and a nice bank account. Do you want to live in Annapolis?" He wasn't sure where it was. It was a long way from Dublin, in any case.

"No. Audrey didn't either, after the war. It's a nice chunk of money. I'll sell the house. This is medical school for both of us," she said, beaming at him. "I won't need my father's permission now. I can pay for it myself." He smiled at her and gave her a hug.

"That's great, but I can't take that from you, Liz. She left it to you, not to both of us. I'll see what's available for veterans in Ireland after the war."

"I want you to come home with me," she said. He had thought of it too. He was going to ask his cousin about how complicated it would be to emigrate to Boston, and if his cousin would sponsor him.

"Let's make sure we're both around to do that," Ed said seriously. The deaths of Pru and Audrey had shaken all of them, and were a brutal reminder of the dangers they faced every day. It was going to be a sad Christmas this year, without them. "Maybe my cousin can help me get whatever papers I'd need to move to Boston," he said, and if for some reason Lizzie didn't survive, he wouldn't want to go to Boston. They had already agreed that they didn't want to make plans before the war ended. They were afraid it would be bad luck for either or both of them. Many others felt as they did and refused to discuss the future.

"If I go back to Boston, I want you to come too," she said firmly. "We could go to medical school together. We'll both be veterans. And now we have the money to pay for it, thanks to Audrey." It was an incredible gift. She was beaming as she said it.

"We're getting ahead of ourselves here," he interrupted her. "Let's get this damn war over and done and dusted, and then we'll make plans. Or are you proposing to me right now?" he teased her. He had thought about it himself, but superstition got the best of him every time.

"No, I'll let you do that when peace is declared," she answered.

"What will your father say? Everyone in your family is a doctor, I'm just a poor boy from Dublin."

"You've saved more lives than my father has. And one day you'll be a great doctor." She smiled at him. He loved the way she believed in him and didn't give a damn about where he came from, or how poor he'd been growing up. Audrey had been that way too, and so was Alex. Emma said the same thing about Pru. They had big hearts and open minds, and none of the narrow thinking that he'd grown up with in Ireland, and Emma had in England, where they were trapped in the class they were born into forever. He liked the idea of moving to America with Lizzie and starting a new life. But peacetime first.

She went back to her barracks then and put the letter safely in her own dresser drawer. Audrey had given her the best Christmas gift of all.

With the unit short of their best and most experienced nurses, Pru and Audrey, the commanding officer of the air evac transport unit called Louise into her office a few days before Christmas, and told her she was being transferred to active transport duty. Her days as hospital relief for patients of her own race, and caring for the German POWs, were over. They didn't say it in so many words, but Louise understood the full meaning of their gesture. Her color had become irrelevant, even here, where she had never been discriminated against as she had been in the States all her life. The color line had been lifted and no longer existed. She was one of their best nurses, they recognized it, and she had proven what she was capable of on the complicated mission to help the French Resistance unit and their leader three months before, and she saved the leader's life. He was the most important freedom fighter in France.

She had never had any feedback from it. They weren't told if the mission had been successful and whether or not the nine people they had rescued had made it safely to the Swiss border, or even whether her patient had survived, or if they'd all been captured and killed. She had never heard from Gonzague again, nor did she expect to. She knew it was one of those rare onetime events in a lifetime. A French Resistance fighter in wartime, who claimed to be a nobleman, had appeared out of the mists, needing her nursing skills, and kissed her like a prince in a fairy tale. She didn't expect to see or hear from him again, but she cherished the memory. It was one of those wartime experiences that she knew she would remember for a lifetime.

Her new job as full-time flying evacuation nurse was to begin on the first of January. She couldn't wait to tell her parents. She had done her job well so far and there was justice in what had just happened. She only wished that Pru and Audrey hadn't died, to leave the places vacant for her. She told the other nurses about it and savored the victory that she would be fully one of them now. They were happy for her. They didn't know, and never would, how much more she'd had to achieve in order to prove herself worthy of what was given to them so easily. But she didn't care how long it took, or what she had to do. It was worth it in the end, and the victory was sweet.

Chapter 15

E mma finished reading Pru's journal the week before Christmas. She then read it again when she had a day off, this time at one sitting. There was so much in it she loved, she didn't want to miss anything. There were so many references to her, and to Pru's parents, and her brothers, and everything she cared about and believed in. Reading it, Pru shone through the pages, and one knew exactly who she was.

A tiny part of Emma wanted to keep it, and never let them know it existed, but she couldn't do that. It wouldn't be fair. It would be selfish of her. She knew that Pru would have wanted her parents to have it, and her older brother to see it. It belonged with them. She thought about mailing it to them, but that seemed so cold and impersonal. She had no one to be with on Christmas, she never did, like Audrey in the end. She had no family. Audrey had had one, but Emma hadn't since she was fifteen, and it was only her drunken mother before that. She was used to spending holidays alone. She always spent them working, which gave someone else a chance to take a day off, someone who had better use for a holiday, and loved ones to spend it with, which Emma didn't.

Lizzie was spending Christmas with Ed, and Louise had volunteered for general duty at the hospital. Alex had volunteered at the psych ward, so Emma wanted to do something special for Pru. She gift wrapped the journal in silver paper she bought, and decided to take a train to Yorkshire. It would probably take forever to get there with wartime disruptions, unreliable train schedules, and bombing raids. But she didn't care how long it took. She had nowhere else to be. She had already visualized it. She would ring the front doorbell, ask to see Pru's mother, Lady Pommery, whom she had heard so much about, and hand her the silver-wrapped journal as a Christmas gift from Pru.

She was sure that Pru would have loved her doing it. Emma smiled every time she thought of it. She had two days off, and she didn't care if she wound up sleeping on a bench in the train station in York on Christmas Eve. She went to the train station near the base at seven A.M. on the morning of Christmas Eve. She waited two hours for a train, and then got one headed north. It stopped several times, and was sidetracked for an hour halfway there, but she reached the station in York at five o'clock, and found an old man who was willing to drive her to Pommery Manor. She offered him some money, but he refused it. He dropped her off in front of the manor and wished her a Merry Christmas. She was holding her precious package close to her chest.

She rang the doorbell of the imposing home, and no one answered for a long time. She was afraid they were out, but she could hear children shouting and laughing from open windows on the top floor. The blackout shades were already up. Finally, after a ten-minute wait in the cold, while she wondered what to do, a tall young man in uniform opened the door. Emma guessed instantly that it was Pru's older brother, Max. He looked like Pru. He was surprised to see her and asked Emma what he could do for her. She had worn her uniform too, with the trousers, coat, and cap, so she'd be warm on the train.

"May I see Lady Pommery?" Emma asked politely, in her least East End voice. She felt self-conscious being there, and she had noticed immediately that the man in the uniform had the same aristocratic diction as Pru. "I have a package for her," Emma explained. "From her daughter." He looked startled at that and opened the door wider.

"Please come in," he said with a smile. "I'm afraid Lord and Lady Pommery are out. They're dining with friends. What sort of package is it?" He hadn't noticed the slim silver-wrapped volume in her hand. She'd added a narrow silver ribbon, to make it look more festive. She hesitated, while standing in the front hall, and then extended it to him.

"I am . . . I was a friend of Pru's. We trained together. I'm a nurse. We were in the same unit, and we were roommates. I loved her very much. We all did and we miss her terribly," she said in a rush, fighting back tears. "I found her journal after I packed up her things. It's wonderful, and there's so much in it about everyone she loved . . . I'm afraid I read it. I thought your mother would like to have it, as sort of a Christmas gift from Pru."

"Are you staying nearby? Perhaps you'd like to come and see my mother tomorrow. I'm sure she'll be very grateful to you," he said graciously, looking Emma over carefully, and she wondered if he had noticed the accent and disapproved.

"No, I'm not staying nearby," Emma said, embarrassed. "I took the train up to bring it to her. I thought Pru might like that," she said, and he narrowed his eyes as he noticed the red hair under her cap. "I'm sorry. I'm Emma Jones," she said, and held out her hand to shake his.

"The firebrand!" he said with a broad grin. "My sister told me all about you last summer, when she was here after . . . after our brother died. She adored you," he said, directing her toward the drawing room. "Can I take your coat? Come in and sit down. You must be freezing after the day on the train." He was stunned that she had brought it herself, and took the gift-wrapped journal from her, while she took off her coat. He led her into the drawing room, where the fire was blazing, and invited her to sit down. He set the journal down on a table, and she hoped he'd remember to give it to his mother. "Would you like something to eat? You must be starving!" She was, but she was too shy to admit it to him. "She called you a firebrand, you know." They both laughed at that. "She admired you so much. You were really her closest friend in the end." They both thought about Pru for a quiet minute, and he smiled at Emma. He had the same warm smile as Pru, that started at his eyes. "I insist that you let me give you something to eat. I have some rather sad-looking sausages, and dreadful potato soup. I was about to eat, myself. I'm afraid rationing has made our menus a bit thin. But my mother made scones today, and I've got some of her home-made jam." He made it so inviting that Emma didn't want to turn it down, and she was hungry. He invited her into the big old-fashioned kitchen, where he put the meal together himself. He reminded her a lot of Pru: practical, down-to-earth, warm and unassuming, with a look of mischief in his eye.

They sat down at the kitchen table together, and he told her funny stories about Pru from their childhood, while they shared the meal. The time passed quickly, and she told him about the journal and how much she had loved reading it.

"My mother will love it, and I'll read it myself. I'm down here for five days, on leave. Christmas and all that, although it's going to be hard this year. Fortunately, we have the children to distract us. I'm sure Pru told you about them."

"Yes, she did," Emma said with a smile, as they heard the front door open and then close hard. A moment later, his mother walked into the kitchen. She was an elegant woman with impeccably groomed white hair, wearing a black velvet dress and a fur coat. She smiled as soon as she saw Emma, and then looked embarrassed.

"Oh, I am sorry. I didn't know you invited a friend," she said to Max. "Oh my God, you've given her that awful soup, and Mr. Jarvis's nasty sausages."

"The scones were delicious," Emma said, feeling like an intruder, but Lady Pommery was so warm and welcoming, and Max had been so kind, that she enjoyed being there, even though she was an uninvited guest.

"This is Emma Jones," Max introduced her to his mother, "a dear friend of Pru's. They were roommates at the base and flew together. She took the train all the way up here to bring you something very special. I left it in the drawing room for you. It's Pru's journal." They were both bowled over that Emma had brought it herself, and gone to so much trouble to do it.

"It didn't seem right to just send it by post," Emma explained.

"What an incredibly nice thing to do. Where are you staying?" Lady Pommery asked her.

"I'm not. I'm going to take the train back tonight."

"You can't possibly. I won't hear of it. On Christmas Eve? You have to at least spend the night. We have plenty of room. The entire third floor is full of children, and they'll wake you at dawn tomorrow, but the second floor is quite civilized. You must spend the night. We'll be devastated if you don't." She went to find the package then, sat down in the drawing room and opened it, and they joined her a few minutes later, after Max put their dishes in the sink. Lord Pommery had settled into his favorite chair by the fire and had lit a pipe. He stood up to greet Emma politely, they shook hands, and he sat down again. Lady Pommery was already reading the first pages of the journal, and she looked up with a smile and damp eyes when Max and Emma walked in, then was engrossed in it again.

"What a dear girl you are to bring this to me. Are you on duty tomorrow? I hope not, since it's Christmas."

"No, I'm not," Emma answered.

"Then you must spend the night. I won't hear of your going back on some dreadful train tonight. You'll get sick."

"I really shouldn't." Emma hesitated.

"Yes, you should," Max said softly, and she looked at him. "Pru would want you to." Emma had the feeling that was true, and she allowed them to convince her. She sat down with them by the fire, and they talked for an hour. Then Pru's parents went up to bed, and Lady Pommery told Max which guest room to put her in.

"I'm sorry to have just dropped in like this on Christmas Eve. I just wanted to drop off Pru's journal," she said after his parents left, and he looked thoughtful.

"You know, I think this is Pru at work from wherever she is. She loved you, and she loved us, and we all loved her. Can't you just imagine her wanting us to be together, especially on Christmas?" The truth was that Emma could imagine it perfectly, and she nodded. "Now, my rakish younger brother is another story. He would have rather been in London, chasing around some beautiful girl, or a flock of them. Yorkshire was far too tame for him. Pru and I loved it here, but Phillip never did, from the time he turned eighteen. And where is your family?" he asked her.

"They're not. My father died in the last war before I was born, and my mother when I was fifteen. I've been on my own since I turned eighteen. I went to nursing school, eventually became a midwife, and then I enlisted. And now here I am. Pru was like a sister to me," she said in a gentle voice.

"She said the same thing about you," he said, startled by her description of her origins, and life on her own. She was a little older than Pru, but not that much, and he was about to turn twenty-eight. He felt like an old man these days.

As the fire died down and the room got chilly, he took her up to the guest room his mother had suggested. Emma noticed that Lady Pommery had taken the journal with her to bed and she was pleased. The gift had been a success, and she had ended up spend-

235

ing the evening with Pru's family, which she hadn't expected and was enjoying more than she'd imagined, with such warm treatment from the Pommerys. The bedroom Max led her to was large and comfortable and looked as though it hadn't been used in a long time.

She fell asleep thinking of Pru and woke to the sound of children laughing and talking, and thundering down the stairs to have breakfast, shepherded by the young women who took care of them.

Emma dressed in her uniform and joined the children in the kitchen. She was playing games with them when Max walked in, looking as impeccably put together as he had the night before. She felt a little bit intimidated by him. He seemed so sophisticated, handsome, and aristocratic, and he had been nothing but welcoming to her since she'd arrived.

"I'm so sorry. Did the little monsters wake you?" He put one of the younger ones on his lap, and Emma had an adorable little girl on hers. They chatted over the din, and one of the babysitters made them coffee, which they agreed was ghastly ever since the war, and they ate some of the leftover scones. His mother joined them shortly after and told the children that Father Christmas had left them some presents in the great hall. Max told Emma when his mother left the room that she had wrapped them all herself. The children followed her like the Pied Piper and Max and Emma could hear the noise in the hall as they opened their gifts. Pru's mother managed to make it a happy day for all of them, despite what the Pommerys had been through that year, losing two children. She thanked Emma profusely again for Pru's journal. She said she had already read half of it.

"You two were quite the naughty girls together, playing tricks on the other nurses, I gather," she teased Emma, and she laughed.

"We had fun."

"Pru was always fun, even as a little girl," she said. "Those were happy times. Life is much harder now, but hopefully it will be over soon."

Emma said she had to leave, after breakfast. She didn't want to overstay, and she said she needed to start the journey back or she wouldn't get to the base, and she was flying the next day.

Lady Pommery hugged her before she left and looked at her with a warm smile. "Thank you for coming, my dear, and thank you for that incomparable gift. Nothing could have pleased me more. Promise me you'll come back and visit soon, and stay longer next time." Emma nodded with tears in her eyes. No one had ever been as kind to her, except Pru. Emma thanked her for letting her spend the night, and Max drove her to the station. She didn't see his father again. Max said his father got up late now, to avoid the children in the kitchen at breakfast.

They were both quiet as they drove to the station.

"I had a really lovely time," Emma said softly. "Thank you."

"I'm so glad you came, and didn't just send the journal by post," he said, and looked as though he meant it. "I'm glad I met the famous firebrand." She almost seemed like a gift from Pru. They both laughed at what he said, and he hugged her before she left. There was a train waiting in the station. She bought a ticket and got on it. He waved as it pulled away, and she leaned out the window and shouted back to him.

"Merry Christmas!"

"And to you, Emma!" he shouted back. They were both smiling as the train left the station. It had been a perfect Christmas, Emma thought, thanks to Pru.

Alex had a letter from Dan Stanley, which arrived on Christmas Eve. She hadn't heard from him since he went back to the front, and he couldn't tell her where he was. He sounded friendly and in good spirits in the letter, and said he had been thinking of her. Alex thought she might not hear from him again, since she hadn't in so long. She was happy when she did. It had been five months. So much had happened since he left. Pru and Audrey had died. The war was raging on, although Paris had been liberated.

The Germans seemed to have an unlimited supply of bombs to drop on Great Britain. And it was hard to believe that Europe was celebrating its sixth wartime Christmas. The war had become a way of life by then. But Dan sounded cheerful in his letter, and suggested to her that when the war finally ended, she come to Paris and celebrate with him, which seemed like a bold thing to say. She wouldn't have admitted it to him, but she liked the idea. She was sure her parents would have been horrified at the thought of her meeting a man in Paris, but she was an adult, and she was in the air forces. She was sure they would be even more horrified if they met him. But he was a good man, and she felt comfortable with him, more than she ever had with her parents' friends, or the men they considered suitable. There was nothing about her life in the air forces that they would approve of, and she knew that when the war was over and she went back to New York, that would have to change. Maybe Dan Stanley would be part of that change. She was surprised to realize that she liked that idea very much.

Lizzie had a Christmas surprise too. Alfred, the wounded boy who had been a patient of hers when she first arrived and had declared undying love for her, and even proposed marriage, was back. He was suffering from tinnitus, a self-inflicted wound in his right foot, and battle fatigue. He was in their psychiatric ward, which was increasingly crowded these days. Alex had volunteered to work Christmas Day there, and told Lizzie that night that Alfred was telling all the nursing staff that he and Lieutenant Hatton were engaged.

"You might want to put a damper on that," Alex said discreetly, particularly if Ed heard about it.

"He wrote to me a few times, and I sent him cheery little notes," Lizzie said, thinking about it. "He actually did ask me to marry him when he was here last time, and of course I said no." Lizzie looked mildly embarrassed by his claims. "How is he?"

Alex looked serious when she answered. "To be honest, Lizzie, he's in terrible shape. He was on Omaha Beach. I think his mind is gone. Something snapped. I suspect the army knows it too. He has delusions in the daytime, like being engaged to you, and nightmares all night. He claims he was shot in the foot by a German soldier, but his commanding officer believes he shot himself. You've never heard anyone scream the way he does at night. They're put-

ting him on the next hospital ship home, and until then, we're ba-
bysitting him here in the psych ward until one shows up. I think
something in him is irreparably broken." They had both seen others
like him, and it was always sad. "I don't know how they're going to
put boys like him back together when they get back to the States.
The war has been hard on everyone, and we'll all have nightmares
about things we'll never forget. But I think some of the men will
never recover from them. The trauma they went through was just
too great for their minds. I think Alfred is one of those. He's just a
kid, but his mind is shot. He says he met Hitler in Berlin."

"Oh God. Maybe I'll go see him," Lizzie said, thinking about it,
and sorry for him again.

"Be careful what you say. He's delusional."

"I'd like him to stop saying we're engaged," Lizzie said quietly.

"No one is taking it seriously," Alex assured her, "any more than
they are about his meeting Hitler."

"The poor kid. He was a sweet boy. He wasn't right in his head
the last time I saw him either. He was desperate for me to agree to
getting engaged. Ed and I aren't even engaged and I'm in love with
him." They both laughed at that.

"Do you think that'll happen?" Alex asked her, and Lizzie
shrugged in answer and looked vague.

"After what happened to Pru and Audrey, you can't count on anything until the war is over. We're not making any plans. We both
want to go to medical school after the war and become doctors, but
he lives in Dublin, I live in Boston."

"Stranger things have happened," Alex encouraged her. She was
thinking that about her own life too, and Dan. Meeting him had

been unexpected, but it had seemed so right, and still did, no matter how different their backgrounds were.

"Everything in wartime is strange," Lizzie said, "and maybe afterwards too, good and bad. The only thing I do know is that you can't count on anything while we're here and the war is still on." They both knew it was true. Alex nodded and left the room after delivering the message about Alfred.

Lizzie went to see him the next day and found him much more delusional than he'd been before. She had no experience with psychiatric nursing, nor training for it, unlike Alex, but his mind was all over the place. He recognized Lizzie immediately, but then he wandered off into dark corners of his mind. He told her in detail about his meeting with Hitler, and that a German officer had shot him in the foot. She saw the notes in his chart about the nightmares he had every night. He had to be sedated and restrained when he had them. When she mentioned that he would be going home soon, he said that no, he was being sent for duty in North Africa as an aide to General de Gaulle. He didn't mention being engaged to her, although the head nurse on the psych ward said he spoke of it all the time, and that he was fixated on it. They were recommending electric shock treatment for him when he got back to the States. The military wasn't going to release him until some semblance of sanity had returned. Lizzie wondered if it ever would or if his mind was blown forever by the rigors of war.

She went to see him another time, and he thought she was his mother, and then he said he was Jesus and she was the Virgin Mary. She wished him a good trip home when she left the ward and didn't go back to see him again. There was no point. He didn't recognize her some of the time, and he came in and out of lucidity. It tore at her heart to see it. The war had destroyed so many minds and bodies and lives. She hoped they could put him back together, but it didn't seem likely. Nothing was sure anymore. They had all been through too much. And boys like Alfred couldn't find their way back from the terrible things they'd seen and done in the war.

Chapter 16

Emma was on her way back to her barracks after flying missions one night in January, when she saw a familiar figure walk toward her. He was wearing an RAF uniform, but she wasn't sure who it was at first. And then she saw that it was Max, Pru's older brother. She was surprised to see him. He smiled as he got closer, and he was carrying something. It was a cold night, and she'd had a hard time keeping the men warm on her last flight back. Her bright red hair was sticking up, and he looked happy to see her.

"What are you doing here?" she asked him, smiling.

"I was looking for you." Being there made him feel guilty that he hadn't visited Pru more often. Now he wished he had.

"Do you want to come in for a cup of tea, or go to the pub?" she suggested.

He looked pleased at the prospect. "A glass of wine might be nice. Have you got time?"

"I just finished. I'm free for the night."

They walked swiftly toward the pub in the cold night air and were happy to find it warm and inviting, with a blazing fire in the hearth. They found a small table and he ordered a glass of red wine for each of them.

"What brings you here?" she asked him.

"My mother asked me to give you this." He handed her his sister's journal, and Emma looked surprised. "She said there's so much of the two of you in here, she thought you should have it." Emma's eyes lit up at the kind gesture. She had sent Lady Pommery a note, thanking her for inviting her to stay on Christmas Eve.

"That's so nice of her." She tucked it into the bag she was carrying and couldn't wait to read it again. She had missed it. The way Pru described things with her keen eye and dry wit brought her back to life. He had felt that way too when he read it.

"So, what have you been up to?" he asked after they each took a sip of the wine.

"Flying men back from the battlefield. I'm so tired of the damn Germans. We got Paris back and they still won't give up."

"They will soon, we're pounding them to bits every night," Max said reassuringly.

"They're pounding us too. Will it ever stop?"

"It will one day. And then what will you do?" he asked her.

"Sleep for about a month, and then I suppose I'll go back to delivering babies in Poplar."

"That must be rough," he said.

"Not after the war. And I'm used to being a midwife in Poplar. Until they figure out what's causing it, I have plenty of work." He laughed.

"Do you enjoy it?"

"There's something beautiful about bringing babies into the world. It never gets old. It's always exciting. Especially after all this." They'd all seen too much death after the last five years. "Midwifery is easier than what we do here, even a complicated delivery is nothing compared to what we see every day. There are some sad ones, but the men we fly back are so damaged. It's a race against time on every flight. A baby is a confirmation of life."

"I don't know how you do it with the evacuations."

"You figure it out as you go, and pray you get it right. I don't always. Pru was brilliant. I could never tell if she was scared. She made it look like she always knew what she was doing."

"From what I read in her journal, she was impressed by you too."

"We were a good team when we worked together, and she gave me good advice. What about you? What comes after the RAF?"

"I'm not sure. Run the farms on the estate? Go back to school? Study law? Give flying lessons?" They were all wondering what they'd do later.

"People keep saying that the world is going to be different now," Emma said thoughtfully. "I wonder if that's true, or if we'll be back in another war twenty years from now. They say there will be women in the workforce now, but as soon as the boys return, they'll want their jobs back, and the women will be at home, scrubbing floors and having babies."

"I'd rather give flying lessons," he said, and she laughed.

"Yeah, me too. I love delivering children. I'm not sure I'd want one of my own."

"Why not?"

"The world seems like such an uncertain place now." He didn't disagree with her.

"I can't figure out if I want to live in London or Yorkshire. The life of a gentleman farmer, or go into business and work in the city, or be a barrister. My father's generation didn't worry about it. Now we've got choices, that can be confusing."

"I've never lived in the country. I grew up in the city," Emma said, thinking about it.

"I wonder what Pru would have done," Max said thoughtfully.

"She wanted to work in a hospital in London. Trauma or something like that."

"I wondered if she'd want London."

"We were going to rent a flat together," Emma said wistfully. "It wouldn't be the same now without her."

"She didn't have a man in her life, did she?"

"She was afraid of what would happen if she did. You fall in love, and the next thing you know, the guy gets shot down over Germany and your heart is broken."

"And instead she's gone, and our hearts are broken," he said, and Emma nodded. "I miss her," he said, and he looked so sad that she reached out to him and touched his hand.

"Me too. She'd be happy that we're here, having a glass of wine, talking about her." He nodded. He was thinking of his brother too. Suddenly, he was an only child.

"If I move to London, will you have dinner with me?" he asked her, and she looked surprised.

"Of course. Do you know one of the things I loved about Pru? She didn't care where I grew up, or that I sound like the East End.

It never mattered to her. As soon as I met her, I thought she'd be a snob when we started working together, and she wasn't. She didn't give a damn where anyone came from."

"I don't give a damn either," he said, and looked at Emma with the same gentle eyes as Pru. And their mother had been just as kind to her.

"I think the war did change some things, or it should have. We're all in this together," she said, and wondered what it would be like to go out with him.

"Would it be all right if I visit you here from time to time?" It was the reason why he had come. The journal had only been the excuse. She looked surprised when he asked her.

"Of course." She smiled at him. "We can talk about Pru."

"We can talk about you too. I want to know more about you . . . the firebrand." The smile in his eyes lit up his face.

Emma laughed. "I don't know why she called me that."

"Because you say what you think. I like that about you. You're not afraid to be who you are, no matter what people think. You're brave, the way she was, and you have a good heart, like hers. I can't believe you took the train all the way to Yorkshire so you could hand my mother Pru's journal in person, and you were going to take the train back the same night. I don't know another woman who would do that."

She thought about it for a minute. "It was the right thing to do."

"Most people don't care what that is. They do what's easy. Pru was like you. She always did the right thing. That's what matters, Emma. That's what makes you different."

"I've never thought about it that way."

"She didn't either. Doing the right thing came naturally to her. That's why everybody loved her. Do you want to have dinner with me next week?" he asked her. "I've got a mission early tomorrow morning, or I'd buy you dinner tonight."

"I'd like that, just do something for me."

"What's that?"

"Stay alive till we're out of this mess. Don't be stupid and be a hero. Your parents need you, and I might too." She looked at him mischievously, and he laughed at her. Her bright red hair was sticking up all over the place after her day's work, and she didn't seem to care. His sister had been that way too. She was beautiful, but had been totally unaware of it, and never really cared how she looked if she was busy.

"I'll try to keep it in mind and not do anything stupid."

"Thank you. I'd appreciate it." He paid for their wine and walked her back to the barracks. He was smiling and so was she. He liked just being with her. There was something calming about her, and fun at the same time. He liked her courage and her spunk.

"I might remind you of the same thing," he told her. "Try not to get shot down or go missing. My sister said you're rubbish at reading maps, and you had her walking all over France, trying to find your way home."

"That wasn't my fault. And maps never make sense to me," she said, embarrassed.

"Good, then keep your ass on the plane, and don't screw up our dinner plans." He sounded just like Pru when he said it, and Emma laughed at him.

"Oh God, you're going to turn out to be just like her, aren't you? She was such a pain in the ass at times, and so stubborn."

"And you're not?" He was laughing again.

"I'm only stubborn when I'm right," she corrected him.

"Which you are most of the time?"

"No, *all* the time!"

"I can see this isn't going to be easy. You're going to be an enormous headache."

"Just do what I say, and everything will be fine," she said, and he pulled her close then and kissed her on the cheek.

"Damn stubborn girl. Behave yourself, and don't get shot out of any damn airplanes, do you hear me?" She nodded and kissed him on the cheek too.

"You too. Goddamn Luftwaffe. See you next week for dinner." He watched her run up the stairs, and she waved at him and disappeared into the building. He was smiling as he walked back to where he had left the car he had borrowed. She was such an interesting girl, and he was looking forward to their dinner.

Alex had another letter from Dan in April. He was vague about his whereabouts again, as he had to be. She knew he was on a ship somewhere, but he said they would be coming into port soon. He reminded her of his earlier invitation to meet him in Paris, and said he might drop by to see her at the base if she couldn't. But Paris still sounded good to her. The Germans had left it eight months before, but the war wasn't over yet. The Allies were reclaiming most of

Europe. There were constant rumors now that the fighting was almost over.

And then suddenly, finally, two weeks later, it was.

On the eighth of May, five years and eight months after war was declared in Europe, almost to the day, the war was over. Sirens blared, church bells were rung, horns honked. They still transported the wounded for another three weeks, but no one was trying to shoot them down now. They didn't need a fighter escort. The bodies could repair and the boys could go home. And the air evac crews could fly them back to the base safely.

The nurses of the air evac transport unit were waiting for their final orders and discharge papers. Their families wanted to know when they would see them again. They didn't know yet.

Dan called Alex from a small hotel where he was staying in Paris. He had a two-week leave and wanted to know if she could join him. And if not, he was sailing back to the States in a few weeks and docking in New York at the end of June. He said she could have her own room if she came to Paris, which made it sound like a good idea to her. She got a weekend off, and Emma said she'd cover for her. They were finally doing fewer runs and flying fewer missions.

They got their orders the day before she left for Paris. There was going to be an award ceremony on the tenth of June to honor the nurses who had been killed in combat. And on the fifteenth they were flying home. Lizzie called her parents to tell them. They were so relieved. They were waiting to hear from Henry. He was still in Okinawa, but he said in his letters that he was sure he'd be home soon.

Alex called her parents, and her mother cried when she told her, which surprised Alex. Louise's parents were going to meet her in New York and fly home with her. Emma was going to start looking for an apartment in London and apply for a job as a midwife in a hospital. Max got his orders the day after she did, and he had decided to look for a job in London too, probably at a bank.

Alex told Dan the good news when she met him at his hotel on the Left Bank. He had taken a room for her, just as he promised, and filled it with flowers for her. They walked down the Champs-Élysées to the Place de la Concorde, and agreed that they'd never seen anything as beautiful. Paris was already recovering from the Occupation, and the city was jubilant, as all of Europe was. The Japanese hadn't surrendered yet, but the war wouldn't last much longer in the Pacific either.

"I think I dock in New York about a week after you get home," Dan told her as they walked to the Trocadero, with its breathtaking view of the Eiffel Tower, and sat down at an outdoor café. "And what happens after that?" he asked her, admiring how beautiful she was. She was still in uniform. They both were. There were American uniforms all over Paris.

"I get a job and an apartment." Alex smiled at him. "I haven't told my parents that yet. But I can't go back to living with them. I'd rather live in an army barracks."

"Am I going to meet them?" he asked her.

"Yes, you are." She had thought about it. Coming to meet him in Paris was a big step for her. It was a promise of things to come if all went well between them. And what better place to begin than

Paris? She wanted her parents to meet him. She was proud to be with him, no matter what they thought. She no longer needed their approval, but she wanted them to meet the man she was falling in love with. "It won't be fun," she warned him.

"Will they hate me?"

"No. But they won't be happy about it. My father will be all right. My mother will be difficult. It's my life, Dan." She knew what she wanted. She wanted a life with him in Pittsburgh, whenever they decided the time was right for it, and she hoped it would be soon. They didn't know each other well enough yet, but he had promised to come to New York as often as he could. They had talked about it as soon as she got to Paris. He wanted to ask her father's permission and get engaged as soon as they got home.

"You know, I thought Omaha Beach was the worst thing that had ever happened to me," he said, thinking about it. "Now it turns out it was the best thing. If I hadn't been sent there, I'd never have met you, and none of this would be happening. I'd be sitting at a café in Paris by myself, watching all the guys with their girls and lonely as hell." He was smiling as he said it, and he leaned over and kissed her. "I want to take you to Twenty-One for dinner, as soon as I dock in New York. Where are we going to go on our honeymoon?" he asked, and she laughed.

"Shouldn't we get engaged first?"

"I feel like we already are." Everything felt so comfortable between them. But she didn't want to rush things. She wanted to savor it and get to know each other.

"So do I." She smiled happily. The hard memories were already starting to fade, all the men she'd seen suffering, and the ones who had died. She was going to miss the nurses she had worked with and lived with. They were bonded forever. Lizzie and Louise, and Emma. They all still missed Pru and Audrey. Those memories would never leave them, and the good times that they'd shared. They had all grown up together.

He took her to dinner at the Hôtel Ritz that night. The Nazi High Command had lived there for the Occupation, but there was no sign of them now. Parisians were treating American soldiers like royalty, and the sight of him kissing a woman in uniform made people who walked past them smile. It was a familiar sight. Everyone in Paris seemed to be kissing someone.

She told him when she left that they were the three happiest days of her life. He was coming back to England for their award ceremony on the tenth, right before he shipped out. His ship was leaving from Southampton on the twelfth of June. She was flying home three days after he sailed. It would give her a few days to prepare her parents before he got there. They were expecting her to come home and settle into the life they wanted for her, and instead she was going to marry a wholesale butcher from Pittsburgh. It was going to be a shock. But whether they liked it or not, she knew that it was the right path for her, and he was the right man. He was different from every man she'd ever known.

He took her to the train for Calais, and from there she would take the ferry back to England. She had already promised Lizzie that she would come up to Boston for a weekend before they both found jobs.

It was going to be hard leaving Emma in England. But she had Max now. Things had been progressing nicely for them for the past five months, since Christmas. And Emma was going to spend time with his family in Yorkshire with him that summer. They all had new lives to begin. They all had plans now, and hope for the future.

There were missing pieces and missing people, but there were friends who would always be part of their lives after what they'd been through together. Louise wanted them to visit her in North Carolina.

Lizzie had slipped away to a hotel in Brighton with Ed the weekend that Alex went to Paris to meet Dan.

They walked down the boardwalk arm in arm and felt the sea breeze on their faces. She was looking out to sea when he slipped down on one knee next to her, and she looked at him in surprise. He'd been planning it for weeks and wanted to wait until their weekend away together.

"What are you doing?" she said, looking startled.

"You said not to ask you till the war was over and we were both alive, so here we are." He smiled at her. "Elizabeth Hatton, will you marry me?"

"I . . . yes," she said softly, and he stood up and kissed her. As soon as they came up for air, she asked him a question. "Where are we going to live?" She didn't want to move to Ireland. She had to go home to Boston, for her parents. They had lost one child, they couldn't lose two, if she moved away. That didn't seem fair now.

"My cousin is going to sponsor me." Ed smiled at her. "He's already started on the paperwork. I want to apply for citizenship. And I can get veterans' benefits, to pay for medical school," he said calmly, and kissed her again, and she was smiling too.

"We have Audrey's money too, don't forget. When are we getting married?"

"As soon as your father says yes. My cousin is sending me a ticket, and he can give me a job at his restaurant. I'll fly to Boston as soon as I get released by the RAF, probably in the next month or two. You can start planning the wedding as soon as you want." She knew her parents would be shocked, but she wasn't going to give them a choice. They were both going to apply to medical school and go through it together. They had so much to look forward to, and they had survived the war. That was the greatest miracle of all. So many hadn't. They walked back to their hotel then, disappeared into their room and closed the door. It was what they had dreamed and hoped for since the day they met, and now it was all within reach. They were just sorry that Pru and Audrey weren't there to share it with them, but their memories would live on forever in their hearts.

Alex went to look for the others as soon as she got back from Paris. She found Lizzie in her room. She had just come back from Brighton.

"I'm going to marry Dan," Alex said as soon as she walked through the door.

"I'm engaged!" Lizzie countered, and they both laughed.

"What are you two sinful women up to? You should be ashamed of yourselves!" Emma said as she stuck her head through the doorway. "Sneaking off to hotels with your men, although it does sound very romantic," she conceded.

"We're getting married!" Lizzie announced.

"To each other? Now that should be interesting," Emma said, grinning at them. She was happy for them, and she wasn't surprised. Louise joined them a few minutes later.

"How was Paris?" she asked Alex. But she could see from the smile on her face and the light in her eyes.

"They're getting married," Emma told her. Louise was happy for them, although they all still felt the absence of their lost friends. Lizzie knew Ed did too. He talked about Pru all the time. And Lizzie missed Audrey. They had been through so much together.

They had dinner in the mess hall that night. And they were flying their last missions in the next week.

The entire squadron was going to attend the award ceremony five days before the American nurses were due to start going back to the States. They were flying back on military transports. There was so much to do, and so many papers to fill out before they left. The dormitory was exploding with life, with women packing and seeing friends, spending time with the men they'd been dating, and promising to visit each other once they got home. They all wondered if there would be enough jobs back home for all the nurses returning from the war. And some had boyfriends at home they hadn't seen in three years. They wondered what that would be like. They had all changed so much. They were grown women now, not girls.

They had all learned so much, and life at home had moved on. Nieces and nephews had been born whom they'd never seen. Parents had died, relatives had gotten married. They had to fit back into a world that many of them had outgrown. Many had plans to marry men they hadn't seen in years. And wartime lovers were being left behind. Soldiers were leaving babies they had spawned or trying to bring women to America to join them, but they would have to wait for their papers. They were leaving their new world and going back to their old one and wondered if they would still fit in after what they'd seen and done for nearly four years. There were so many who would never come home again and had died overseas in Normandy, and England, Italy, and Germany, and in the Pacific, like Lizzie's brother. The world would never be the same again. War had changed all of them, and the returning men and women were going home as the new people they had become, while their friends and families waited for the old ones to return. It was going to be an adjustment for all.

Louise was walking back to the barracks from the airstrip after her last mission, wondering if her world had changed or if she was going home to the same prejudices and restrictions, when she saw a tall man watching her from the end of the airstrip. She had seen him as she came down the ladder in her flight suit. There was something familiar about him. She wondered if he was one of the men they'd saved, who had come to thank her and say goodbye. Many had. And as she walked toward him, he smiled at her, and then she saw the piercing blue eyes and knew who it was. She would have known those eyes anywhere.

"Bonsoir, Louise," he said to her in French when she reached him. "I told you I would come and find you. We made it safely to Switzerland after we left you. You saved my life." It was Gonzague.

"Oh my God," was all she could say as he pulled her close to him. She felt as though she were dreaming.

"They tell me that you're going home. I will go home soon too. Come, let us sit. We have a lot to talk about."

They found a log under a tree and sat on it. He held her hand and kissed her. He wanted to know everything. When she was leaving, where she was going, what she would do now.

"You don't know me. But I know you. I knew you that night, and everything I needed to know." It had been ten months since she'd seen him, and it suddenly felt like only days. She had been so sure she would never see him again, that it was only a dream. "The Germans took my home and have been living there for the entire Occupation. I'm going home to reclaim it," he explained to her. "I'm sure the German pigs who lived there didn't treat it with respect. I go now to make it livable again. But I wanted to see you first. And then I want you to come and see it, to tell me if you think you could be happy there. It's in the country, near Provence. My family built it three hundred years ago. And you live where?"

"In North Carolina. Raleigh. My father is a doctor. And my mother runs a school. I'm a nurse," she said, not knowing where to start, and he laughed.

"I know. I remember. You are very good at what you do. And you wish to continue? Would you live in France with me? Married, of course." He scarcely knew her, but he had no doubt in his mind. He had known it the night they met, when she got him on his feet to escape the Germans and saved him. "I've been asked to work with the new government, with General de Gaulle. Some of my skills and experience of the past six years could be useful to them in the

Department of the Interior, as a minister of the government, which means some time in Paris, and some time at home in Provence. I would like to meet your family." She was frowning, wondering how realistic he was about the problems he would face with a woman like her. It all felt like a dream, and maybe he was dreaming too. He sounded certain about her, even though he barely knew her. He was going purely on instinct and his powerful attraction to her. He had been living by his wits for nearly six years, and trusted what he felt for her.

"Gonzague," she said quietly, and loved the sound of his name. It was wonderfully old-fashioned and lyrical, as he was in a way, like a prince in a fairy tale, but this was real life. "I'm Black," she said, and he looked at her as though for the first time.

"I didn't know," he said simply, with those piercing eyes, and then she laughed. "Perhaps you don't remember. I was shot in the leg. I am not blind. So? You think I am afraid of that?"

"So what happens here? Where I live it would be a very hard thing. Impossible, or almost. They would punish us for being to-gether. Terrible things would happen, our children would suffer, and so would we." Just describing it to him made her feel sick. And it was what she was going back to now.

"That's very wrong. It would not be that way in France. You are a very beautiful woman, but I'm not interested in your color. I care about your mind, and your heart. You are a woman of purpose. You are not afraid. You were not afraid when you came to help me. I saw your eyes, your face, your heart. Nothing frightened you then. Are you afraid now?" He waited for her answer. It all rested on that and what she would say.

"No, I'm not," she said in a clear voice. "Are you?"

"Not at all. I am afraid of other things, of a world that allows a travesty to exist like the one we just lived, where brother betrays brother and nothing is safe or true or right. We allowed that to happen. We gave our country away. We allowed evil to exist and to prosper. France had poison in her veins for these years. I am not interested in the color of skin. What happened here must never happen again. That is important to me. And so is life with a good woman at my side. An extraordinary woman, which you are. Your color means nothing." He was as beautiful and exciting and mysterious and strong as he had been when she met him. She had fallen in love with him on the spot, and believed she could never have him, and would never see him again. But she was wrong. He was a man of his word and he was here now. It wasn't a fairy tale. It was real. And so was he, and he loved her just as she was.

"Do you have family? Parents? Brothers?" She wanted to know all about him too now.

"I had three brothers and a father. All dead in the Resistance. My mother died when I was a child. I have no one now. I have you, if you wish it to be so. You are going home soon, I believe." He had made discreet inquiries to find her. "I must deal with my house, and get the men started working on it. Then I would like to visit you and your family in . . . Carolina?"

"North Carolina."

"Yes. And then I would like you and your family to visit me, and then you will decide what you wish. Is that right for you?"

"Very right." She would have a lot to explain to her parents, about how they met and why she thought this was the right path for her, with a French count she had met in the Resistance. It was a big leap from Raleigh.

"Will they be unhappy?"

"Surprised."

"Yes, so was I when I met you. You are a very surprising woman." She smiled.

"I'm not the one with surprises here, Gonzague." He was no ordinary man. He was unusual in a thousand different ways, and she was sure there was a part of him and his war history that she would never know, but maybe it was just as well.

"Do we have a good plan? I will visit you, and then you and your parents will come to visit me, and then we will make our plans."

"I think that's a very good plan." She smiled at him.

"Good." He stood up then and pulled her to her feet, and they walked to her barracks. He was courteous and gentlemanly, but beneath that, she sensed the force of a hurricane. Life with him would never be predictable or boring, but it was the life and the man she wanted. They had much to discover about each other, but they knew enough. She was sure. And so was he. He had done exactly what he said. He had found her, and he had come back. It was all she needed to know for now.

"There's an award ceremony," she explained to him. "Will you stay?"

"If you wish."

"I do." She didn't want him to be her secret lover or mystery man. If they loved each other, she wanted their relationship to be in the open, with her proud to be at his side, and he at hers.

The award ceremony would be in two days, and he said he would be there. He had business in London and promised to come back. She wanted to introduce him to her friends. He had been her dream for nearly a year, now he had stepped out into the light, and she wanted to share her life with him. The award ceremony would be part of the world she was leaving behind, the life she had lived for four years, and the people she had lived with at Down Ampney.

He kissed her in front of the barracks, and it was a searing kiss like the one she remembered the very first time.

"We will have an interesting life," he said as he smiled down at her. Of that she had no doubt.

She sensed correctly that there was an element of danger about him. She wasn't wrong. He had killed many men in his years in the Resistance, and had managed not to be killed by being smarter than they were. He had helped to save France, and had won the admiration of the British in the process. And the one thing she knew with absolute certainty was that Gonzague de Lafayette was her soulmate, and the love of her life. They had both known it the instant they met. The rest they could discover in time.

Chapter 17

The nurses of the Medical Air Evacuation Transport Squadron wore their dress uniforms for the ceremony. The base commander was there, and a representative from the Army Air Forces, the Flight Nurses' Corps, and the RAF on the British side. The roll was called and each of them was given a medal for distinguished service and bravery in combat, which they hadn't expected. Six women were named posthumously for service to their country and bravery in combat, among them were Lieutenant Prudence Pommery and Lieutenant Audrey Anne Parker. Max accepted the medal for Pru, and Lizzie for Audrey. Lizzie couldn't stop crying when she accepted it, and she was going to deliver it herself to the cemetery in Annapolis to be put on display.

Max had come to the ceremony to be with Emma, and Pru's parents had come too. Ed was there with Lizzie. Dan was there for Alex. And Gonzague had come for Louise. He was proud of her when she received her medal. He had come in a dark suit and looked very proper. He was to be decorated soon by General de Gaulle as a Commander of the Legion of Honour. They all stayed together in a group at the reception afterwards, after all the speeches, and photographs were taken, and the London *Times* had covered it.

The others were intrigued by Gonzague. Louise had told them the story. She was the only one who would be returning to Europe again soon, to live in France with him, as his wife. She wanted the marriage to take place in France. It would have been illegal in North Carolina, nothing had changed. And in France, she would be a countess as Gonzague's wife. Her parents would come to France, after Gonzague went to meet them in North Carolina. The others had their lives waiting for them in the States, except for Emma, who was going to stay with the Pommerys in Yorkshire for a month. Max had a month's leave before he was to be discharged.

It was a special event on a golden day they would never forget. Gonzague spent another day with Louise afterwards, and then left for Provence. The nurses were leaving in five days. Each moment seemed precious and fleeting in their final hours together.

They were all in Lizzie's room with her the next day, when she was asked to come downstairs to the sitting room, and they all went with her, as though they sensed danger in their midst for a last time. An air forces commander was waiting for her, and she started to cry as soon as she saw him. She knew what it meant, and so did her friends. They had been through it too often. It didn't seem possible that tragedy could strike again, but it had.

In the last great battle of the war in the Pacific, her brother Henry had been killed at the Battle of Okinawa. She had lost both her brothers to the war, and her parents had given both sons. It had happened to others and seemed unthinkably cruel. Audrey's brother had been among the very first casualties, and now Lizzie's brother was the last. She was her parents' only surviving child now. Just like the Pommerys with Max. It was too much to give and too much to lose in a war that would leave none of them the same and had taken too much from everyone. She went back to her room, and cried all day, with her friends around her for support.

Lizzie spoke to her parents that night. She was coming home to them. They were devastated by another immense blow. She felt dazed during her remaining days in England, and her friends never left her for an instant. They took turns sleeping in Audrey's empty bed in her room. She was going home to console her parents and Ed would be joining her soon. He comforted her in the loss of her brother, as he had with the first one. And now he was her future. Their losses had brought them closer, as it had dome for so many.

Five days after they received their medals, they were at the airport. Lizzie, Louise, and Alex were ready to leave, and ten other nurses were flying home on the same flight. There was a crowd of nurses from the air evacuation squadron who had come to say goodbye. There was hugging and kissing and tears and promises to meet again. Leaving each other was like leaving home again. They had become a family and were returning to an unfamiliar world with their losses as battle scars, and the bond they shared one of pure love. They had brought each other safety and comfort in a place where there was none.

This was the last time they would all be together. They were going home now, forever changed, forever different, and stronger than when they arrived, forever bonded to each other. Their comrades in war never to be forgotten, the experiences they shared a part of them, their memories treasured.

Alex, Lizzie, and Louise climbed the stairs together to the transport plane waiting on the tarmac. They waved to their friends and a cheer went up from the crowd. When the doors closed, the plane lumbered down the runway, and took to the skies. Their friends on the ground watched them until the plane disappeared. The Flying Angels were homebound at last, with their losses and all they had gained and learned from each other engraved on their hearts.

About the Author

DANIELLE STEEL has been hailed as one of the world's best-selling authors, with almost a billion copies of her novels sold. Her many international bestsellers include *The Butler, Complications, Nine Lives, Finding Ashley, The Affair, Neighbors, All That Glitters, Royal, Daddy's Girls,* and other highly acclaimed novels. She is also the author of *His Bright Light,* the story of her son Nick Traina's life and death; *A Gift of Hope,* a memoir of her work with the homeless; *Expect a Miracle,* a book of her favorite quotations for inspiration and comfort; *Pure Joy,* about the dogs she and her family have loved; and the children's books *Pretty Minnie in Paris* and *Pretty Minnie in Hollywood.*

daniellesteel.com
Facebook.com/DanielleSteelOfficial
Twitter: @daniellesteel
Instagram: @officialdaniellesteel

About the Type

This book was set in Charter, a typeface designed in 1987 by Matthew Carter (b. 1937) for Bitstream, Inc., a digital type-foundry that he cofounded in 1981. One of the most influential typographers of our time, Carter designed this versatile font to feature a compact width, squared serifs, and open letterforms. These features give the typeface a fresh, highly legible, and unencumbered appearance.